Grass for his Pillow

LIAN HEARN

Grass for his Pillow

Tales of the Otori

Book Two

MACMILLAN

First published 2003 by Macmillan
an imprint of Pan Macmillan Ltd
Pan Macmillan, 20 New Wharf Road, London N1 9RR
Basingstoke and Oxford
www.panmacmillan.com
Associated companies throughout the world

ISBN 1 4050 0582 3 (HB)
ISBN 1 4050 0583 1 (TPB)

Yamanoue no Okura poem reprinted by kind permission of
Columbia University Press

Manyoshu poem from *The Country of Eight Islands* by Hiroaki Sato and
Burton Watson copyright 1981 by Hiroaki Sato and Burton Watson.
By permission of Columbia University Press.

The Fulling Block, by Zeami, can be found in *Japanese No Drama* translated
and edited by Royall Tyler, Penguin Classics 1992

1 3 5 7 9 8 6 4 2

A CIP catalogue record for this book is available from the British Library.

Typeset by Intype Libra Ltd
Printed and bound in Great Britain by Mackays of Chatham plc, Kent

for D

Tales of the Otori

Characters

The Clans

The Otori
(Middle Country; castle town: Hagi)

Otori Shigeru . . . . rightful heir to the clan

Otori Takeshi . his younger brother, murdered by the Tohan clan

Otori Takeo . . . . (born Tomasu) his adopted son

Otori Shigemori . . . . Shigeru's father, killed at
the battle of Yaegahara (d.)

Otori Ichiro . . . . a distant relative, Shigeru
and Takeo's teacher

Chiyo ⎫
Haruka ⎭ . . . . maids in the household

Shiro . . . . a carpenter

Otori Shoichi . . . . . . Shigeru's uncle, now lord of the clan

Otori Masahiro . . . . his younger brother

Otori Yoshitomi . . . . Masahiro's son

Miyoshi Kahei ⎫
Miyoshi Gemba ⎭ . . . . brothers, friends of Takeo

Miyoshi Satoru . . . . their father, captain of the
guard in Hagi castle

Endo Chikara . . . . a senior retainer

Terada Fumifusa . . . . a pirate

Terada Fumio . . . . his son, friend of Takeo

Ryoma . . . . a fisherman, Masahiro's illegitimate son

The Tohan
(The East; castle town: Inuyama)

Iida Sadamu . . . . lord of the clan
Iida Nariaki . . . . his cousin

Ando ⎫
Abe ⎭ . . . . Iida's retainers

Lord Noguchi . . . . an ally
Lady Noguchi . . . . his wife
Junko . . . . a servant in Noguchi castle

The Seishuu
(an alliance of several ancient families in the West. Main castle towns: Kumamoto and Maruyama)

Arai Daiichi . . . . a warlord

Niwa Satoru . . . . a retainer
Akita Tsutomu . . . . a retainer
Sonoda Mitsuru . . . . Akita's nephew

Maruyama Naomi . . . . head of the Maruyama domain, Shigeru's lover
Mariko . . . . her daughter
Sachie . . . . her maid

Sugita Haruki . . . . a retainer
Sugita Hiroshi . . . . his nephew
Sakai Masaki . . . . Hiroshi's cousin

Lord Shirakawa
Kaede . . . . his eldest daughter, Lady Maruyama's cousin

Ai ⎫
Hana ⎭ . . . . his daughters

Ayame
Manami } . . . . *maids in the household*
Akane

Amano Tenzo . . . . *a Shirakawa retainer*

Shoji Kiyoshi . . . . *senior retainer to Lord Shirakawa*

The Tribe

The Muto Family

Muto Kenji . . . . *Takeo's teacher, the Master*

Muto Shizuka . . . . *Kenji's niece, Arai's mistress and Kaede's companion*

Zenko
Taku } . . . . *her sons*

Muto Seiko . . . . *Kenji's wife*

Muto Yuki . . . . *their daughter*

Muto Yuzuru . . . . *a cousin*

Kana
Miyabi } . . . . *maids*

The Kikuta Family

Kikuta Isamu . . . . *Takeo's real father (d.)*

Kikuta Kotaro . . . . *his cousin, the Master*

Kikuta Gosaburo . . . . *Kotaro's younger brother*

Kikuta Akio . . . . *their nephew*

Kikuta Hajime . . . . *a wrestler*

Sadako . . . . *a maid*

The Kuroda Family

Kuroda Shintaro . . . . *a famous assassin*
Kondo Kiichi

Imai Kazuo

Kudo Keiko

Others

Lord Fujiwara . . . . . a nobleman, exiled from the capital

Mamoru . . . . his protégé and companion

Ono Rieko . . . . his cousin

Murita . . . . a retainer

Matsuda Shingen . . . . the Abbot at Terayama

Kubo Makoto . . . . a monk, Takeo's closest friend

Jin-emon . . . . a bandit

Jiro . . . . a farmer's son

Jo-An . . . . an outcaste

Horses

Raku . . . . grey with black mane and tail.
Takeo's first horse, given by him to Kaede

Kyu . . . . . black, Shigeru's horse, disappeared in Inuyama

Aoi . . . . black (half-brother to Kyu)

Ki . . . . Amano's chestnut

Shun . . . . Takeo's bay. A very clever horse

bold = main characters

(d.) = character died before the start of Book 1

THE THREE COUNTRIES

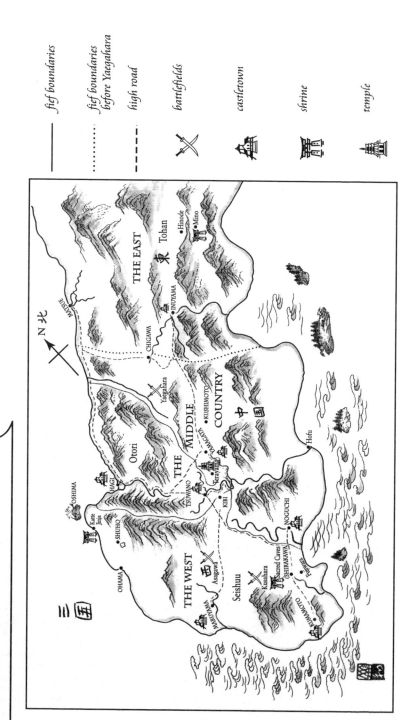

三国

THE WEST 西

THE MIDDLE COUNTRY 中国

THE EAST 東

N 北

MATSUE

Legend:
- fief boundaries
- fief boundaries before Yaegahara
- high road
- battlefields
- castletown
- shrine
- temple

OHAMA

MARUYAMA

Seishuu

Asagawa

Kumamoto

Sacred Caves

Kushara

SHIRAKAWA

Hidan River

NOGUCHI

KIBI

Hofu

SHUHO

Kano Jinja

OSHIMA

HAGI

Otori

TSUWANO

Terayama

YAMAGATA

Yaegahara

KUSHIMOTO

CHIGAWA

INUYAMA

Tohan

Hinode

Mino

On nights when, wind mixing in, the rain falls,
On nights when, rain mixing in, the snow falls

Yamanoue no Okura: 'A Dialogue on Poverty'

From 'The Country of Eight Islands'
Trans: Hiroaki Sato

Foreword

These events took place in the year following the death of Otori Shigeru in the Tohan stronghold of Inuyama. The leader of the Tohan clan, Iida Sadamu, was killed in revenge by Shigeru's adopted son, Otori Takeo, or so it was widely believed, and the Tohan overthrown by Arai Daiichi, one of the Seishuu clan from Kumamoto, who took advantage of the chaos following the fall of Inuyama to seize control of the Three Countries. Arai had hoped to form an alliance with Takeo and arrange his marriage to Shirakawa Kaede, now the heir to the Maruyama and Shirakawa domains.

However, torn between Shigeru's last commands and the demands of his real father's family, the Kikuta of the Tribe, Takeo gave up his inheritance and marriage with Kaede, with whom he was deeply in love, to go with the Tribe, feeling himself bound to them by blood and by oath.

Otori Shigeru was buried at Terayama, a remote mountain temple in the heart of the Middle Country. After the battles of Inuyama and Kushimoto Arai visited the temple to pay his respects to his fallen ally and to confirm the new alliances. Here Takeo and Kaede met for the last time.

One

Shirakawa Kaede lay deeply asleep in the state close to unconsciousness that the Kikuta can deliver with their gaze. The night passed, the stars paled as dawn came, the sounds of the temple rose and fell around her, but she did not stir. She did not hear her companion, Shizuka, call anxiously to her from time to time, trying to wake her. She did not feel Shizuka's hand on her forehead. She did not hear Lord Arai Daiichi's men as they came with increasing impatience to the veranda, telling Shizuka that the warlord was waiting to speak to Lady Shirakawa. Her breathing was peaceful and calm, her features as still as a mask's.

Towards evening the quality of her sleep seemed to change. Her eyelids flickered and her lips appeared to smile. Her fingers, which had been curled gently against her palms, spread.

Be patient. He will come for you.

Kaede was dreaming that she had been turned to ice. The words echoed lucidly in her head. There was no fear in the dream, just the feeling of being held by something cool and white in a world that was silent, frozen and enchanted.

Her eyes opened.

It was still light. The shadows told her it was evening. A wind bell rang softly, once, and then the air was still.

The day she had no recollection of must have been a warm one. Her skin was damp beneath her hair. Birds were chattering from the eaves, and she could hear the clip of the swallows' beaks as they caught the last insects of the day. Soon they would fly south. It was already autumn.

The sound of the birds reminded her of the painting Takeo had given her, many weeks before, at this same place, a sketch of a wild forest bird that had made her think of freedom; it had been lost along with everything else she possessed, her wedding robes, all her other clothes, when the castle at Inuyama burned. She possessed nothing. Shizuka had found some old robes for her at the house they had stayed in, and had borrowed combs and other things. She had never been in such a place before, a merchant's house, smelling of fermenting soy, full of people, who she tried to keep away from, though every now and then the maids came to peep at her through the screens.

She was afraid everyone would see what had happened to her on the night the castle fell. She had killed a man, she had lain with another, she had fought alongside him, wielding the dead man's sword. She could not believe she had done these things. Sometimes she thought she was bewitched, as people said. They said of her that any man who desired her died – and it was true. Men had died. But not Takeo.

Ever since she had been assaulted by the guard when she was a hostage in Noguchi castle, she had been afraid of all men. Her terror of Iida had driven her to defend herself against him; but she had had no fear of Takeo. She had only wanted to hold him closer. Since their first meeting in Tsuwano her body had longed for his. She had wanted him to touch her, she had wanted the feel of his skin against hers. Now, as she remembered that night, she understood with renewed clarity that she could marry no one but him, she would love no one but him. *I will be patient*, she promised. But where had those words come from?

She turned her head slightly and saw Shizuka's outline, on the edge of the veranda. Beyond the woman rose the ancient trees of the shrine. The air smelled of cedars and dust. The temple bell tolled the evening hour. Kaede did not speak. She did not want to talk to anyone, or hear any voice. She wanted to go back to that place of ice where she had been sleeping.

Then, beyond the specks of dust that floated in the last rays of the sun, she saw something: a spirit, she thought, yet not only a spirit for it had substance; it was there, undeniable and real, gleaming like fresh snow. She stared, half rose, but in the moment that she recognized her, the White Goddess, the all-compassionate, the all-merciful, was gone.

'What is it?' Shizuka heard the movement and ran to her side. Kaede looked at Shizuka and saw the deep concern in her eyes. She realized how precious this woman had become to her, her closest, indeed her only, friend.

'Nothing. A half dream.'

'Are you all right? How do you feel?'

'I don't know. I feel . . .' Kaede's voice died away. She gazed at Shizuka for several moments. 'Have I been asleep all day? What happened to me?'

'He shouldn't have done it to you,' Shizuka said, her voice sharp with concern and anger.

'It was Takeo?'

Shizuka nodded. 'I had no idea he had that skill. It's a trait of the Kikuta family.'

'The last thing I remember is his eyes. We gazed at each other and then I fell asleep.'

After a pause Kaede went on, 'He's gone, hasn't he?'

'My uncle, Muto Kenji, and the Kikuta master, Kotaro, came for him last night,' Shizuka replied.

'And I will never see him again?' Kaede remembered her desperation the previous night, before the long, deep sleep. She had begged Takeo not to leave her. She had been terrified of her future without him; angry and wounded by his rejection of her. But all that turbulence had been stilled.

'You must forget him,' Shizuka said, taking Kaede's hand in hers and stroking it gently. 'From now on his life and yours cannot touch.'

Kaede smiled slightly. *I cannot forget him*, she was thinking. *Nor can he ever be taken from me. I have slept in ice. I have seen the White Goddess.*

'Are you all right?' Shizuka said again, with urgency. 'Not many people survive the Kikuta sleep. They are usually dispatched before they wake. I don't know what it has done to you.'

'It hasn't harmed me. But it has altered me in some way. I feel as if I don't know anything. As if I have to learn everything anew.'

Shizuka knelt before her, puzzled, her eyes searching Kaede's face. 'What will you do now? Where will you go? Will you return to Inuyama with Arai?'

'I think I should go home to my parents. I must see my mother. I'm so afraid she will have died while we were delayed in Inuyama for all that time. I will leave in the morning. I suppose you should inform Lord Arai.'

'I understand your anxiety,' Shizuka replied. 'But Arai may be reluctant to let you go.'

'Then I shall have to persuade him,' Kaede said calmly. 'First I must eat something. Will you ask them to prepare some food? And bring me some tea, please.'

'Lady.' Shizuka bowed to her and stepped off the veranda. As she walked away, Kaede heard the plaintive notes of a flute, played by some unseen person in the garden behind the temple. She thought she knew the player, one of the young monks, from the time when they had first visited the temple to view the famous Sesshu paintings, but she could not recall his name. The music spoke to her of the inevitability of suffering and loss. The trees stirred as the wind rose, and owls began to hoot from the mountain.

Shizuka came back with the tea and poured a cup for Kaede. She drank as if she were tasting it for the first time, every drop having its own distinct, smoky flavour against her tongue. And when the old woman, who looked after guests, brought rice and vegetables cooked with bean curd, it was as if she had never tasted food before. She marvelled silently at the new powers that had been awakened within her.

'Lord Arai wishes to speak with you before the end of the day,' Shizuka said. 'I told him you were not well, but he insisted. If you do not feel like facing him now, I will go and tell him again.'

'I am not sure we can treat Lord Arai in that fashion,' Kaede said. 'If he commands me, I must go to him.'

'He is very angry,' Shizuka said in a low voice. 'He is offended and outraged by Takeo's disappearance. He sees in it the loss of two important alliances. He will almost certainly have to fight the Otori now, without Takeo on his side. He'd hoped for a quick marriage between you—'

'Don't speak of it,' Kaede interrupted. She finished the

5

last of the rice, placed the eating sticks down on the tray and bowed in thanks for the food.

Shizuka sighed. 'Arai has no real understanding of the Tribe, how they work, what demands they place on those who belong to them.'

'Did he never know that you were from the Tribe?'

'He knew I had ways of finding things out, of passing on messages. He was happy enough to make use of my skills in forming the alliance with Lord Shigeru and Lady Maruyama. He had heard of the Tribe but like most people he thought they were little more than a guild. That they should have been involved in Iida's death shocked him profoundly, even though he profited from it.' She paused, and then said quietly, 'He has lost all trust in me – I think he wonders how he slept with me so many times without being assassinated himself. Well, we will certainly never sleep together again. That is all over.'

'Are you afraid of him? Has he threatened you?'

'He is furious with me,' Shizuka replied. 'He feels I have betrayed him, worse, made a fool out of him. I do not think he will ever forgive me.' A bitter note crept into her voice. 'I have been his closest confidante, his lover, his friend, since I was hardly more than a child. I have borne him two sons. Yet he would have me put to death in an instant were it not for your presence.'

'I will kill any man who tries to harm you,' Kaede said.

Shizuka smiled. 'How fierce you look when you say that!'

'Men die easily,' Kaede's voice was flat. 'From the prick of a needle, the thrust of a knife. You taught me that.'

'But you are yet to use those skills, I hope,' Shizuka

replied. 'Though you fought well at Inuyama. Takeo owes his life to you.'

Kaede was silent for a moment. Then she said in a low voice, 'I did more than fight with the sword. You do not know all of it.'

Shizuka stared at her. 'What are you telling me? That it was you who killed Iida?' she whispered.

Kaede nodded. 'Takeo took his head, but he was already dead. I did what you told me. He was going to rape me.'

Shizuka grasped her hands. 'Never let anyone know that! Not one of these warriors, not even Arai, would let you live.'

'I feel no guilt or remorse,' Kaede said. 'I never did a less shameful deed. Not only did I protect myself but the deaths of many were avenged: Lord Shigeru, my kinswoman, Lady Maruyama, and her daughter, and all the other innocent people whom Iida tortured and murdered.'

'Nevertheless, if this became generally known, you would be punished for it. Men will think the world has turned upside down if women start taking up arms and seeking revenge.'

'My world is already turned upside down,' Kaede said. 'Still, I must go and see Lord Arai. Bring me—' she broke off and laughed. 'I was going to say, "Bring me some clothes," but I have none. I have nothing!'

'You have a horse,' Shizuka replied. 'Takeo left the grey for you.'

'He left me Raku?' Kaede smiled, a true smile that illuminated her face. She stared into the distance, her eyes dark and thoughtful.

'Lady?' Shizuka touched her on the shoulder.

'Comb out my hair, and send a message to Lord Arai to say I will visit him directly.'

It was almost completely dark by the time they left the women's rooms, and went towards the main guest rooms where Arai and his men were staying. Lights gleamed from the temple and, further up the slope, beneath the trees, men stood with flaring torches round Lord Shigeru's grave. Even at this hour people came to visit it, bringing incense and offerings, placing lamps and candles on the ground around the stone, seeking the help of the dead man who every day became more of a god to them.

He sleeps beneath a covering of flame, Kaede thought, herself praying silently to Shigeru's spirit for guidance while she pondered what she should say to Arai. She was the heir to both Shirakawa and Maruyama; she knew Arai would be seeking some strong alliance with her, probably a marriage that would bind her into the power he was amassing. They had spoken a few times during her stay at Inuyama, and again on the journey, but Arai's attention had been taken up with securing the countryside and his strategies for the future. He had not shared these with her, beyond expressing his desire for the Otori marriage to take place. Once, a lifetime ago it seemed now, she had wanted to be more than a pawn in the hands of the warriors who commanded her fate. Now, with the new-found strength that the icy sleep had given her, she resolved again to take control of her life. *I need time*, she thought. *I must do nothing rashly. I must go home before I make any decisions.*

One of Arai's men – she remembered his name was Niwa – greeted her at the veranda's edge and led her to the doorway. The shutters all stood open. Arai sat at the end of the room, three of his men next to him. Niwa spoke her name and the warlord looked up at her. For a moment they studied each other. She held his gaze, and felt power's strong pulse in her veins. Then she dropped to her knees and bowed to him, resenting the gesture, yet knowing she had to appear to submit.

He returned her bow, and they both sat up at the same time. Kaede felt his eyes on her. She raised her head and gave him the same unflinching look. He could not meet it. Her heart was pounding at her audacity. In the past she had both liked and trusted the man in front of her. Now she saw changes in his face. The lines had deepened around his mouth and eyes. He had been both pragmatic and flexible, but now he was in the grip of his intense desire for power.

Not far from her parents' home the Shirakawa flowed through vast limestone caves, where the water had formed pillars and statues. As a child she had been taken there every year to worship the goddess who lived within one of these pillars under the mountain. The statue had a fluid, living shape – as though the spirit that dwelt within were trying to break out from beneath the covering of lime. She thought of that stone covering now. Was power a limey river calcifying those who dared to swim in it?

Arai's physical size and strength made her quail inwardly, reminding her of that moment of helplessness in Iida's arms, of the strength of men who could force women in any way they wanted. *Never let them use that strength*, came the thought, and then, *Always be armed*. A taste came into her mouth, as sweet as persimmon, as strong as blood, the knowledge and taste of power. Was this what drove men to clash endlessly with each other, to enslave and destroy each other? Why should a woman not have that too?

She stared at the places on Arai's body where the needle and the knife had pierced Iida, had opened him up to the world he'd tried to dominate and let his life's blood leak away. *I must never forget it,* she told herself. *Men also can be killed by women. I killed the most powerful warlord in the Three Countries.*

All her upbringing had taught her to defer to men, to submit to their will and their greater intelligence. Her heart was beating so strongly she thought she might faint. She breathed deeply, using the skills Shizuka had taught her, and felt the blood settle in her veins.

'Lord Arai, tomorrow I will leave for Shirakawa. I would be very grateful if you will provide men to escort me home.'

'I would prefer you to stay in the East,' he said, slowly. 'But that is not what I want to talk to you about first.' His eyes narrowed as he stared at her. 'Otori's disappearance. Can you shed any light on this extraordinary occurrence? I believe I have established my right to power. I was already in alliance with Shigeru. How can young Otori ignore all obligations to me and to his dead father? How can he disobey and walk away? And where has he gone? My men have been searching the district all day, as far as Yamagata. He's completely vanished.'

'I do not know where he is,' she replied.

'I'm told he spoke to you last night before he left.'

'Yes,' she said simply.

'He must have explained to you at least . . .'

'He was bound by other obligations.' Kaede felt sorrow build within her as she spoke. 'He did not intend to insult you.' Indeed she could not remember Takeo mentioning Arai to her, but she did not say this.

'Obligations to the so-called Tribe?' Arai had been controlling his anger, but now it burst fresh into his voice, into his eyes. He moved his head slightly, and she guessed he was looking past her to where Shizuka knelt in the shadows on the veranda. 'What do you know of them?'

'Very little,' she replied. 'It was with their help that Lord Takeo climbed into Inuyama. I suppose we are all in their debt in that respect.'

Speaking Takeo's name made her shiver. She recalled the feel of his body against hers, at that moment when they both expected to die. Her eyes darkened, her face softened. Arai was aware of it, without knowing the reason and, when he spoke again, she heard something else in his voice besides rage.

'Another marriage can be arranged for you. There are other young men of the Otori, cousins to Shigeru. I will send envoys to Hagi.'

'I am in mourning for Lord Shigeru,' she replied. 'I cannot consider marriage to anyone. I will go home and recover from my grief.' *Will anyone ever want to marry me, knowing my reputation?* she wondered, and could not help following with the thought, *Takeo did not die.* She had thought Arai would argue further but after a moment he concurred.

'Maybe it's best that you go to your parents. I will send for you when I return to Inuyama. We will discuss your marriage then.'

'Will you make Inuyama your capital?'

'Yes, I intend to rebuild the castle.' In the flickering light his face was set and brooding. Kaede said nothing. He spoke again abruptly. 'But to return to the Tribe. I had

11

not realized how strong their influence must be. To make Takeo walk away from such a marriage, such an inheritance, and then to conceal him completely. To tell you the truth, I had no idea what I was dealing with.' He glanced again towards Shizuka.

He will kill her, she thought. *It's more than just anger at Takeo's disobedience. His self-esteem has been deeply wounded too. He must suspect Shizuka has been spying on him for years.* She wondered what had happened to the love and desire that had existed between them. Had it all dissolved overnight? Did the years of service, the trust and loyalty all come to nothing?

'I shall make it my business to find out about them,' he went on, almost as if he were speaking to himself. 'There must be people who know, who will talk. I cannot let such an organization exist. They will undermine my power just as the white ant chews through wood.'

Kaede said, 'I believe it was you who sent Muto Shizuka to me, to protect me. I owe my life to that protection. And I believe I kept faith with you in Noguchi castle. Strong bonds exist between us and they shall be unbroken. Whoever I marry will swear allegiance to you. Shizuka will remain in my service, and will come with me to my parents' home.'

He looked at her then, and again she met his gaze with ice in her eyes. 'It's barely thirteen months since I killed a man for your sake,' he said. 'You were hardly more than a child. You have changed . . .'

'I have been made to grow up,' she replied. She made an effort not to think of her borrowed robe, her complete lack of possessions. *I am the heir to a great domain,* she told herself. She continued to hold his eyes until he reluctantly inclined his head.

'Very well. I will send men with you to Shirakawa, and you may take the Muto woman.'

'Lord Arai.' Only then did she drop her eyes and bow.

Arai called to Niwa to make arrangements for the following day, and Kaede bade him goodnight, speaking with great deference. She felt she had come out of the encounter well; she could afford to pretend that all power lay on his side.

She returned to the women's rooms with Shizuka, both of them silent. The old woman had already spread out the beds, and now she brought sleeping garments for them before helping Shizuka undress Kaede. Wishing them goodnight, she retired to the adjoining room.

Shizuka's face was pale and her demeanour more subdued than Kaede had ever known it. She touched Kaede's hand and whispered, 'Thank you,' but said nothing else. When they were both lying beneath the cotton quilts, as mosquitoes whined around their heads and moths fluttered against the lamps, Kaede could feel the other woman's body rigid next to hers, and knew Shizuka was struggling with grief. Yet she did not cry.

Kaede reached out and put her arms around Shizuka, holding her closely, without speaking. She shared the same deep sorrow but no tears came to her eyes. She would allow nothing to weaken the power that was coming to life within her.

Two

The next morning palanquins and an escort had been prepared for the women. They left as soon as the sun was up. Remembering the advice of her kinswoman, Lady Maruyama, Kaede stepped delicately into the palanquin, as though she were as frail and powerless as most women, but she made sure the grooms brought Takeo's horse from the stable and, once they were on the road, she opened the waxed paper curtains so she could look out.

The swaying movement was intolerable to her; even being able to see did not prevent sickness coming over her. At the first rest stop, at Yamagata, she was so dizzy she could hardly walk. She could not bear to look at food, and when she drank a little tea it made her vomit immediately. Her body's weakness infuriated her, seeming to undermine her newly discovered feeling of power. Shizuka led her to a small room in the rest house, bathed her face with cold water, and made her lie down for a while. The sickness passed as quickly as it had come, and she was able to drink some red bean soup and a bowl of tea.

The sight of the black palanquin, however, made her feel queasy again. 'Bring me the horse,' she said. 'I will ride.'

The groom lifted her onto Raku's back, and Shizuka

mounted nimbly behind her, and so they rode for the rest of the morning, saying little, each wrapped in her own thoughts, but taking comfort from the other's closeness.

After they left Yamagata the road began to climb steeply. In places it was stepped with huge, flat stones. There were already signs of autumn, though the sky was clear blue and the air warm. Beech, sumac and maple were beginning to turn gold and vermilion. Strings of wild geese flew high above them. The forest deepened, still and airless. The horse walked delicately, its head low as it picked its way up the steps. The men were alert and uneasy. Since the overthrow of Iida and the Tohan the countryside was filled with masterless men of all ranks who resorted to banditry rather than swear new allegiances.

The horse was strong and fit. Despite the heat and the climb its coat was hardly darkened with sweat when they stopped again at a small rest house at the top of the pass. It was a little past midday. The horses were led away to be fed and watered, the men retired to the shade trees around the well, and an old woman spread mattresses on the floor of a matted room so Kaede might rest for an hour or two.

Kaede lay down, thankful to be able to stretch out. The light in the room was dim and green. Huge cedars shut out most of the glare. In the distance she could hear the cool trickle of the spring, and voices: the men talking quietly, occasionally a ripple of laughter, Shizuka chatting to someone in the kitchen. At first Shizuka's voice was bright and gossipy, and Kaede was glad that she seemed to be recovering her spirits, but then it went low, and the person to whom she was speaking responded in the same vein. Kaede could no longer make out anything they said.

After a while the conversation ceased. Shizuka came quietly into the room, and lay down next to Kaede.

'Who were you talking to?'

Shizuka turned her head so she could speak directly into Kaede's ear. 'A cousin of mine works here.'

'You have cousins everywhere.'

'That's how it is with the Tribe.'

Kaede was silent for a moment. Then she said, 'Don't other people suspect who you are and want to . . .'

'Want to what?'

'Well, get rid of you.'

Shizuka laughed. 'No one dares. We have infinitely more ways of getting rid of them. And no one ever knows anything about us for sure. They have their suspicions. But you may have noticed, both my uncle Kenji and I can appear in many different guises. The Tribe are hard to recognize, in addition to possessing many other arts.'

'Will you tell me more about them?' Kaede was fascinated by this world that lay in the shadows of the world she knew.

'I can tell you a little. Not everything. Later, when we cannot be overheard.'

From outside a crow called harshly.

Shizuka said, 'I learned two things from my cousin. One is that Takeo has not left Yamagata. Arai has search parties out and guards on the highway. They will be concealing him within the town.'

The crow cried again. *Aah! Aah!*

I might have passed his hiding place today, Kaede thought. After a long moment she said, 'What was the second thing?'

'An accident may occur on the road.'

'What sort of accident?'

'To me. It seems Arai does want to get rid of me, as you put it. But it is planned to look like an accident, a brigand attack, something like that. He cannot bear that I should live, but he does not wish to offend you outright.'

'You must leave.' Kaede's voice rose with urgency. 'As long as you are with me he knows where to find you.'

'Shush,' Shizuka warned. 'I'm only telling you so you won't do anything foolish.'

'What would be foolish?'

'To use your knife, to try to defend me.'

'I would do that,' Kaede said.

'I know. But you must keep your boldness and those skills hidden. Someone is travelling with us who will protect me. More than one probably. Leave the fighting to them.'

'Who is it?'

'If my lady can guess I'll give her a present!' Shizuka said lightly.

'What happened to your broken heart?' Kaede asked, curious.

'I mended it with rage,' Shizuka replied. Then she spoke more seriously. 'I may never love a man as much again. But I have done nothing shameful. I am not the one who has acted with dishonour. Before, I was bound to him, a hostage to him. In cutting me off from him he has set me free.'

'You should leave me,' Kaede said again.

'How can I leave you now? You need me more than ever.'

Kaede lay still. 'Why more than ever now?'

'Lady, you must know. Your bleeding is late, your face is softer, your hair thicker. The sickness, followed by hunger . . .' Shizuka's voice was soft, filled with pity.

Kaede's heart began to race. The knowledge lay beneath her skin, but she could not bring herself to face it.

'What will I do?'

'Whose child is it? Not Iida's?'

'I killed Iida before he could rape me. If it's true there is a child, it can only be Takeo's.'

'When?' Shizuka whispered.

'The night Iida died. Takeo came to my room. We both expected to die.'

Shizuka breathed out. 'I sometimes think he is touched by madness.'

'Not madness. Bewitchment, maybe,' Kaede said. 'It's as if we were both under a spell ever since we met in Tsuwano.'

'Well, my uncle and I are partly to blame for that. We should never have brought you together.'

'There was nothing you or anyone could have done to prevent it,' Kaede said. Despite herself a quiet intimation of joy stirred within her.

'If it were Iida's child, I would know what to do,' Shizuka said. 'I would not hesitate. There are things I can give you that will get rid of it. But Takeo's child is my own kin, my own blood.'

Kaede said nothing. *The child may inherit Takeo's gifts,* she was thinking. *Those gifts that make him valuable. Everyone wanted to use him for some purpose of their own. But I love him for himself alone. I will never get rid of his child. And I will never let the Tribe take it from me. But would Shizuka try? Would she so betray me?*

She was silent for so long Shizuka sat up to see if she had fallen asleep. But Kaede's eyes were open, staring at the green light beyond the doorway.

18

'How long will the sickness last?' Kaede said.

'Not long. And you will not show for three or four months.'

'You know about these things. You said you have two sons?'

'Yes. Arai's children.'

'Where are they?'

'With my grandparents. He does not know where they are.'

'Hasn't he acknowledged them?'

'He was interested enough in them until he married and had a son by his legal wife,' Shizuka said. 'Then, since my sons are older, he began to see them as a threat to his heir. I realized what he was thinking and took them away to a hidden village the Muto family have. He must never know where they are.'

Kaede shivered, despite the heat. 'You think he would harm them?'

'It would not be the first time a lord, a warrior, had done so,' Shizuka replied bitterly.

'I am afraid of my father,' Kaede said. 'What will he do to me?'

Shizuka whispered, 'Suppose Lord Shigeru, fearing Iida's treachery, insisted on a secret marriage at Terayama, the day we visited the temple. Your kinswoman, Lady Maruyama, and her companion, Sachie, were the witnesses, but they did not live.'

'I cannot lie to the world in that way,' Kaede began.

Shizuka hushed her. 'You do not need to say anything. It has all been hidden. You are following your late husband's wishes. I will let it be known, as if inadvertently. You'll see how these men can't keep a secret among themselves.'

'What about documents, proof?'

'They were lost when Inuyama fell, along with everything else. The child will be Shigeru's. If it is a boy, it will be the heir to the Otori.'

'That is too far in the future to think about,' Kaede said quickly. 'Don't tempt fate.' For Shigeru's real unborn child came into her mind, the one that had perished silently within its mother's body in the waters of the river at Inuyama. She prayed that its ghost would not be jealous, she prayed her own child would live.

Before the end of the week the sickness had eased a little. Kaede's breasts swelled, her nipples ached, and she became suddenly urgently hungry at unexpected times, but otherwise she began to feel well, better than she had ever felt in her life. Her senses were heightened almost as if the child shared its gifts with her. She noted with amazement how Shizuka's secret information spread through the men as, one by one, they began to address her as Lady Otori, in lowered voices and with averted eyes. The pretence made her uneasy, but she went along with it, not knowing what else to do.

She studied the men carefully, trying to discern which was the member of the Tribe who would protect Shizuka when the moment came. Shizuka had regained her cheerfulness and laughed and joked with them all equally, and they all responded with different emotions ranging from appreciation to desire, but not one of them seemed to be particularly vigilant.

Because they rarely looked at Kaede directly they would have been surprised at how well she came to know them. She could distinguish each of them in the dark by his tread or his voice, sometimes even by his smell. She gave them names: Scar, Squint, Silent, Long Arm.

Long Arm's smell was of the hot spiced oil that the men used to flavour their rice. His voice was low, roughly accented. He had a look about him that suggested insolence to her, a sort of irony that annoyed her. He was of medium build, with a high forehead and eyes that bulged a little and were so black he seemed to have no pupils. He had a habit of screwing them up, and then sniffing with a flick of his head. His arms were abnormally long, and his hands big. If anyone were going to murder a woman, Kaede thought, it would be him.

In the second week a sudden storm delayed them in a small village. Confined by the rain to the narrow, uncomfortable room, Kaede was restless. She was tormented by thoughts of her mother. When she sought her in her mind she met nothing but darkness. She tried to recall her face, but could not. Nor could she summon up her sisters' appearance. The youngest would be almost nine. If her mother, as she feared, was dead, she would have to take her place, be a mother to her sisters, run the household – overseeing the cooking, cleaning, weaving and sewing that were the year-round chores of women, taught to girls by their mothers and aunts and grandmothers. She knew nothing of such things. When she had been a hostage she had been neglected by the Noguchi family. They had taught her so little; all she had learned was how to survive on her own in the castle while she ran around like a maid, waiting on the armed men. Well, she would have to learn these practical skills. The child gave her feelings and instincts she had not known before: the instinct to take care of her people. She thought of the Shirakawa retainers, men like Shoji Kiyoshi and Amano Tenzo, who had come with her father when he had visited her at Noguchi castle, and the servants of the house like Ayame, whom she had missed almost as much as her mother when she had been taken away at seven years old. Was Ayame still alive? Would she still remember the girl she had looked after? Kaede was returning, ostensibly married and widowed, another man dead on her account, and she was pregnant. What would her welcome be at her parents' home?

The delay irritated the men too. She knew they were anxious to be done with this tiresome duty, impatient to return to the battles that were their real work, their life. They wanted to be part of Arai's victories over the Tohan in the East, not far away from the action in the West, looking after women.

Arai was only one of them, she thought wonderingly. How had he suddenly become so powerful? What did he have that made these men, each of them adult, physically strong, want to follow and obey him? She remembered again his swift ruthlessness when he had cut the throat of the guard who had attacked her in Noguchi castle. He would not hesitate to kill any one of these men in the same way. Yet it was not fear that made them obey him. Was it a sort of trust in that ruthlessness, in that willingness to act immediately, whether the act was right or wrong? Would they ever trust a woman in that way? Could she command men as he did? Would warriors like Shoji obey her?

The rain stopped and they moved on. The storm had cleared the last of the humidity and the days that followed were brilliant, the sky huge and blue above the mountain peaks where every day the maples showed more red. The nights grew cooler, already with a hint of the frost to come.

The journey wound on and the days became long and

tiring. Finally one morning Shizuka said, 'This is the last pass. Tomorrow we will be at Shirakawa.'

They were descending a steep path, so densely carpeted with pine needles the horses' feet made no noise. Shizuka was walking alongside Raku while Kaede rode. Beneath the pines and cedars it was dark, but a little ahead of them the sun slanted through a bamboo grove, casting a dappled, greenish light.

'Have you been on this road before?' Kaede asked.

'Many times. The first time was years ago. I was sent to Kumamoto to work for the Arai family when I was younger than you are now. The old lord was still alive then. He kept his sons under an iron rule, but the oldest, Daiichi is his given name, still found ways to take the maids to bed. I resisted him for a long time – it's not easy, as you know, for girls living in castles. I was determined he would not forget me as quickly as he forgot most of them. And naturally I was also under instructions from my family, the Muto.'

'So you were spying on him all that time,' Kaede murmured.

'Certain people were interested in the Arai allegiances. Particularly in Daiichi, before he went to the Noguchi.'

'Certain people meaning Iida?'

'Of course. It was part of the settlement with the Seishuu clan after Yaegahara. Arai was reluctant to serve Noguchi. He disliked Iida and thought Noguchi a traitor, but he was compelled to obey.'

'You worked for Iida?'

'You know who I work for,' Shizuka said quietly. 'Always in the first instance for the Muto family, for the Tribe. Iida employed many of the Muto at that time.'

'I'll never understand it,' Kaede said. The alliances of

her class were complex enough, with new ones being formed through marriage, old ones maintained by hostages, allegiances being broken by sudden insults or feuds or sheer opportunism. Yet these seemed straightforward compared with the intrigues of the Tribe. The unpleasant thought that Shizuka only stayed with her on orders from the Muto family came to her again.

'Are you spying on me?'

Shizuka made a sign with her hand to silence her. The men rode ahead and behind, out of earshot, Kaede thought.

'Are you?'

Shizuka put her hand on the horse's shoulder. Kaede looked down on the back of her head, the white nape of her neck beneath the dark hair. Her head was turned away so Kaede could not see her face. Shizuka kept pace with the horse as it stepped down the slope, swinging its haunches to keep its balance. Kaede leaned forwards and tried to speak quietly. 'Tell me.'

Then the horse startled and plunged suddenly. Kaede's forwards movement turned into a sudden downwards dive.

I'm going to fall, she thought in amazement, and the ground rushed up towards her as she and Shizuka fell together.

The horse was jumping sideways as it tried not to step on them. Kaede was aware of more confusion, a greater danger.

'Shizuka!' she cried.

'Keep down,' the girl replied, and pushed her to the ground, but Kaede struggled to look.

There were men on the path ahead, two of them, wild bandits by the look of them, with drawn swords. She felt for her knife, longed for a sword or a pole at least, remembered her promise, all in a split second before she heard the thrum of a bowstring. An arrow flew past the horse's ears, making it jump and buck again.

There was a brief cry and one man fell at her feet, blood streaming from where the arrow had pierced his neck.

The second man faltered for a moment. The horse plunged sideways, knocking him off balance. He swung his sword in a desperate sideways slice at Shizuka, then Long Arm was on him, coming up under the blow with almost supernatural speed, his sword's tip seeming to find its own way into the man's throat.

The men in front turned and ran back, those behind came milling forward. Shizuka had caught the horse by the bridle and was calming it.

Long Arm helped Kaede to her feet. 'Don't be alarmed, Lady Otori,' he said, in his rough accent, the smell of pepper oil strong on his breath. 'They were just brigands.'

Just brigands? Kaede thought. They had died so suddenly and with so much blood. *Brigands, maybe, but in whose pay?*

The men took their weapons and drew lots for them, then threw the bodies into the undergrowth. It was impossible to tell if any one of them had anticipated the attack, or was disappointed in its failure. They seemed to show more deference to Long Arm, and she realized they were impressed by the swiftness of his reaction and his fighting skills, but otherwise they acted as if it was a normal occurrence, one of the hazards of travel. One or two of them joked with Shizuka that the bandits wanted her as a wife, and she answered in the same vein, adding that the forest was full of such desperate men, but even a bandit had more chance with her than any of the escort.

'I would never have picked your defender,' Kaede said later. 'In fact, quite the opposite. He was the one I suspected would kill you with those big hands of his.'

Shizuka laughed. 'He's quite a clever fellow, and a ruthless fighter. It's easy to misjudge or underestimate him. You were not the only person surprised by him. Were you afraid at that moment?'

Kaede tried to remember. 'No, mainly because there was no time. I wished I had a sword.'

Shizuka said, 'You have the gift of courage.'

'It's not true. I am often afraid.'

'No one would ever guess,' Shizuka murmured. They had come to an inn in a small town on the border of the Shirakawa domain. Kaede had been able to bathe in the hot spring, and she was now in her night attire waiting for the evening meal to be brought. Her welcome at the inn had been perfunctory, and the town itself made her uneasy. There seemed to be little food, and the people were sullen and dispirited.

She was bruised down one side from the fall, and she feared for the child. She was also nervous about meeting her father. Would he believe she had married Lord Otori? She could not imagine his fury if he discovered the truth.

'I don't feel very brave at the moment,' she confessed.

Shizuka said, 'I'll massage your head. You look exhausted.'

But even as she leaned back and enjoyed the feeling of the girl's fingers against her scalp, Kaede's misgivings increased. She remembered what they had been talking about at the moment of the attack.

'You will be home tomorrow,' Shizuka said, feeling her tension, 'The journey is nearly over.'

'Shizuka, answer me truthfully. What's the real reason you stay with me? Is it to spy on me? Who employs the Muto now?'

'No one employs us at the moment. Iida's downfall has thrown the whole of the Three Countries into confusion. Arai is saying he will wipe out the Tribe. We don't know yet if he is serious or if he will come to his senses and work with us. In the meantime my uncle, Kenji, who admires Lady Shirakawa greatly, wants to be kept informed of her welfare and her intentions.'

And of my child, Kaede thought, but did not speak it. Instead she asked, 'My intentions?'

'You are heir to one of the richest and most powerful domains in the West, Maruyama, as well as to your own estate of Shirakawa. Whoever you marry will become a key player in the future of the Three Countries. At the moment everyone assumes you will maintain the alliance with Arai, strengthening his position in the West while he settles the Otori question: your destiny is closely linked with the Otori clan and with the Middle Country too.'

'I may marry no one,' Kaede said, half to herself. *And in that case*, she was thinking, *why should I not become a key player myself?*

Three

The sounds of the temple at Terayama, the midnight bell, the chanting of the monks, faded from my hearing, as I followed the two masters, Kikuta Kotaro and Muto Kenji, down a lonely path, steep and overgrown, alongside the stream. We went swiftly, the noise of the tumbling water hiding our footsteps. We said little and we saw no one.

By the time we came to Yamagata it was nearly dawn and the first cocks were crowing. The streets of the town were deserted, though the curfew was lifted and the Tohan were no longer there to patrol them. We came to a merchant's house in the middle of the town, not far from the inn where we had stayed during the Festival of the Dead. I already knew the street from when I had explored the town at night. It seemed a lifetime ago.

Kenji's daughter, Yuki, opened the gate as though she had been waiting for us all night, even though we came so silently that not a dog barked. She said nothing, but I caught the intensity in the look she gave me. Her face, her vivid eyes, her graceful muscular body, brought back all too clearly the terrible events at Inuyama the night Shigeru died. I had half-expected to see her at Terayama for it was she who had travelled day and night to take Shigeru's head to the temple and break the news of his death. There were many things I would have liked to have questioned her about: her journey, the uprising at Yamagata, the overthrow of the Tohan. As her father and the Kikuta master went ahead into the house, I lingered a little so that she and I stepped up onto the veranda together. A low light was burning by the doorway.

She said, 'I did not expect to see you alive again.'

'I did not expect to live.' Remembering her skill and her ruthlessness, I added, 'I owe you a huge debt. I can never repay you.'

She smiled. 'I was repaying debts of my own. You owe me nothing. But I hope we will be friends.'

The word did not seem strong enough to describe what we already were. She had brought Shigeru's sword, Jato, to me and had helped me in his rescue and revenge: the most important and most desperate acts of my life. I was filled with gratitude for her, mingled with admiration.

She disappeared for a moment and came back with water. I washed my feet, listening to the two masters talking within the house. They planned to rest for a few hours, then I would travel on with Kotaro. I shook my head wearily. I was tired of listening.

'Come,' she said, and led me into the centre of the house where, as in Inuyama, there was a concealed room as narrow as an eel's bed.

'Am I a prisoner again?' I said, looking around at the windowless walls.

'No, it's only for your own safety, to rest for a few hours. Then you will travel on.'

'I know; I heard.'

'Of course,' she said, 'I forget you hear everything.'

'Too much,' I said, sitting down on the mattress that was already spread out on the floor.

'Gifts are hard. But it's better to have them than not. I'll get you some food, and tea is ready.'

She came back in a few moments. I drank the tea but could not face food. 'There's no hot water for bathing,' she said. 'I'm sorry.'

'I'll live.' Twice already she had bathed me, once here in Yamagata when I did not know who she was and she had scrubbed my back and massaged my temples, and then again in Inuyama when I could barely walk. The memory came flooding over me. Her gaze met mine, and I knew she was thinking of the same thing. Then she looked away and said quietly, 'I'll leave you to sleep.'

I placed my knife close to the mattress and slid beneath the quilt without bothering to undress. I thought of what Yuki had said, about gifts. I did not think I would ever be as happy again as I had been in the village where I was born, Mino – but in Mino I was a child, and now the village was destroyed, my family all dead. I knew I must not dwell on the past. I had agreed to come to the Tribe. It was because of my gifts that they wanted me so badly, and it was only with the Tribe that I would learn to develop and control the skills I had been given.

I thought of Kaede whom I had left sleeping at Terayama. Hopelessness came over me, followed by resignation. I would never see her again. I would have to forget her. Slowly the town started to wake around me. Finally, as the light brightened beyond the doors, I slept.

I woke suddenly to the sound of men and horses in the street beyond the walls of the house. The light in the room had changed, as though the sun had crossed above the roof, but I had no idea how long I'd slept. A man was shouting and in reply a woman was complaining, growing angry. I caught the gist of the words. The men were Arai's, going from house to house, looking for me.

I pushed back the quilt and felt for the knife. As I picked it up, the door slid open, and Kenji came silently into the room. The false wall was locked into place behind him. He looked at me briefly, shook his head and sat down cross-legged on the floor in the tiny space between the mattress and the wall.

I recognized the voices – the men had been at Terayama with Arai. I heard Yuki calming the angry woman down, offering the men a drink.

'We're all on the same side now,' she said, and laughed. 'Do you think if Otori Takeo were here we'd be able to hide him?'

The men drank quickly and left. As their footsteps died away Kenji snorted through his nose and gave me one of his disparaging looks. 'No one can pretend not to have heard of you in Yamagata,' he said. 'Shigeru's death made him a god, Iida's has turned you into a hero. It's a story the people are wild about.' He sniffed and added, 'Don't let it go to your head. It's extremely annoying. Now Arai's mounted a full-scale search for you. He's taking your disappearance as a personal insult. Luckily your face is not too well known here, but we'll have to disguise you.' He studied my features, frowning. 'That Otori look . . . you'll have to conceal it.'

He was interrupted by a sound outside, as the wall was lifted away. Kikuta Kotaro came in followed by Akio, the young man who had been one of my captors in Inuyama. Yuki stepped after them, bringing tea.

The Kikuta master gave me a nod as I bowed to him. 'Akio has been out in the town, listening to the news.'

Akio dropped to his knees before Kenji, and inclined

31

his head slightly to me. I responded in the same way. When he and the other Tribe members had kidnapped me in Inuyama, they had been doing their best to restrain me without hurting me. I had been fighting in earnest. I had wanted to kill him. I had cut him. I could see now that his left hand still bore a half-healed scar, red and inflamed. We had hardly spoken before – he had reprimanded me for my lack of manners and had accused me of breaking every rule of the Tribe. There had been little goodwill between us. Now when our eyes met I felt his deep hostility.

'It seems Lord Arai is furious that this person left without permission, and refused a marriage that the lord desired. Lord Arai has issued orders for this person's arrest, and he intends to investigate the organization known as the Tribe, which he considers illegal and un-desirable.' He bowed again to Kotaro and said stiffly, 'I'm sorry, but I do not know what this person's name is to be.'

The master nodded and stroked his chin, saying nothing. We had talked about names before and he had told me to continue using Takeo, though, as he'd said, it had never been a Tribe name. Was I to take the family name of Kikuta now? And what would my given name be? I did not want to give up Takeo, the name Shigeru had given me, but if I was no longer to be one of the Otori, what right did I have to it?

'Arai is offering rewards for information,' Yuki said, placing a bowl of tea on the matting in front of each of us.

'No one in Yamagata will dare to volunteer information,' Akio said. 'They'll be dealt with if they do!'

'It's what I was afraid of,' Kotaro said to Kenji. 'Arai

has had no real dealings with us, and now he fears our power.'

'Should we eliminate him?' Akio said eagerly. 'We . . .'

Kotaro made a movement with his hand, and the young man bowed again, and fell silent.

'With Iida gone there is already a lack of stability. If Arai should perish too, who knows what anarchy would break out?'

Kenji said, 'I don't see Arai as any great danger. Threats and bluster, perhaps, but no more than that in the long run. As things have turned out now, he is our best hope for peace.' He glanced at me. 'That's what we desire above all. We need some degree of order for our work to flourish.'

'Arai will return to Inuyama and make that his capital,' Yuki said. 'It is easier to defend and more central than Kumamoto, and he has claimed all Iida's lands by right of conquest.'

'Unh,' Kotaro grunted. He turned to me. 'I had planned for you to return to Inuyama with me. I have matters to attend to there for the next few weeks, and you would have begun your training there. However, it may be better if you remain here for a few days. We will then take you north, beyond the Middle Country, to another of the Kikuta houses, where no one has heard of Otori Takeo, where you will start a new life. Do you know how to juggle?'

I shook my head.

'You have a week to learn. Akio will teach you. Yuki and some of the other actors will accompany you. I will meet you in Matsue.'

I bowed, saying nothing. I looked from under my lowered eyelids at Akio. He was staring downwards, frowning, the line deep between his eyes. He was only three or four years older than me but at that moment it was possible to see what he would be like as an old man. So he was a juggler. I was sorry I had cut his clever juggler's hand, but I thought my actions perfectly justified. Still, the fight lay between us, along with other feelings, unresolved, festering.

Kotaro said, 'Kenji, your association with Lord Shigeru has singled you out in this affair. Too many people know that this is your main place of residence. Arai will certainly have you arrested if you stay here.'

'I'll go to the mountains for a while,' Kenji replied. 'Visit the old people, spend some time with the children.' He smiled, looking like my harmless old teacher again.

'Excuse me, but what is this person to be called?' Akio said.

'He can take a name as an actor for the time being,' Kotaro said. 'What his Tribe name is, depends . . .'

There was some meaning behind his words that I did not understand but Akio all too clearly did. 'His father renounced the Tribe!' he burst out. 'He turned his back on us.'

'But his son has returned, with all the gifts of the Kikuta,' the master replied. 'However, for now, in everything, you are his senior. Takeo, you will submit to Akio and learn from him.'

A smile played on his lips. I think he knew how hard that would be for me. Kenji's face was rueful, as if he also could foresee trouble.

'Akio has many skills,' Kotaro went on. 'You are to master them.' He waited for my acceptance, then told Akio and Yuki to leave. Yuki refilled the tea bowls before she left, and the two older men drank noisily. I could smell food cooking. It seemed like days since I'd last eaten. I was sorry I had not accepted Yuki's offer of food the previous night; I was faint with hunger.

Kotaro said, 'I told you I was first cousin to your father. I did not tell you that he was older than me, and would have become master at our grandfather's death. Akio is my nephew and my heir. Your return raises questions of inheritance and seniority. How we deal with them depends on your conduct in the next few months.'

It took me a couple of moments to grasp his meaning. 'Akio was brought up in the Tribe,' I said slowly. 'He knows everything I don't know. There must be many others like that. I've no wish to take his or anyone else's place.'

'There are many,' Kotaro replied, 'and all of them more obedient, better trained and more deserving than you. But none has the Kikuta gift of hearing to the extent that you have it and no one else could have gone alone into Yamagata castle as you did.'

That episode seemed like something from a past life. I could hardly remember the impulse that had driven me to climb into the castle and release into death the Hidden who were encaged in baskets and hung from the castle walls: the first time I had killed. I wished I had never done it – if I had not drawn the Tribe's attention to myself so dramatically maybe they would not have taken me before ... before ... I shook myself. There was no point in endlessly trying to unravel the threads that had woven Shigeru's death.

'However, now I've said that,' Kotaro continued, 'you must know that I cannot treat you in any way differently from the others of your generation. I cannot have favourites. Whatever your skills, they are useless to us unless we also have your obedience. I don't have to remind you that you have already pledged this to me. You will stay here for a week. You must not go outside or let anyone know you are here. In that week you must learn enough to pass as a juggler. I will meet you at Matsue before winter. It's up to you to go through the training with complete obedience.'

'Who knows when I will meet you again?' Kenji said, regarding me with his usual mixture of affection and exasperation. 'My work with you is done,' he went on. 'I found you, taught you, kept you alive somehow and brought you back to the Tribe. You'll find Akio tougher than I was.' He grinned, showing the gaps between his teeth. 'But Yuki will look after you.'

There was something in the way he said it that made the colour rise in my face. We had done nothing, had not even touched each other, but something existed between us and Kenji was aware of it.

Both masters were grinning as they stood up and embraced me. Kenji gave me a cuff round the head. 'Do as you're told,' he said. 'And learn to juggle.'

I wished Kenji and I could have spoken alone. There was so much still unresolved between us. Yet maybe it was better that he should bid me farewell as though he truly were an affectionate teacher whom I had outgrown. Besides, as I was to learn, the Tribe do not waste time on the past and do not like to be confronted with it.

After they'd left, the room seemed gloomier than ever, airless and stuffy. I could hear through the house the sounds of their departure. Not for them the elaborate preparations, the long goodbyes of most travellers. Kenji and Kotaro just walked out of the door, carrying everything they needed for the road in their hands – light

36

bundles in wrapping cloths, a spare pair of sandals, some rice cakes flavoured with salted plums. I thought about them and the roads they must have walked, tracing and retracing their way across the Three Countries, and beyond for all I knew, following the vast web the Tribe spun from village to village, town to town. Wherever they went they would find relatives; they would never be without shelter or protection.

I heard Yuki say she would walk with them to the bridge and heard the woman who'd been angry with the soldiers reply.

'Take care of yourselves,' the woman called after them. The footsteps faded down the street.

The room seemed even more depressing and lonely. I couldn't imagine being confined in it for a week. Almost without realizing what I was doing, I was already planning to get out. Not to escape. I was quite resigned to staying with the Tribe. Just to get out. Partly to look at Yamagata again by night, partly to see if I could.

Not long after, I heard someone approaching. The door slid back and a woman stepped in. She was carrying a tray of food: rice, pickles, a small piece of dried fish, a bowl of soup. She knelt, placing the tray on the floor.

'Here, eat, you must be hungry.'

I was famished. The smell of the food made me dizzy. I fell on it like a wolf. She sat and watched me while I ate.

'So you're the one who's been causing my poor old husband so much trouble,' she remarked as I was polishing the bowl for the last grains of rice.

Kenji's wife. I shot a look at her and met her gaze. Her face was smooth, as pale as his, with the similarity that many long-married couples attain. Her hair was still thick and black, with just a few white hairs appearing at the centre of her scalp. She was thickset and solid, a true townswoman, with square, short-fingered capable hands. The only thing I could remember Kenji saying about her was that she was a good cook, and indeed the food was delicious.

I told her so, and as the smile moved from her lips to her eyes I saw in an instant that she was Yuki's mother. Their eyes were the same shape and when she smiled the expression was the same.

'Who'd have thought that you'd have turned up after all these years,' she went on, sounding garrulous and motherly. 'I knew Isamu, your father, well. And no one knew anything about you until that incident with Shintaro. Imagine you hearing and outwitting the most dangerous assassin in the Three Countries! The Kikuta family were delighted to discover Isamu had left a son. We all were. And one with such talents too!'

I didn't reply. She seemed a harmless old woman – but then Kenji had appeared a harmless old man. I felt in myself a faint echo of the mistrust I'd had when I first saw Kenji in the street in Hagi. I tried to study her without appearing to, and she stared openly at me. I felt she was challenging me in some way, but I had no intention of responding until I'd found out more about her and her skills.

'Who killed my father?' I said instead.

'No one's ever found out. It was years before we even knew for certain that he was dead. He'd found an isolated place to hide himself in.'

'Was it someone from the Tribe?'

That made her laugh, which angered me. 'Kenji said you trusted no one. It's good, but you can trust me.'

'Like I could trust him,' I muttered.

'Shigeru's scheme would have killed you,' she said mildly. 'It's important for the Kikuta, for the whole Tribe, to keep you alive. It's so rare these days to find such a wealth of talent.'

I grunted at that, trying to discern some hidden meaning beneath her flattery. She poured tea, and I drank it at a gulp. My head ached from the stuffy room.

'You're tense,' she said, taking the bowl from my hands, and placing it on the tray. She moved the tray to one side, and came closer to me. Kneeling behind me she began to massage my neck and shoulders. Her fingers were strong, pliant and sensitive all at the same time. She worked over my back, and then, saying, 'Close your eyes,' began on my head. The sensation was exquisite. I almost groaned aloud. Her hands seemed to have a life of their own. I gave my head to them, feeling as though it were floating off my neck.

Then I heard the door slide. My eyes snapped open. I could still feel her fingers in my scalp, but I was alone in the room. A shiver ran down my spine. Kenji's wife might look harmless but her powers were probably as great as her husband's or her daughter's.

She'd also taken away my knife.

I was given the name of Minoru, but hardly anyone called me by it. When we were alone Yuki occasionally called me Takeo, letting the word form in her mouth as if she were granting herself a gift. Akio only said 'you', and always in the form used when addressing inferiors. He was entitled to. He was my senior in years, training and knowledge, and I'd been ordered to submit to him. It rankled though; I hadn't realized how much I had become accustomed to being treated with respect as an Otori warrior and Shigeru's heir.

My training began that afternoon. I had not known that the muscles in my hands could ache so much. My right wrist was still weak from my first fight with Akio. By the end of the day it was throbbing again. We started with exercises to make the fingers deft and supple. Even with his damaged hand Akio was far faster and far more dexterous than me. We sat opposite each other and time and again he rapped my hands before I could move them.

He was so quick; I could not believe that I could not even see the movement. At first the rap was no more than a light tap, but as the afternoon turned to evening and we both grew tired and frustrated by my clumsiness, he began to hit me in earnest.

Yuki, who had come into the room to join us, said quietly, 'If you bruise his hands it will take longer.'

'Maybe I should bruise his head,' Akio muttered, and the next time, before I could move my hands away, he seized both of them in his right hand, and with his left, hit me on the cheek. It was a real blow, strong enough to make my eyes water.

'Not so bold without a knife,' he said, releasing my hands and holding his own ready again.

Yuki said nothing. I could feel anger simmering inside me. It was outrageous to me that he should hit an Otori lord. The confined room, the deliberate teasing, Yuki's indifference all combined to drive me towards loss of control. The next time Akio made the same move with opposite hands. The blow was even harder, making my neck snap back. My sight went black, then red. I felt the rage erupt just as it had with Kenji. I hurled myself at him.

It's been many years since I was seventeen, since the

40

fury seized me and threw me beyond self-control. But I still recall the way the release felt, as though my animal self had been unleashed, and then I'd have no memory of what happened after that, just the blind feeling of not caring if I lived or died, of refusing to be forced or bullied any longer.

After the first moment of surprise, when I had my hands round Akio's throat, the two of them restrained me easily. Yuki did her trick of pressing into my neck and, as I began to black out, she hit me harder than I would have thought possible in the stomach. I doubled over, retching. Akio slid out from beneath me and pinioned my arms behind my back.

We sat on the matting, as close as lovers, breathing heavily. The whole episode had lasted no more than a minute. I couldn't believe Yuki had hit me so hard. I'd thought she would have been on my side. I stared at her with rancour in my heart.

'That's what you have to learn to control,' she said calmly.

Akio released my arms and knelt in readiness. 'Let's start again.'

'Don't hit me in the face,' I said.

'Yuki's right, it's best not to bruise your hands,' he replied. 'So be quicker.'

I vowed inwardly I would not let him hit me again. The next time, though I did not get close to rapping him, I moved head and hands away before he could touch me. Watching him I began to sense the slightest intimation of movement. I finally managed to graze the surface of his knuckles. He said nothing, nodded as if satisfied, but barely, and we moved on to working with juggling balls.

So the hours went: passing the ball from one palm to

the other, from palm to mat to palm. By the end of the second day I could juggle three balls in the ancient style, by the end of the third day, four. Akio still sometimes managed to catch me off-guard and slap me, but mostly I learned to avoid it, in an elaborate dance of balls and hands.

By the end of the fourth day I was seeing balls behind my eyelids, and I was bored and restless beyond words. Some people, and I guessed Akio was one, work persistently at these skills because they are obsessed by them and by their desire to master them. I quickly realized I was not among them. I couldn't see the point to juggling. It didn't interest me. I was learning in the hardest of ways and for the worst of reasons – because I would be beaten if I did not. I submitted to Akio's harsh teaching because I had to, but I hated it, and I hated him. Twice more his goading led to the same outburst of fury but just as I was learning to anticipate him, so he and Yuki came to know the signs, and were ready to restrain me before anyone got hurt.

That fourth night, once the house was silent and everyone slept, I decided to go exploring. I was bored, I could not sleep, I was longing to breathe some fresh air, but above all I wanted to see if I could. For obedience to the Tribe to make sense, I had to find out if I could be disobedient. Forced obedience seemed to have as little point as juggling. They might as well tie me up day and night like a dog, and I would growl and bite on command.

I knew the layout of the house. I had mapped it when I had nothing else to do but listen. I knew where everyone slept at night. Yuki and her mother were in a room at the back of the building, with two other women whom I had not seen, though I had heard them. One served in the shop, joking loudly with the customers in the local accent.

Yuki addressed her as 'Aunty'. The other was more of a servant. She did the cleaning and most of the food preparation, always first up in the morning and the last to lie down at night. She spoke very little, in a low voice with a northern accent. Her name was Sadako. Everyone in the household bullied her cheerfully and took advantage of her; her replies were always quiet and deferential. I felt I knew these women, though I'd never set eyes on either of them.

Akio and the other men, three of them, slept in a loft in the roof space above the shop. Every night they took it in turns to join the guards at the back of the house. Akio had done it the night before, and I'd suffered for it, as sleeplessness added an extra edge to his teasing. Before the maid went to bed, while the lamps were still lit, I would hear one or other of the men help her close the doors and the outer shutters, the wooden panels sliding into place with a series of dull thumps that invariably set the dogs barking.

There were three dogs, each with its own distinctive voice. The same man fed them every night, whistling to them through his teeth in a particular way that I practised when I was alone, thankful that no one else had the Kikuta gift of hearing.

The front doors of the house were barred at night, and the rear gates guarded, but one smaller door was left unbarred. It led into a narrow space between the house and the outer wall, at the end of which was the privy. I was escorted there three or four times a day. I'd been out in the yard after dark a couple of times, to bathe in the small bath house which stood in the back yard, between the end of the house and the gates. Though I was kept hidden, it was, as Yuki said, for my own safety. As far as

43

I could tell, no one seriously expected me to try and escape: I was not under guard.

I lay for a long time, listening to the sounds of the house. I could hear the breathing of the women in the downstairs room, the men in the loft. Beyond the walls the town gradually quietened. I had gone into a state I recognized. I could not explain it, but it was as familiar to me as my own skin. I did not feel either fear or excitement. My brain switched off. I was all instinct, instinct and ears. Time altered and slowed. It did not matter how long it took to open the door of the concealed room. I knew I would do it eventually, and I would do it soundlessly. Just as I would get to the outer door silently.

I was standing by this outer door, aware of every noise around me, when I heard footsteps. Kenji's wife got up, crossed the room where she'd been sleeping and went towards the concealed room. The door slid, a few seconds passed. She came out of the room and, a lamp in her hand, walked swiftly but not anxiously towards me. Briefly I thought of going invisible, but I knew there was no point. She would almost certainly be able to discern me, and if she couldn't she would raise the household.

Saying nothing I jerked my head in the direction of the door that led to the privy and went back to the hidden room. As I passed her I was aware of her eyes on me. She didn't say anything either, just nodded at me, but I felt she knew I was trying to get out.

The room was stuffier than ever. Sleep now seemed impossible. I was still deep within my state of silent instinct. I tried to discern her breathing, but could not hear it. Finally I convinced myself that she must be asleep again. I got up, slowly opened the door, and stepped out into the room. The lamp still burned. Kenji's wife sat there next to it. Her eyes were closed, but she opened them and saw me standing in front of her.

'Going to piss again?' she said in her deep voice.

'I can't sleep.'

'Sit down. I'll make some tea.' She got to her feet in one movement – despite her age and size she was as lithe as a girl. She put her hand on my shoulder and pushed me gently down onto the matting.

'Don't run away!' she warned, mockery in her voice.

I sat, but I was not really thinking. I was still bent on getting outside. I heard the kettle hiss as she blew on the embers, heard the chink of iron and pottery. She came back with the tea, knelt to pour it, and handed me a bowl, which I leaned forward to take. The light glowed between us. As I took the bowl I looked into her eyes, saw the amusement and mockery in them, saw that she had been flattering me before: she did not really believe in my talents. Then her eyelids flickered and closed. I dropped the bowl, caught her as she swayed and set her down, already deeply asleep, on the matting. In the lamplight the spilled tea steamed.

I should have been horrified, but I wasn't. I just felt the cold satisfaction that the skills of the Tribe bring with them. I was sorry that I hadn't thought of this before, but it had never occurred to me that I would have any power at all over the wife of the Muto master. I was mainly relieved that now nothing was going to stop me getting outside.

As I slipped through the side door into the yard I heard the dogs stir. I whistled to them, high and quiet so only they and I would hear. One came padding up to investigate me, tail wagging. In the way of all dogs, he liked me. I put out my hand. He laid his head on it. The moon was low in the sky, but it gave enough light to make his eyes shine yellow. We stared at each other for a few moments, then he yawned, showing his big white teeth, lay down at my feet and slept.

Inside my head the thought niggled, *A dog is one thing, the Muto master's wife is quite another*, but I chose not to listen. I crouched down and stroked the dog's head a couple of times while I looked at the wall.

Of course, I had neither weapons nor tools. The overhang of the wall's roof was wide and so pitched that, without grapples, it was impossible to get a handhold. In the end I climbed onto the roof of the bath house and jumped across. I went invisible, crept along the top of the wall away from the rear gate and the guards, and dropped into the street just before the corner. I stood against the wall for a few moments, listening. I heard the murmur of voices from the guards. The dogs were silent and the whole town seemed to sleep.

As I had done before, the night I climbed into Yamagata castle, I worked my way from street to street, heading in a zigzag direction towards the river. The willow trees still stood beneath the setting moon. The branches moved gently in the autumn wind, the leaves already yellow, one or two floating down into the water.

I crouched in their shelter. I had no idea who controlled this town now: the lord whom Shigeru had visited, Iida's ally, had been overthrown along with the Tohan when the town erupted at the news of Shigeru's death, but presumably Arai had installed some kind of interim governor. I could not hear any sound of patrols. I stared at the castle, unable to make out if the heads of the Hidden whom I had released from torture into death had been removed or not. I could hardly believe my own memory:

it was as if I had dreamed it, or been told the story of someone else who had done it.

I was thinking about that night and how I had swum beneath the surface of the river when I heard footsteps approaching along the bank: the ground was soft and damp and the footfall was muffled, but whoever it was, was quite close. I should have left then but I was curious to see who would come to the river at this time of night, and I knew he would not see me.

He was a man of less than average height and very slight: in the darkness I could make out nothing else. He looked around furtively, and then knelt at the water's edge, as if he were praying. The wind blew off the river, bringing the tang of water and mud, and along with it the man's own smell.

His scent was somehow familiar. I sniffed the air like a dog, trying to place it. After a moment or two it came to me: it was the smell of the tannery. This man must be a leather worker, therefore an outcaste. I knew then who he was: the man who had spoken to me after I had climbed into the castle. His brother had been one of the tortured Hidden to whom I had brought the release of death. I had used my second self on the river bank and this man had thought he had seen an angel and had spread the rumour of the Angel of Yamagata. I could guess why he was there praying. He must also be from the Hidden, maybe hoping to see the angel again. I remembered how the first time I saw him I had thought I had to kill him, but had not been able to bring myself to do so. I gazed on him now with the troubled affection you have for someone whose life you have spared.

I felt something else too, a pang of loss and regret for the certainties of my childhood, for the words and rituals that had comforted me then, seeming as eternal as the turn of the seasons and the passage of the moon and the stars in the sky. I had been plucked from my life among the Hidden when Shigeru had saved me at Mino. Since then I had kept my origins concealed, never speaking of them to anyone, never praying openly. But sometimes at night I still prayed after the manner of the faith I was raised in, to the secret god that my mother worshipped, and now I felt a yearning to approach this man and talk to him.

As an Otori lord, even as a member of the Tribe, I should have shunned a leather worker, for they slaughter animals and are considered unclean, but the Hidden believe all men are created equal by the secret god, and so I had been taught by my mother. Still, some vestige of caution kept me out of sight beneath the willow, though as I heard his whispered prayer I found my tongue repeating the words along with him.

I would have left it like that – I was not a complete fool even though that night I was behaving like one – if I had not caught the sound of men approaching over the nearest bridge. It was a patrol of some sort, probably Arai's men, though I had no way of knowing for sure. They must have stopped on the bridge and gazed down the river.

'There's that lunatic,' I heard one say, 'Makes me sick having to see him there night after night.' His accent was local, but the next man who spoke sounded as if he came from the West.

'Give him a beating, he'll soon give up coming.'
'We've done that. Makes no difference.'
'Comes back for more, does he?'
'Let's lock him up for a few nights.'

'Let's just chuck him in the river.'

They laughed. I heard their footsteps grow louder as they began to run, and then fade a little as they passed behind a row of houses. They were still some way off; the man on the bank had heard nothing. I was not going to stand by and watch while the guards threw my man into the river. My man: he already belonged to me.

I slipped out from beneath the branches of the willow and ran towards him. I tapped him on the shoulder and, when he turned, I hissed at him, 'Come, hide quickly!'

He recognized me at once and with a great gasp of amazement, threw himself at my feet, praying incoherently. In the distance I could hear the patrol approaching down the street that ran along the river. I shook the man, lifted his head, put my finger to my lips and, trying to remember not to look him in the eye, pulled him into the shelter of the willows.

I should leave him here, I thought. *I can go invisible and avoid the patrol,* but then I heard them tramping around the corner and realized I was too late.

The breeze ruffled the water and set the willow leaves quivering. In the distance a cock crowed, a temple bell sounded.

'Gone!' a voice exclaimed, not ten paces from us.

Another man swore, 'Filthy outcastes.'

'Which is worse, do you reckon, outcastes or Hidden?'

'Some are both! That's the worst.'

I heard the slicing sigh of a sword being drawn. One of the soldiers slashed at a clump of reeds and then at the willow itself. The man next to me tensed. He was trembling but he made no sound. The smell of tanned leather was so strong in my nostrils I was sure the guards would catch it, but the rank smell of the river must have masked it.

I was thinking I might attract their attention away from the outcaste, split my self and somehow evade them, when a pair of ducks, sleeping in the reeds, suddenly flew off quacking loudly, skimming the surface of the water and shattering the quiet of the night. The men shouted in surprise, then jeered at each other. They joked and grumbled for a little longer, threw stones at the ducks, then left in the opposite direction to the one they'd come from. I heard their footsteps echo through the town, fading until even I could hear them no more. I began to scold the man.

'What are you doing out at this time of night? They'd have thrown you in the river if they'd found you.'

He bent his head to my feet again.

'Sit up,' I urged him. 'Speak to me.'

He sat, glanced briefly upwards at my face, and then dropped his eyes. 'I come every night I can,' he muttered. 'I've been praying to God for one more sight of you. I can never forget what you did for my brother, for the rest of them.' He was silent for a moment, then whispered, 'I thought you were an angel. But people say you are Lord Otori's son. You killed Lord Iida in revenge for his death. Now we have a new lord, Arai Daiichi from Kumamoto. His men have been combing the town for you. I thought they must know you were here. So I came tonight again to see you. Whatever form you choose to come in you must be one of God's angels to do what you did.'

It was a shock to hear my story repeated by this man. It brought home to me the danger I was in. 'Go home. Tell no one you saw me.' I prepared to leave.

He did not seem to hear me. He was in an almost

exalted state, his eyes glittering, flecks of spittle shimmering on his lips. 'Stay, lord,' he urged me. 'Every night I bring food for you, food and wine. We must share them together, then you must bless me and I will die happy.'

He took up a small bundle. Unwrapping the food and placing it on the ground between us he began to say the first prayer of the Hidden. The familiar words made my neck tingle and when he'd finished I responded quietly with the second prayer. Together we made the sign over the food and over ourselves, and I began to eat.

The meal was pitifully sparse, a millet cake with a trace of smoked fish skin buried in it, but it had all the elements of the rituals of my childhood. The outcaste brought out a small flask and poured from it into a wooden bowl. It was some home-brewed liquor, far rougher than wine, and we had no more than a mouthful each, but the smell reminded me of my home. I felt my mother's presence strongly and tears pricked my eyelids.

'Are you a priest?' I whispered, wondering how he had escaped the Tohan persecution.

'My brother was our priest. The one you released in mercy. Since his death I do what I can for our people – those who are left.'

'Did many die under Iida?'

'In the East, hundreds. My parents fled here many years ago, and under the Otori there was no persecution. But in the ten years since Yaegahara no one has been safe here. Now we have a new overlord, Arai: no one knows which way he will jump. They say he has other fish to gut. We may be left alone while he deals with the Tribe.' His voice dropped to a whisper at this last word, as though just to utter it was to invite retribution. 'And that would only be justice,' he went on, 'For it's they who are the murderers and the assassins. Our people are harmless. We are forbidden to kill.' He shot me an apologetic look. 'Of course, lord, your case was different.'

He had no idea how different, or how far I had gone from my mother's teaching. Dogs were barking in the distance, roosters announced the coming day. I had to go, yet I was reluctant to leave.

'You're not afraid?' I asked him.

'Often I am terrified. I don't have the gift of courage. But my life is in God's hands. He has some plan for me. He sent you to us.'

'I am not an angel,' I said.

'How else would one of the Otori know our prayers?' he replied. 'Who but an angel would share food with someone like me?'

I knew the risk I was taking but I told him anyway. 'Lord Shigeru rescued me from Iida at Mino.'

I did not have to spell it out. He was silent for a moment as if awed. Then he whispered, 'Mino? We thought no one survived from there. How strange are the ways of God. You have been spared for some great purpose. If you are not an angel, you are marked by the Secret One.'

I shook my head. 'I am the least of beings. My life is not my own. Fate, that led me away from my own people, has now led me away from the Otori.' I did not want to tell him I had become one of the Tribe.

'You need help?' he said. 'We will always help you. Come to us at the outcastes' bridge.'

'Where is that?'

'Where we tan the hides, between Yamagata and Tsuwano. Ask for Jo-An.' He then said the third prayer, giving thanks for the food.

'I must go,' I said.

'First would you give me a blessing, lord?'

I placed my right hand on his head, and began the prayer my mother used to say to me. I felt uncomfortable, knowing I had little right to speak these words, but they came easily off my tongue. Jo-An took my hand and touched his forehead and lips to my fingers. I realized then how deeply he trusted me. He released my hand and bowed his head to the ground. When he raised it again I was on the far side of the street. The sky was paling, the dawn air cool.

I slipped back from doorway to doorway. The temple bell rang out. The town was stirring: the first of the shutters were taken down, and the smell of smoke from kitchen fires wafted through the streets. I had stayed far too long with Jo-An. I had not used my second self all night, but I felt split in half, as if I had left my true self permanently beneath the willow tree with him. The self that was returning to the Tribe was hollow.

When I came to the Muto house the nagging thought that had been at the back of my mind all night surfaced. How was I going to get across the overhang of the wall from the street? The white plaster, the grey tiles both shone in the dawn light, mocking me. I crouched in the shelter of the house opposite, deeply regretting my own rashness and stupidity. I'd lost my focus and concentration: my hearing was as acute as ever, but the inner certainty, the instinct was gone.

I couldn't stay where I was. In the distance I heard the tramp of feet, the pad of hoofs. A group of men was approaching. Their voices floated towards me. I thought I recognized the Western accent that would mark them as Arai's men. I knew that if they found me my life with the

Tribe would be over – my life would probably be over altogether if Arai was as insulted as had been said.

I had no choice but to run to the gate and shout to the guards to open it, but as I was about to cross the street, I heard voices from beyond the wall. Akio was calling quietly to the guards. There was a creak and a thud as the gate was unbarred.

The patrol turned into the far end of the street. I went invisible, ran to the gate and slipped inside.

The guards did not see me but Akio did, just as he had forestalled me at Inuyama when the Tribe first seized me. He stepped into my path and grabbed both arms.

I braced myself for the blows I was certain would follow, but he did not waste any time. He pulled me swiftly towards the house.

The horses of the patrol were moving faster now, coming down the street at a trot. I stumbled over the dog. It whimpered in its sleep. The riders shouted to the guards at the gate, 'Good morning!'

'What've you got there?' one of the guards replied.

'None of your business!'

As Akio pulled me up into the house I looked back. Through the narrow space between the bath house and the wall, I could just see the open gate and the street beyond.

Behind the horses two men on foot were dragging a captive between them. I could not see him clearly but I could hear his voice. I could hear his prayers. It was my outcaste, Jo-An.

I must have made a lunge off the step towards the gate, for Akio pulled me back with a force that almost dislocated my shoulder. Then he did hit me, silently and efficiently on the side of the neck. The room spun sickeningly. Still without speaking he dragged me into the main room where the maid was sweeping the matting. She took no notice of us at all.

He called out to the kitchen as he opened the wall of the hidden room, and pushed me inside. Kenji's wife came into the room and Akio slid the door shut.

Her face was pale and her eyes puffy, as though she were still fighting sleep. I could feel her fury before she spoke. She slapped me twice across the face. 'You little bastard! You half-bred idiot! How dare you do that to me.'

Akio pushed me to the floor, still holding my arms behind my back. I lowered my head in submission. There didn't seem to be any point in saying anything.

'Kenji warned me you'd try to get out. I didn't believe him. Why did you do it?'

When I didn't reply, she knelt too and raised my head so she could see my face. I kept my eyes turned away.

'Answer me! Are you insane?'

'Just to see if I could.'

She sighed in exasperation, sounding like her husband.

'I don't like being shut in,' I muttered.

'It's madness,' Akio said angrily, 'He's a danger to us all. We should . . .'

She interrupted him swiftly. 'That decision can only be taken by the Kikuta master. Until then our task is to try and keep him alive and out of Arai's hands.' She gave me another cuff round the head, but a less serious one. 'Who saw you?'

'No one. Just an outcaste.'

'What outcaste?'

'A leather worker. Jo-An.'

'Jo-An? The lunatic? The one who saw the angel?' She took a deep breath. 'Don't tell me he saw you.'

'We talked for a while,' I admitted.

'Arai's men have already picked the outcaste up,' Akio said.

'I hope you realize just what a fool you are,' she said.

I bowed my head again. I was thinking about Jo-An, wishing I'd seen him home – if he had any home in Yamagata – wondering if I could rescue him, demanding silently to know what his god's purpose was for him now. *I am often afraid*, he had said. *Terrified*. Pity and remorse twisted my heart.

'Find out what the outcaste gives away,' Kenji's wife said to Akio.

'He won't betray me,' I said.

'Under torture, everyone betrays,' he replied briefly.

'We should bring forward your journey,' she went on. 'Perhaps you should even leave today.'

Akio was still kneeling behind me, holding me by the wrists. I felt the movement as he nodded.

'Is he to be punished?' he said.

'No, he has to be able to travel. Besides, as you should have realized by now, physical punishment makes no impression on him. However, make sure he knows exactly what the outcaste suffers. His head may be stubborn but his heart is soft.'

'The masters say it is his main weakness,' Akio remarked.

'Yes, if it weren't for that we might have another Shintaro.'

'Soft hearts can be hardened,' Akio muttered.

'Well, you Kikuta know best how to do that.'

I remained kneeling on the floor while they discussed

me as coldly as if I were some commodity, a vat of wine perhaps that might turn out to be a particularly fine one, or might be tainted and worthless.

'What now?' Akio said, 'Is he to be tied up until we leave?'

'Kenji said you chose to come to us,' she said to me. 'If that's true, why do you try to escape?'

'I came back.'

'Will you try again?'

'No.'

'You will go to Matsue with the actors and do nothing to endanger them or yourself?'

'Yes.'

She thought for a moment and told Akio to tie me up anyway. After he'd done so, they left me to make the preparations for our departure. The maid came with a tray of food and tea, and helped me to eat and drink without saying a word. After she had taken away the bowls no one came near me. I listened to the sound of the house and thought I discerned all the harshness and cruelty that lay beneath its everyday song. A huge weariness came over me. I crawled to the mattress, made myself as comfortable as I could, thought hopelessly of Jo-An and my own stupidity, and fell asleep.

I woke suddenly, my heart pounding, my throat dry. I had been dreaming of the outcaste, a terrible dream in which, from far away, an insistent voice, as small as a mosquito's, was whispering something only I could hear.

Akio must have had his face pressed up against the outside wall. He described every detail of Jo-An's torture at the hands of Arai's men. It went on and on in a slow monotone, making my skin crawl and my stomach turn.

Now and then he would fall silent for long periods; I would think with relief it was over, then his voice would begin again.

I could not even put my fingers in my ears. There was no escape from it. Kenji's wife was right; it was the worst punishment she could have devised for me. I wished above all I had killed the outcaste when I first saw him on the river bank. Pity had stayed my hand then but that pity had had fatal results. I would have given Jo-An a swift and merciful death. Now because of me he was suffering torment.

When Akio's voice finally died away, I heard Yuki's tread outside. She stepped into the room carrying a bowl, scissors and a razor. The maid, Sadako, followed her with an armful of clothes, placed them on the floor, and then went silently out of the room. I heard Sadako tell Akio that the midday meal was ready, heard him get to his feet and follow her to the kitchen. The smell of food floated through the house, but I had no appetite.

'I have to cut your hair,' Yuki said. I still wore it in the warrior style, restrained as Ichiro, my former teacher in Shigeru's household, had insisted, but unmistakable, the forehead shaved, the back hair caught up in a topknot. It had not been trimmed for weeks, nor had I shaved my face, though I still had very little beard.

Yuki untied my hands and legs and made me sit in front of her. 'You are an idiot,' she said, as she began to cut.

I didn't answer. I was already aware of that but also knew I would probably do the same thing again.

'My mother was so angry. I don't know which surprised her more, that you'd been able to put her to sleep or that you dared to.'

Bits of hair were falling around me. 'At the same time she was almost excited,' Yuki went on. 'She says you remind her of Shintaro when he was your age.'

'She knew him?'

'I'll tell you a secret: she burned for him. She'd have married him, but it didn't suit the Tribe, so she married my father instead. Anyway, I don't think she could bear for anyone to have that power over her. Shintaro was a master of the Kikuta sleep: no one was safe from him.'

Yuki was animated, more chatty than I'd ever known her. I could feel her hand trembling slightly against my neck as the scissors snipped cold on my scalp. I remembered Kenji's dismissive words about his wife, the girls he'd slept with. Their marriage was, like most, an arranged alliance between two families.

'If she'd married Shintaro I would have been someone else,' Yuki said pensively. 'I don't think she ever stopped loving him, in her heart.'

'Even though he was a murderer?'

'He wasn't a murderer! No more than you are.'

Something in her voice told me the conversation was moving onto dangerous ground. I found Yuki very attractive. I knew she had strong feelings for me. But I did not feel for her what I had felt for Kaede, and I did not want to be talking about love.

I tried to change the subject. 'I thought the sleep thing was something only Kikuta do. Wasn't Shintaro from the Kuroda family?'

'On his father's side. His mother was Kikuta. Shintaro and your father were cousins.'

It chilled me to think that the man whose death I'd caused, whom everyone said I resembled, should have been a relative.

'What exactly happened the night Shintaro died?' Yuki said curiously.

'I heard someone climbing into the house. The window of the first floor was open because of the heat. Lord Shigeru wanted to take him alive but when he seized him we all three fell into the garden. The intruder struck his head on a rock, but we thought he also took poison in the moment of the fall. Anyway, he died without regaining consciousness. Your father confirmed it was Kuroda Shintaro. Later we learned that Shigeru's uncles, the Otori lords, had hired him to assassinate Shigeru.'

'It's extraordinary,' Yuki said, 'that you should have been there and no one knew who you were.'

I answered her unguardedly, disarmed perhaps by the memories of that night. 'Not so extraordinary. Shigeru was looking for me when he rescued me at Mino. He already knew of my existence and knew my father had been an assassin.' Lord Shigeru had told me this when we had talked in Tsuwano. I had asked him if that was why he had sought me out and he had told me it was the main reason, but not the only one. I had never found out what the other reasons might have been, and now I never would.

Yuki's hands had gone still. 'My father was not aware of that.'

'No, he was allowed to believe that Shigeru acted on an impulse, that he saved my life and brought me back to Hagi purely by chance.'

'You can't be serious?'

Too late her intensity aroused my suspicions. 'What does it matter now?'

'How did Lord Otori find out something that even the Tribe had not suspected? What else did he tell you?'

'He told me many things,' I said impatiently. 'He and Ichiro taught me almost everything I know.'

'I mean about the Tribe!'

I shook my head as if I did not understand. 'Nothing. I know nothing about the Tribe other than what your father taught me, and what I've learnt here.'

She stared at me. I avoided looking at her directly. 'There's a whole lot more to learn,' she said finally. 'I'll be able to teach you on the road.' She ran her hands over my cropped hair and stood in one movement like her mother. 'Put these on. I'll bring you something to eat.'

'I'm not hungry,' I said, reaching over and picking up the clothes. Once brightly coloured, they had faded to dull orange and brown. I wondered who had worn them and what had befallen him on the road.

'We have many hours of travel ahead,' she said. 'We may not eat again today. Whatever Akio and I tell you to do, you do. If we tell you to brew the dirt under our fingernails and drink it, you do it. If we say eat, you eat. And you don't do anything else. We learned this sort of obedience when we were children. You have to learn it now.'

I wanted to ask her if she had been obedient when she'd brought Shigeru's sword, Jato, to me in Inuyama, but it seemed wiser to say nothing. I changed into the actor's clothes, and when Yuki came back with food, I ate without question.

She watched me silently, and when I'd finished she said, 'The outcaste is dead.'

They wanted my heart hardened. I did not look at her or reply.

'He said nothing about you,' she went on. 'I did not know an outcaste would have such courage. He had no poison to release himself. Yet he said nothing.'

I thanked Jo-An in my heart, thanked the Hidden who take their secrets with them . . . where? Into Paradise? Into another life? Into the silencing fire, the silent grave? I wanted to pray for him, after the fashion of our people. Or light candles and burn incense for him as Ichiro and Chiyo had taught me in Shigeru's house in Hagi. I thought of Jo-An going alone into the dark. What would his people do without him?

'Do you pray to anyone?' I asked Yuki.

'Of course,' she said, surprised.

'Who to?'

'The Enlightened One, in all his forms. The gods of the mountain, the forest, the river: all the old ones. This morning I took rice and flowers to the shrine at the bridge to ask for a blessing on our journey. I'm glad we're leaving today after all. It's a good day for travelling, all the signs are favourable.' She looked at me as if she were thinking it all over, then shook her head. 'Don't ask things like that. It makes you sound so different. No one else would ask that.'

'No one else has lived my life.'

'You're one of the Tribe now. Try and behave like it.'

She took a small bag from inside her sleeve and passed it to me. 'Here. Akio said to give you these.'

I opened it and felt inside, then tipped the contents out. Five juggler's balls, smooth and firm, packed with rice grain, fell onto the floor. Much as I hated juggling, it was impossible not to pick them up and handle them. With three in my right hand and two in my left, I stood up. The feel of the balls, the actor's clothes had already turned me into someone else.

'You are Minoru,' Yuki said. 'These would have been

62

given to you by your father. Akio is your older brother, I'm your sister.'

'We don't look very alike,' I said, tossing up the balls.

'We will become alike enough,' Yuki replied. 'My father said you could change your features to some extent.'

'What happened to our father?' Round and back the balls went, the circle, the fountain . . .

'He's dead.'

'Convenient.'

She ignored me. 'We're travelling to Matsue for the autumn festival. It will take five or six days depending on the weather. Arai still has men looking for you, but the main search here is over. He has already left for Inuyama. We travel in the opposite direction. At night we have safe houses to go to. But the road belongs to no one. If we meet any patrols you'll have to prove who you are.'

I dropped one of the balls, and bent to retrieve it.

'You can't drop them,' Yuki said. 'No one of your age ever drops them. My father also said you could impersonate well. Don't bring any of us into danger.'

We left from the back entrance. Kenji's wife came out to bid us farewell. She looked me over, checked my hair and clothes. 'I hope we meet again,' she said, 'but knowing your recklessness I hardly expect it.'

I bowed to her, saying nothing. Akio was already in the yard with a handcart like the one I'd been bundled into in Inuyama. He told me to get inside and I climbed in among the props and costumes. Yuki handed me my knife. I was pleased to see it again and tucked it away inside my clothes.

Akio lifted the cart handles and began to push. I

rocked through the town in semi-darkness, listening to its sounds and to the speech of the actors. I recognized the voice of the other girl from Inuyama, Keiko. There was one other man with us too: I'd heard his voice in the house but had not set eyes on him.

When we were well beyond the last houses, Akio stopped, opened the side of the cart and told me to get out. It was about the second half of the hour of the Goat, and still very warm, despite the onset of autumn. Akio gleamed with sweat. He had removed most of his clothes to push the cart. I could see how strong he was. He was taller than me, and much more muscular. He went to drink from the stream that ran beside the road, and splashed water onto his head and face. Yuki, Keiko and the older man were squatting by the side of the road. I would hardly have recognized any of them. They were completely transformed into a troupe of actors, making a precarious living from town to town, existing on their wits and talents, always on the verge of starvation or crime.

The older man gave me a grin, showing his missing teeth. His face was lean, expressive and slightly sinister. Keiko ignored me. Like Akio she had half-healed scars on one hand, from my knife.

I took a deep breath. Hot as it was, it was infinitely better than the room I'd been shut up in and the stifling cart. Behind us lay the town of Yamagata, the castle white against the mountains, which were still mostly green and luxuriant, with splashes of colour here and there where the leaves had started to turn. The rice fields were turning gold too. It would soon be harvest time. To the south-west I could see the steep slope of Terayama, but the roofs of the temple were invisible behind the cedars. Beyond lay

64

fold after fold of mountains, turning blue in the distance, shimmering in the afternoon haze. Silently I said farewell to Shigeru, reluctant to turn away and break my last tie with him and with my life as one of the Otori.

Akio gave me a blow on the shoulder. 'Stop dreaming like an imbecile,' he said, his voice changed into a rougher accent and dialect. 'It's your turn to push.'

By the time evening came I'd conceived the deepest hatred possible for that cart. It was heavy and unwieldy, blistering the hands and straining the back. Pulling it uphill was bad enough, as the wheels caught in potholes and ruts and it took all of us to get it free, but hanging onto it downhill was even harder. I would happily have let go and sent it hurtling into the forest. I thought longingly of my horse, Raku.

The older man, Kazuo, walked alongside me, helping me to adjust my accent and telling me the words I needed to know in the private language of actors. Some Kenji had already taught me, the dark street slang of the Tribe, some were new to me. I mimicked him, as I'd mimicked Ichiro, my Otori teacher, in a very different kind of learning, and tried to think myself into becoming Minoru.

Towards the end of the day when the light was beginning to fade we descended a slope towards a village. The road levelled out and the surface grew smoother. A man walking home called the evening greeting to us.

I could smell wood smoke and food cooking. All around me rose the sounds of the village at the end of the day: the splash of water as the farmers washed, children playing and squabbling, women gossiping as they cooked, the crackle of the fires, the chink of axe on wood, the shrine bell, the whole web of life that I'd been raised in.

And I caught something else: the clink of a bridle, the muffled stamp of a horse's feet.

'There's a patrol ahead,' I said to Kazuo.

He held up his hand for us to stop, and called quietly to Akio. 'Minoru says there's a patrol.'

Akio squinted at me against the setting sun. 'You heard them?'

'I can hear horses. What else would it be?'

He nodded and shrugged as if to say, *As good now as any time*. 'Take the cart.'

As I took Akio's place Kazuo began to sing a rowdy comic song. He had a good voice. It rang out into the still evening air. Yuki reached into the cart and took out a small drum which she threw to Akio. Catching it, he began to beat out the rhythm of the song. Yuki also brought out a one-stringed instrument which she twanged as she walked beside us. Keiko had spinning tops, like the ones that had captured my attention at Inuyama.

Singing and playing, we rounded the corner and came to the patrol. They had set up a bamboo barrier just before the first houses of the village. There were about nine or ten men, most of them sitting on the ground eating. They wore Arai's bear crest on their jackets; the setting sun banners of the Seishuu had been erected on the bank. Four horses grazed beneath them.

A swarm of children hung around and when they saw us they ran towards us shouting and giggling. Kazuo broke off his song to direct a couple of riddles at them and then shouted impudently to the soldiers, 'What's going on, lads?'

Their commander rose to his feet and approached us. We all immediately dropped to the dust.

'Get up,' he said. 'Where've you come from?' He had

a squarish face with heavy brows, a thin mouth and a clenched jaw. He wiped the rice from his lips on the back of his hand.

'Yamagata.' Akio handed the drum to Yuki and held out a wooden tablet. It had our names inscribed on it, the name of our guild and our licence from the city. The commander gazed at it for a long time, deciphering our names, every now and then looking across at each of us in turn, scanning our faces. Keiko was spinning the tops. The men watched her with more than idle interest. Players were the same as prostitutes as far as they were concerned. One of them made a mocking suggestion to her; she laughed back.

I leaned against the cart, and wiped the sweat from my face.

'Minoru, what's he do?' the commander said, handing the tablet back to Akio.

'My younger brother? He's a juggler. It's the family calling.'

'Let's see him,' the commander said, his thin lips parting in a sort of smile.

Akio did not hesitate for a moment. 'Hey, little brother. Show the lord.'

I wiped my hands on my headband and tied it back round my head. I took the balls from the bag, felt their smooth weight, and in an instant became Minoru. This was my life. I had never known any other: the road, the new village, the suspicious hostile stares. I forgot my tiredness, my aching head and blistered hands. I was Minoru, doing what I'd done since I was old enough to stand.

The balls flew in the air. I did four first, then five. I'd just finished the second sequence of the fountain when

Akio jerked his head at me. I let the balls flow in his direction. He caught them effortlessly, throwing the tablet into the air with them. Then he sent them back to me. The sharp edge of the tablet caught my blistered palm. I was angry with him, wondering what his intention was: to show me up? To betray me? I lost the rhythm. Tablet and balls fell into the dust.

The smile left the commander's face. He took a step forward. In that moment a mad impulse came into my mind: to give myself up to him, throw myself on Arai's mercy, escape the Tribe before it was too late.

Akio seemed to fly towards me. 'Idiot!' he yelled, giving me a cuff round the ear. 'Our father would cry out from his grave!'

As soon as he raised his hand to me, I knew my disguise would not be penetrated. It would have been unthinkable for an actor to strike an Otori warrior. The blow turned me into Minoru again, as nothing else could have done.

'Forgive me, older brother,' I said, picking up the balls and the tablet; I kept them spinning in the air until the commander laughed and waved us forward.

'Come and see us tonight!' Keiko called to the soldiers.

'Yes, tonight,' they called back.

Kazuo began to sing again, Yuki to beat the drum. I threw the tablet to Akio and put the balls away. They were darkened with blood. I picked up the handles of the cart. The barrier was lifted aside and we walked through to the village beyond.

Four

Kaede set out on the last day of her journey home on a perfect autumn morning, the sky clear blue, the air cool and thin as spring water. Mist hung in the valleys and above the river, silvering spiders' webs and the tendrils of wild clematis. But just before noon the weather began to change. Clouds crept over the sky from the north-west and the wind swung. The light seemed to fade early and before evening it began to rain.

The rice fields, vegetable gardens and fruit trees had all been severely damaged by storms. The villages seemed half-empty, and the few people around stared sullenly at her, bowing only when threatened by the guards and then with bad grace. She did not know if they recognized her or not; she did not want to linger among them, but she could not help wondering why the damage was un-repaired, why the men were not working in the fields to salvage what they could of the harvest.

Her heart did not know how to behave. Sometimes it slowed in foreboding, making her feel she might faint, and then it sped up, beating frantically in excitement and fear. The miles left to travel seemed endless, and yet the horses' steady step ate them up all too quickly. She was afraid above all of what faced her at home.

She kept seeing views she thought were familiar and her heart would leap in her throat, but when they came at last to the walled garden and the gates of her parents' home she did not recognize any of it. Surely this was not where she lived? It was so small; it was not even fortified and guarded. The gates stood wide open. As Raku stepped through them, Kaede could not help gasping.

Shizuka had already slid from the horse's back. She looked up. 'What is it, lady?'

'The garden,' Kaede exclaimed. 'What happened to it?'

Everywhere were signs of the ferocity of the storms. An uprooted pine tree lay across the stream. In its fall it had knocked over and crushed a stone lantern. Kaede had a flash of memory: the lantern, newly erected, a light burning in it, evening, the Festival of the Dead perhaps; a lamp floated away downstream and she felt her mother's hand against her hair.

She gazed, uncomprehending, at the ruined garden. It was more than storm damage. Obviously it had been months since anyone had tended the shrubs or the moss, cleared out the pools or pruned the trees. Was this her house, one of the key domains of the West? What had happened to the once powerful Shirakawa?

The horse lowered his head and rubbed it against his foreleg. He whinnied, impatient and tired, expecting now that they had stopped to be unsaddled and fed.

'Where are the guards?' Kaede said, 'Where is everyone?'

The man she called Scar, the captain of the escort, rode his horse up to the veranda, leaned forward and shouted, 'Hello! Anyone within?'

'Don't go in,' she called to him. 'Wait for me. I will go inside first.'

Long Arm was standing by Raku's head, holding the

bridle. Kaede slid from the horse's back into Shizuka's arms. The rain had turned to a fine, light drizzle that beaded their hair and clothes. The garden smelled rankly of dampness and decay, sour earth and fallen leaves. Kaede felt the image of her childhood home, kept intact and glowing in her heart for eight long years, intensify unbearably, and then vanish for ever.

Long Arm gave the bridle to one of the foot soldiers and, drawing his sword, went in front of Kaede. Shizuka followed them.

As she stepped out of her sandals onto the veranda, it seemed the feel of the wood was faintly familiar to her feet. But she did not recognize the smell of the house at all. It was a stranger's home.

There was a sudden movement from within and Long Arm leaped forward into the shadows. A girl's voice cried out in alarm. The man pulled her onto the veranda.

'Let go of her,' Kaede commanded in fury. 'How dare you touch her?'

'He is only protecting you,' Shizuka murmured, but Kaede was not listening. She stepped towards the girl, taking her hands and staring into her face. She was almost the same height as Kaede, with a gentle face and light brown eyes like their father's.

'Ai? I am your sister, Kaede. Don't you remember me?'

The girl gazed back. Her eyes filled with tears. 'Sister? Is it really you? For a moment, against the light . . . I thought you were our mother.'

Kaede took her sister in her arms, feeling tears spring into her own eyes. 'She's dead, isn't she?'

'Over two months ago. Her last words were of you. She longed to see you, but the knowledge of your marriage brought her peace.' Ai's voice faltered and she drew back from Kaede's embrace. 'Why have you come here? Where is your husband?'

'Have you had no news from Inuyama?'

'We have been battered by typhoons this year. Many people died and the harvest was ruined. We've heard so little – only rumours of war. After the last storm an army swept through, but we hardly understood who they were fighting for or why.'

'Arai's army?'

'They were Seishuu from Maruyama and further south. They were going to join Lord Arai against the Tohan. Father was outraged, for he considered himself an ally to Lord Iida. He tried to stop them passing through here. He met them near the Sacred Caves. They attempted to reason with him but he attacked them.'

'Father fought them? Is he dead?'

'No, he was defeated, of course, and most of his men were killed, but he still lives. He thinks Arai a traitor and an upstart. He had sworn allegiance, after all, to the Noguchi, when you went as a hostage.'

'The Noguchi were overthrown, I am no longer a hostage, and I am in alliance with Arai,' Kaede said.

Her sister's eyes widened. 'I don't understand. I don't understand any of it.' She seemed conscious for the first time of Shizuka and the men outside. She made a helpless gesture. 'Forgive me, you must be exhausted. You have come a long way. The men must be hungry.' She frowned, suddenly looking like a child. 'What shall I do?' she whispered. 'We have so little to offer you.'

'Are there no servants left?'

'I sent them to hide in the forest when we heard the horses. I think they will come back before nightfall.'

'Shizuka,' Kaede said. 'Go to the kitchen and see what

there is. Prepare food and drink for the men. They may rest here tonight. I shall need at least ten to stay on with me.' She pointed at Long Arm. 'Let him pick them. The others must return to Inuyama. If they harm any of my people or my possessions in any way, they will answer with their lives.'

Shizuka bowed. 'Lady.'

'I'll show you the way,' Ai said, and led Shizuka towards the back of the house.

'What is your name?' Kaede said to Long Arm.

He dropped to his knees before her. 'Kondo, lady.'

'Are you one of Lord Arai's men?'

'My mother was from the Seishuu. My father, if I may trust you with my secrets, was from the Tribe. I fought with Arai's men at Kushimoto, and was asked to enter his service.'

She looked down at him. He was not a young man. His hair was grey streaked, the skin on his neck lined. She wondered what his past had been, what work he had done for the Tribe, how far she could trust him. But she needed a man to handle the soldiers and the horses and defend the house; Kondo had saved Shizuka, he was feared and respected by Arai's other men, and he had the fighting skills she required.

'I may need your help for a few weeks,' she said. 'Can I depend on you?'

He looked up at her then. In the gathering darkness she could not make out his expression. His teeth gleamed white as he smiled, and when he spoke his voice had a ring of sincerity, even devotion. 'Lady Otori can depend on me as long as she needs me.'

'Swear it then,' she said, feeling herself flush as she pretended an authority she was not sure she possessed.

The lines around his eyes crinkled momentarily. He

touched his forehead to the matting and swore allegiance to her and her family, but she thought she detected a note of irony in his voice. *The Tribe always dissemble*, she thought, chilled. *Moreover they answer only to themselves.*

'Go and select ten men you can trust,' she said, 'See how much feed there is for the horses, and if the barns provide shelter enough.'

'Lady Otori,' he replied, and again she thought she heard irony. She wondered how much he knew, how much Shizuka had told him.

After a few moments Ai returned, took Kaede's hand and said quietly, 'Should I tell Father?'

'Where is he? What is his condition? Was he wounded?'

'He was wounded slightly. But it is not the injury . . . Our mother's death, the loss of so many men . . . sometimes his mind seems to wander, and he does not seem to know where he is. He talks to ghosts and apparitions.'

'Why did he not take his life?'

'When he was first brought back he wanted to.' Ai's voice broke completely and she began to weep. 'I prevented him. I was so weak. Hana and I clung to him and begged him not to leave us. I took away his weapons.' She turned her tear-streaked face to Kaede. 'It's all my fault. I should have had more courage. I should have helped him to die and then killed myself and Hana, as a warrior's daughter should. But I couldn't do it. I couldn't take her life, and I couldn't leave her alone. So we live in shame, and it is driving Father mad.'

Kaede thought, *I also should have killed myself, as soon as I heard Lord Shigeru had been betrayed. But I did not. Instead I killed Iida.* She touched Ai on the cheek, felt the wetness of tears.

'Forgive me,' Ai whispered. 'I have been so weak.'

'No,' Kaede replied. 'Why should you die?' Her sister was only thirteen; she had committed no crime. 'Why should any of us choose death?' she said. 'We will live instead. Where is Hana now?'

'I sent her to the forest with the women.'

Kaede had rarely felt compassion before. Now it woke within her, as painful as grief. She remembered how the White Goddess had come to her. The All-Merciful One had consoled her, had promised that Takeo would return to her. But together with the goddess's promise had come the demands of compassion, that Kaede should live to take care of her sisters, her people, her unborn child. From outside she could hear Kondo's voice giving orders, the men shouting in reply. A horse whinnied and another answered. The rain had strengthened, beating out a pattern of sound that seemed familiar to her.

'I must see Father,' she said. 'Then we must feed the men. Will anyone help from the villages?'

'Just before Mother died the farmers sent a delegation. They were complaining about the rice tax, the state of the dykes and fields, the loss of the harvest. Father was furious. He refused even to talk to them. Ayame persuaded them to leave us alone because Mother was sick. Since then everything has been in confusion. The villagers are afraid of Father – they say he is cursed.'

'What about our neighbours?'

'There is Lord Fujiwara. He used to visit Father occasionally.'

'I don't remember him. What sort of a man is he?'

'He's strange. Rather elegant and cold. He is of very high birth, they say, and used to live in the capital.'

'Inuyama?'

'No, the real capital, where the Emperor lives.'

'He is a nobleman, then?'

'I suppose he must be. He speaks differently from people round here. I can hardly understand him. He seems a very erudite man. Father liked talking to him about history and the classics.'

'Well, if he ever calls on Father again, perhaps I will seek his advice.' Kaede was silent for a moment. She was fighting weariness. Her limbs ached and her belly felt heavy. She longed to lie down and sleep. And somewhere within herself she felt guilty that she was not grieving more. It was not that she did not suffer anguish for her mother's death and her father's humiliation, but she had no space left in her soul for any more grief and no energy to give to it.

She looked round the room. Even in the twilight she could see the matting was old, the walls water-stained, the screens torn. Ai followed her gaze. 'I'm ashamed,' she whispered. 'There's been so much to do. And so much I don't know how to do.'

'I almost seem to remember how it used to be,' Kaede said. 'It had a glow about it.'

'Mother made it like that,' Ai said, stifling a sob.

'We will make it like that again,' Kaede promised.

From the direction of the kitchen there suddenly came the sound of someone singing. Kaede recognized Shizuka's voice, and the song as the one she had heard the first time she met her, the love ballad about the village and the pine tree.

How does she have the courage to sing now? she thought, and then Shizuka came quickly into the room carrying a lamp in each hand.

'I found these in the kitchen,' she said, 'and luckily the

fire was still burning. Rice and barley are cooking. Kondo has sent men to the village to buy whatever they can. And the household women have returned.'

'Our sister will be with them,' Ai said, breathing a sigh of relief.

'Yes, she has brought an armful of herbs and mushrooms that she insists on cooking.'

Ai blushed. 'She has become half wild,' she began to explain.

'Let me see her,' Kaede said. 'Then you must take me to Father.'

Ai went out, Kaede heard a few words of argument from the kitchen, and seconds later Ai returned with a girl of about nine years old.

'This is our older sister, Kaede. She left home when you were a baby,' Ai said to Hana, and then, prompting her, 'greet your older sister properly.'

'Welcome home,' Hana whispered, then dropped to her knees and bowed to Kaede. Kaede knelt in front of her, took her hands and raised her. She looked into her face.

'I was younger than you are now when I left home,' she said, studying the fine eyes, the perfect bone structure beneath the childish roundness.

'She is like you, lady,' Shizuka said.

'I hope she will be happier,' Kaede replied, and drawing Hana to her, hugged her. She felt the slight body begin to shake, and realized the child was crying.

'Mother! I want Mother!'

Kaede's own eyes filled with tears.

'Hush, Hana, don't cry, little sister.' Ai tried to soothe her. 'I'm sorry,' she said to Kaede. 'She is still grieving. She has not been taught how to behave.'

77

Well, she will learn, Kaede thought, *as I had to. She will learn not to let her feelings show, to accept that life is made up of suffering and loss, to cry in private if she cries at all.*

'Come,' Shizuka said, taking Hana by the hand, 'you have to show me how to cook the mushrooms. I don't know these local ones.'

Her eyes met Kaede's above the child's head and her smile was warm and cheerful.

'Your woman is wonderful,' Ai said, as they left. 'How long has she been with you?'

'She came to me a few months ago, just before I left Noguchi castle,' Kaede replied. The two sisters remained kneeling on the floor, not knowing what to say to each other. The rain fell heavily now, streaming from the eaves like a curtain of steel arrows. It was nearly dark. Kaede thought, *I cannot tell Ai that Lord Arai himself sent Shizuka to me, as part of the conspiracy to overthrow Iida, or that Shizuka is from the Tribe. I cannot tell her anything. She is so young, she has never left Shirakawa, she knows nothing of the world.*

'I suppose we should go to Father,' she said.

But at that moment she heard his voice calling from a distant part of the house. 'Ai! Ayame!' His footsteps approached. He was complaining softly. 'Ah, they've all gone away and left me. These worthless women!'

He came into the room, and stopped short when he saw Kaede.

'Who's there? Do we have visitors? Who's come at this time of night in the rain?'

Ai stood and went to him. 'It's Kaede: your oldest daughter. She has returned. She's safe.'

'Kaede?' He took a step towards her. She did not stand

78

but, remaining where she was, bowed deeply, touching her forehead to the floor.

Ai helped her father down. He knelt in front of Kaede. 'Sit up, sit up,' he said impatiently. 'Let us see the worst in each other.'

'Father?' she questioned as she raised her head.

'I am a shamed man,' he said. 'I should have died. I did not. I am hollow now, only partly alive. Look at me, daughter.'

It was true that terrible changes had been wrought in him. He had always been so controlled and dignified. Now he seemed a husk of his former self. There was a half-healed slash from temple to left ear: the hair had been shaved away from the wound. His feet were bare and his robe stained, his jaw dark with stubble.

'What happened to you?' she said, trying to keep the anger out of her voice. She had come seeking refuge, looking for the lost childhood home she had spent eight years mourning, only to find it almost destroyed.

Her father made a weary gesture. 'What does it matter? Everything is lost, ruined. Your return is the final blow. What happened to your marriage to Lord Otori? Don't tell me he is dead.'

'Through no fault of mine,' she said bitterly. 'Iida murdered him.'

His lips tightened and his face paled. 'We have heard nothing here.'

'Iida is also dead,' she went on. 'Arai's forces have taken Inuyama. The Tohan are overthrown.'

The mention of Arai's name obviously disturbed him. 'That traitor,' he muttered, staring into the darkness as though ghosts gathered there. 'He defeated Iida?' After a pause he went on, 'I seem to have once again found myself on the losing side. My family must be under some curse. For the first time I am glad I have no son to inherit from me. Shirakawa can fade away, regretted by no one.'

'You have three daughters!' Kaede responded, stung into anger.

'And my oldest is also cursed, bringing death to any man connected with her!'

'Iida caused Lord Otori's death! It was a plot from the start. My marriage was designed to bring him to Inuyama and into Iida's hands.' The rain drummed hard against the roof, cascading from the eaves. Shizuka came in silently with more lamps, placed them on the floor and knelt behind Kaede. *I must control myself,* Kaede thought. *I must not tell him everything.*

He was staring at her, his face puzzled. 'So are you married or not?'

Her heart was racing. She had never lied to her father. Now she found she could not speak. She turned her head away, as if overcome by grief.

Shizuka whispered. 'May I speak, Lord Shirakawa?'

'Who is she?' he said to Kaede.

'She is my maid. She came to me at Noguchi castle.'

He nodded in Shizuka's direction. 'What do you have to say?'

'Lady Shirakawa and Lord Otori were married secretly at Terayama,' Shizuka said in a low voice. 'Your kinswoman was witness, but she also died at Inuyama, along with her daughter.'

'Maruyama Naomi is dead? Things get worse and worse. The domain will be lost to her stepdaughter's family now. We may as well hand over Shirakawa to them too.'

'I am her heir,' Kaede said. 'She entrusted everything to me.'

80

He gave a short mirthless laugh. 'They have disputed the domain for years. The husband is a cousin of Iida's, and is supported by many from both the Tohan and the Seishuu. You are mad if you think they will let you inherit.'

Kaede felt rather than heard Shizuka stir slightly behind her. Her father was just the first man of many, an army, a whole clan, maybe even all the Three Countries, who would try to thwart her.

'All the same, I intend to.'

'You'll have to fight for it,' he said with scorn.

'Then I will fight.' They sat for a few moments in silence in the darkened room with the rain-drenched garden beyond.

'We have few men left,' her father said, his voice bitter. 'Will the Otori do anything for you? I suppose you must marry again. Have they suggested anyone?'

'It is too early to think of that,' Kaede said. 'I am still in mourning.' She took a breath, so deep she was sure he must hear it. 'I believe I am carrying a child.'

His eyes turned again to her, peering through the gloom. 'Shigeru gave you a child?'

She bowed in confirmation, not daring to speak.

'Well, well,' he said, suddenly inappropriately jovial. 'We must celebrate! Another man may have died but his seed lives. A remarkable achievement!' They had been talking in lowered voices, but now he shouted surprisingly loudly. 'Ayame!'

Kaede jumped despite herself. She saw how his mind was loosened, swinging between lucidity and darkness. It frightened her, but she tried to put the fear aside. As long as he believed her for the time being, she would face whatever came afterwards.

81

The woman, Ayame, came in and knelt before Kaede. 'Lady, welcome home. Forgive us for such a sad homecoming.'

Kaede stood, took her hands and raised her to her feet. They embraced. The solid indomitable figure that Kaede remembered had dwindled to a woman who was almost old. Yet she thought she recalled her scent: it aroused sudden memories of childhood.

'Go and bring wine,' Kaede's father commanded. 'I want to drink to my grandchild.'

Kaede felt a shiver of dread, as though by giving the child a false identity she had made its life false. 'It is still so early,' she said in a low voice. 'Do not celebrate yet.'

'Kaede!' Ayame exclaimed, using her name as she would to a child. 'Don't say such things, don't tempt fate.'

'Fetch wine,' her father said loudly. 'And close the shutters. Why do we sit here in the cold?'

As Ayame went towards the veranda they heard the sound of footsteps, and Kondo's voice called, 'Lady Otori!'

Shizuka went to the doorway and spoke to him.

'Tell him to come up,' Kaede said.

Kondo stepped onto the wooden floor and knelt in the entrance. Kaede was conscious of the swift glance he gave round the room, taking in, in a moment, the layout of the house, assessing the people in it. He spoke to her, not to her father.

'I've been able to get some food from the village. I've chosen the men you requested. A young man turned up, Amano Tenzo: he's taken charge of the horses. I'll see that the men get something to eat now, and set guards for the night.'

'Thank you. We'll speak in the morning.'

Kondo bowed again and left silently.

'Who's that fellow?' her father demanded. 'Why did he not speak to me to ask my opinion or permission?'

'He works for me,' Kaede replied.

'If he's one of Arai's men I'll not have him in this house.'

'I said he works for me.' Her patience was wearing thin. 'We are in alliance with Lord Arai now. He controls most of the Three Countries. He is our overlord. You must accept this, Father. Iida is dead and everything has changed.'

'Does that mean daughters may speak to their fathers so?'

'Ayame,' Kaede said, 'take my father to his room. He will eat there tonight.'

Her father began to remonstrate. She raised her voice against him for the first time in her life. 'Father, I am tired. We will talk tomorrow.'

Ayame gave her a look that she chose to ignore. 'Do as I say,' she said coldly, and after a moment the older woman obeyed and led her father away.

'You must eat, lady,' Shizuka said. 'Sit down, I'll bring you something.'

'Make sure everyone is fed,' Kaede said. 'And close the shutters now.'

Later she lay listening to the rain. Her household and her men were sheltered, fed after a fashion, safe, if Kondo could be trusted. She let the events of the day run through her mind, the problems she would have to deal with: her father, Hana, the neglected estate of Shirakawa, the disputed domain of Maruyama. How was she going to claim and keep what was hers?

If only I were a man, she thought. *How easy it would be. If I were Father's son, what would he not do for me?*

She knew she had the ruthlessness of a man. When she was still a hostage in Noguchi castle, she had stabbed a guard without thinking, but Iida she had killed deliberately. She would kill again, rather than let any man crush her. Her thoughts drifted to Lady Maruyama. *I wish I had known you better*, she thought. *I wish I had been able to learn more from you. I am sorry for the pain I caused you. If only we had been able to talk freely.* She felt she saw the beautiful face before her, and heard her voice again. *I entrust my land and my people to you. Take care of them.*

I will, she promised. *I will learn how.* The meagreness of her education depressed her, but that could be remedied. She resolved she would find out how to run the estate, how to speak to the farmers, how to train men and fight battles, everything a son would have been taught from birth. *Father will have to teach me,* she thought. *It will give him something to think about apart from himself.*

She felt a twinge of emotion, fear or shame or, maybe, a combination of both. What was she turning into? Was she unnatural? Had she been bewitched or cursed? She was sure no woman had ever thought the way she did now. Except Lady Maruyama. Holding onto the lifeline of her promise to her kinswoman she fell asleep at last.

The next morning she bade farewell to Arai's men, urging them to leave as soon as possible. They were happy to go, eager to return to the campaigns in the East before the onset of winter. Kaede was equally keen to get rid of them, fearing she could not afford to feed them for even one more night. Next she organized the household women to start cleaning the house and repairing the damage to the garden. Shamefaced, Ayame confided in her that there was nothing to pay workmen with. Most of the Shirakawa treasures and all the money were gone.

'Then we must do what we can ourselves,' Kaede said, and when the work was underway she went to the stables with Kondo.

A young man greeted her with a deference that could not hide his delight. It was Amano Tenzo, who had accompanied her father to Noguchi castle, and whom she had known when they were both children. He was now about twenty years old.

'This is a fine horse,' he said as he brought Raku forward and saddled him.

'He was a gift from Lord Otori's son,' she said, stroking the horse's neck.

Amano beamed. 'Otori horses are renowned for their stamina and good sense. They say they run them in the water meadows, and they're fathered by the river spirit. With your permission, we'll put our mares to him and get his foals next year.'

She liked the way he addressed her directly and talked to her of such things. The stable area was in better condition than most of the grounds, clean and well maintained, though, apart from Raku, Amano's own chestnut stallion and four horses belonging to Kondo and his men, there were only three other war horses, all old and one lame. Horse skulls were fixed to the eaves and the wind moaned through the empty eye sockets. She knew they were placed there to protect and calm the animals below, but at present the dead outnumbered the living.

'Yes, we must have more horses,' she said. 'How many mares do we have?'

'Only two or three at the moment.'

'Can we get more before winter?'

He looked glum. 'The war, the famine . . . this year has been disastrous for Shirakawa.'

'You must show me the worst,' she said. 'Ride out with me now.'

Raku's head was held high and his ears pricked forwards. He seemed to be looking and listening. He whinnied softly at her approach but continued gazing into the distance.

'He misses someone – his master, I suppose,' Amano said. 'Don't let it worry you. He'll settle in with us and get over it.'

She patted the horse's pale grey neck. *I miss him too,* she whispered silently. *Will either of us ever get over it?* She felt the bond between herself and the little horse strengthen.

She rode out every morning, exploring her domain with Kondo and Amano. After a few days an older man turned up at the door and was greeted by the maids with tears of joy. It was Shoji Kiyoshi, her father's senior retainer, who had been wounded and feared dead. His knowledge of the estate, the villages and the farmers was vast. Kaede swiftly realized he could tell her much of what she needed to know. At first he humoured her, finding it strange and slightly comical that a girl should have such interests, but her quick grasp of affairs and her memory surprised him. He began to discuss problems with her and, though she never lost the feeling that he disapproved of her, she felt she could trust him.

Her father took little interest in the day-to-day management of the estate, and Kaede suspected he had been careless, even unjust, though it seemed disloyal to think it. He occupied the days with reading and writing in his rooms. She went to him every afternoon and sat watching him patiently. He spent a lot of time staring into the garden, saying nothing as Ayame and the maids worked tirelessly in it, but sometimes mumbling to himself, complaining about his fate.

She asked him to teach her, pleading, 'Treat me as if I were your son,' but he refused to take her seriously.

'A wife should be obedient and, if possible, beautiful. Men don't want women who think like them.'

'They would always have someone to talk to,' she argued.

'Men don't talk to their wives, they talk to each other,' he retorted. 'Anyway you have no husband. You would spend your time better marrying again.'

'I will marry no one,' she said. 'That's why I must learn. All the things a husband would do for me, I must do for myself.'

'Of course you will marry,' he replied shortly. 'Something will be arranged.' But to her relief he made no efforts in that direction.

She continued to sit with him every day, kneeling beside him as he prepared the ink stone and the brushes, watching every stroke. She could read and write the flowing script that women used, but her father wrote in men's language, the shapes of the characters as impenetrable and solid as prison bars.

She watched patiently, until one day he handed her the brush and told her to write the characters for *man*, *woman* and *child*.

Because she was naturally left-handed she took the brush in that hand but, seeing him frown, transferred it to the right. Using her right hand meant, as always, that she had to put more effort into her work. She wrote boldly, copying his arm movements. He looked at the result for a long time.

'You write like a man,' he said finally.

'Pretend I am one.' She felt his eyes on her and raised her own to meet his gaze. He was staring at her as if he did not know her, as if she alarmed and fascinated him at the same time, like some exotic animal.

'It would be interesting,' he said, 'to see if a girl could be taught. Since I have no son, nor will I ever have one now . . .'

His voice trailed off and he stared into the distance with unseeing eyes. It was the only time he alluded even faintly to her mother's death.

From then on Kaede's father taught her everything that she would have learned already had she been born male. Ayame disapproved strongly; so did most of the household and the men, especially Shoji, but Kaede ignored them. She learned quickly, though much of what she learned filled her with despair.

'All Father tells me is why men rule the world,' she complained to Shizuka. 'Every text, every law explains and justifies their domination.'

'That is the way of the world,' Shizuka replied. It was night and they lay side by side, whispering. Ai, Hana and the other women were asleep in the adjoining room. The night was still, the air cold.

'Not everyone believes that. Maybe there are other countries where they think differently. Even here there are people who dare to think in other ways. Lady Maruyama, for instance . . .' Kaede's voice went even quieter. 'The Hidden . . .'

'What do you know about the Hidden?' Shizuka said, laughing softly.

'You told me about them, a long time ago, when you first came to me at Noguchi castle. You said they believed everyone was created equal by their god. I remember that I thought you, and they, must have been mad. But now when I learn that even the Enlightened One speaks badly of women – or at least his priests and monks do – it makes me question why it should be so.'

'What do you expect?' Shizuka said. 'It's men who write histories and sacred texts. Even poetry. You can't change the way the world is. You have to learn how to work within it.'

'There are women writers,' Kaede said. 'I remember hearing their tales at Noguchi castle. But Father says I should not read them, that they will corrupt my mind.'

Sometimes she thought her father selected works for her to read simply because they said such harsh things about women, and then she thought perhaps there were no other works. She particularly disliked K'ung Fu-Tzu, whom her father admired intensely. She was writing the thoughts of the sage to her father's dictation one afternoon, when a visitor arrived.

The weather had changed in the night. The air was damp with a cold edge to it. Wood smoke and mist hung together in the valleys. In the garden the heavy heads of the last chrysanthemums drooped with moisture. The women had spent the last weeks preparing the winter clothes and Kaede was grateful for the quilted garments she now wore under her robes. Sitting writing and reading made her hands and feet cold. Soon she would have to arrange for braziers . . . she feared the onset of winter for which they were still so unprepared.

Ayame came bustling to the door and said in a voice tinged with alarm, 'Lord Fujiwara is here, sir.'

Kaede said, 'I will leave you,' placed the brush down and stood.

'No, stay. It will amuse him to meet you. No doubt he's come to hear whatever news you may have brought from the East.'

Her father went to the doorway and stepped out to welcome his guest. He turned and beckoned to Kaede and then dropped to his knees.

The courtyard was filled with men on horseback and other attendants. Lord Fujiwara was descending from a palanquin that had been set down beside the huge flat rock that had been transported to the garden expressly for that purpose – Kaede remembered the day from her childhood. She marvelled briefly that anyone should so travel by choice, and hoped guiltily that the men had brought their own food with them. Then she dropped to her knees as one of the attendants loosened the nobleman's sandals and he stepped out of them into the house.

She managed to look at him before she cast her eyes downwards. He was tall and slender, his face white and sculpted like a mask, the forehead abnormally high. His clothes were subdued in colour, but elegant and made of exquisite fabric. He gave out a seductive fragrance that suggested boldness and originality. He returned her father's bow graciously, and responded to his greeting in courteous, flowery language.

Kaede remained motionless as he stepped past her into the room, the scent filling her nostrils.

'My eldest daughter,' her father said casually, as he followed his guest inside. 'Otori Kaede.'

'Lady Otori,' she heard him say and then, 'I would like to look at her.'

'Come in, daughter,' her father said impatiently and she went in on her knees.

'Lord Fujiwara,' she murmured.

'She is very beautiful,' the nobleman remarked. 'Let me see her face.'

She raised her eyes and met his gaze.

'Exquisite.'

In his narrowed, appraising eyes she saw admiration but no desire. It surprised her and she smiled slightly, but unguardedly. He seemed equally surprised and the sternly held line of his lips softened.

'I am disturbing you,' he apologized, his glance taking in the writing instruments and the scrolls. Curiosity got the better of him. One eyebrow went up. 'A lesson?'

'It's nothing,' her father replied, embarrassed. 'A girl's foolishness. You will think me a very indulgent father.'

'On the contrary, I am fascinated.' He picked up the page she had been writing on. 'May I?'

'Please, please,' her father said.

'Quite a fine hand. One would not believe it to be a girl's.'

Kaede felt herself blush. She was reminded again of her boldness in daring to learn men's affairs.

'Do you like K'ung Fu-Tzu?' Lord Fujiwara addressed her directly, confusing her even more.

'I'm afraid my feelings towards him are mixed,' she replied. 'He seems to care so little for me.'

'Daughter,' her father remonstrated, but Fujiwara's lips moved again into something approaching a smile.

'He cannot have anticipated such a close acquaintance,' he replied lightly. 'You have arrived lately from Inuyama, I believe. I must confess my visit is partly to find out what news there is.'

'I came nearly a month ago,' she replied. 'Not directly from Inuyama, but from Terayama, where Lord Otori is buried.'

'Your husband? I had not heard. My condolences.'

His glance ran over her form. *Nothing escapes him,* she thought. *He has eyes like a cormorant.*

'Iida brought about his death,' she said quietly, 'and was killed in turn by the Otori.'

Fujiwara went on to express his sympathy further, and she spoke briefly of Arai and the situation at Inuyama, but beneath his formal elegant speech she thought she discerned a hunger to know more. It disturbed her a little but at the same time she was tempted by it. She felt she could tell him anything and that nothing would shock him, and she was flattered by his obvious interest in her.

'This is the Arai who swore allegiance to the Noguchi,' her father said, returning with anger to his main grudge. 'Because of his treachery I found myself fighting men from the Seishuu clan on my own land – some of them my own relatives. I was betrayed and outnumbered.'

'Father!' Kaede tried to silence him. It was none of Lord Fujiwara's concern, and the less said about the disgrace the better.

The nobleman acknowledged the disclosure with a slight bow. 'Lord Shirakawa was wounded, I believe.'

'Too slightly,' he replied. 'Better I had been killed. I should take my own life but my daughters weaken me.'

Kaede had no desire to hear any more. Luckily they were interrupted by Ayame bringing tea and small pieces of sweetened bean paste. Kaede served the men and then excused herself, leaving them to talk further. Fujiwara's eyes followed her as she left and she found herself hoping she might talk with him again but without her father present.

She could not suggest such a meeting directly but from

time to time she tried to think of ways to make it happen. A few days later, however, her father told her a message had come from the nobleman inviting Kaede to visit him and to view his collection of paintings and other treasures.

'You have aroused his interest in some way,' he said, a little surprised.

Pleased, though somewhat apprehensive, Kaede told Shizuka to go to the stables and ask Amano to get Raku ready and to ride with her to Fujiwara's residence, which was a little more than an hour's journey away.

'You must go in the palanquin,' Shizuka replied firmly.

'Why?'

'Lord Fujiwara is from the court. He is a nobleman. You can't go and visit him on a horse, like a warrior.' Shizuka looked stern and then spoilt the effect by giggling and adding, 'Now if you were a boy and rode up on Raku, he would probably never let you go! But you have to impress him as a woman; you must be presented perfectly.' She looked critically at Kaede. 'He'll think you too tall, no doubt.'

'He already said I was beautiful,' Kaede replied, stung.

'He needs to find you flawless. Like a piece of celadon, or a painting by Sesshu. Then he'll feel the desire to add you to his collection.'

'I don't want to be part of his collection,' she exclaimed.

'What *do* you want?' Shizuka's voice had turned serious.

Kaede answered in a similar tone. 'I want to restore my land and claim what is mine. I want to have power as men have.'

'Then you need an ally,' Shizuka replied. 'If it is to be

93

Lord Fujiwara you must be perfect for him. Send a message to say you had a bad dream and that the day seems inauspicious. Tell him you will attend on him the day after tomorrow. That should give us time.'

The message was sent and Kaede submitted herself to Shizuka's efforts. Her hair was washed, her eyebrows plucked, her skin scrubbed with bran, massaged with lotions and scrubbed again. Shizuka went through all the garments in the house and selected some of Kaede's mother's robes for her to wear. They were not new, but the materials were of high quality and the colours – grey like a dove's wing and the purple of bush clover – brought out Kaede's ivory skin and the blue-black lights in her hair.

'You are certainly beautiful enough to attract his interest,' Shizuka said, 'but you must also intrigue him. Don't tell him too much. I believe he is a man who loves secrets. If you share your secrets with him be sure he pays a fair price for them.'

The nights had turned cold with the first frosts, but the days were clear. The mountains that encircled her home were brilliant with maple and sumac, as red as flames against the dark green cedars and the blue sky. Kaede's senses were heightened by her pregnancy and as she stepped from the palanquin in the garden of the Fujiwara residence the beauty before her moved her deeply. It was a perfect moment of autumn, and would so soon vanish for ever, driven away by the storm winds that would come howling from the mountains.

The house was larger than her own and in much better repair. Water flowed through the garden, trickling over ancient stones and through pools where gold and red carp swam lazily. The mountains seemed to rise directly from the garden, and a distant waterfall both echoed and mirrored the stream. Two great eagles soared above in the cloudless sky.

A young man greeted her at the step and led the way across a wide veranda to the main room where Lord Fujiwara was already sitting. Kaede stepped inside the doorway and sank to her knees, touching her forehead to the floor. The matting was fresh and new, the colour still pale green, the scent poignant.

Shizuka remained outside, kneeling on the wooden floor. Within the room there was silence. Kaede waited for him to speak, knowing he was studying her, trying to see as much as she could of the room without moving her eyes or her head. It was a relief when he finally addressed her and begged her to sit up.

'I am very pleased you could come,' he said, and they exchanged formalities, she keeping her voice soft and low, he speaking in such flowery language that sometimes she could only guess at the meaning of the words. She hoped that, if she said as little as possible, he would find her enigmatic, rather than dull.

The young man returned with tea utensils and Fujiwara himself made tea, whisking the green powder into a foaming brew. The bowls were rough, pink-brown in colour, pleasing to both eye and hand. She turned hers, admiring it.

'It's from Hagi,' he said. 'From Lord Otori's hometown. It is my favourite of all the teaware.' After a moment he went on, 'Will you go there?'

Of course, I should, Kaede thought rapidly. *If he really were my husband and I were carrying his child I would go to his house, to his family.*

'I cannot,' she said simply, raising her eyes. As always

95

the memory of Shigeru's death and the role she had played in it and in the act of revenge brought her almost to tears, darkening her eyes, making them glow.

'There are always reasons,' he said obliquely. 'Take my own situation. My son, my wife's grave are in the capital. You may not have heard this: I myself was asked to leave. My writings displeased the regent. After my exile the city was subjected to two huge earthquakes and a series of fires. It was generally believed to be Heaven's displeasure at such unjust treatment of a harmless scholar. Prayers were offered and I was begged to return, but for the time being my life here pleases me, and I find reasons not to obey immediately, though, of course, eventually I must.'

'Lord Shigeru has become a god,' she said. 'Hundreds of people go every day to pray at his shrine, at Terayama.'

'Lord Shigeru, alas for us all, is dead, however, and I am still very much alive. It is too early for me to become a god.'

He had told her something of himself and now she felt moved to do the same. 'His uncles wanted him dead,' she said, 'That is why I will not go to them.'

'I know little of the Otori clan,' he said, 'apart from the beautiful pottery they produce in Hagi. They have the reputation of skulking there. It's quite inaccessible, I believe. And they have some ancient connection with the imperial family.' His voice was light, almost bantering, but when he went on it changed slightly. The same intensity of feeling that she had noticed previously had entered it again. 'Forgive me if I am intruding, but how did Lord Shigeru die?'

She had spoken so little of the terrible events at Inuyama that she longed to unburden herself to him now, but as he leaned towards her, she felt his hunger again, not for her, but to know what she had suffered.

'I cannot speak of it,' she said in a low voice. She would make him pay for her secrets. 'It is too painful.'

'Ah.' Fujiwara looked down at the bowl in his hand. Kaede allowed herself to study him, the sculpted bones of his face, the sensuous mouth, the long, delicate fingers. He placed the bowl on the matting and glanced up at her. She deliberately held his gaze, let tears form in her eyes, then looked away.

'Maybe one day . . .' she said softly.

They sat without moving or speaking for several moments.

'You intrigue me,' he said finally. 'Very few women do. Let me show you my humble place, my meagre collection.'

She placed the bowl on the floor and stood gracefully. He watched every movement she made but with none of the predatory desire of other men. Kaede realized what Shizuka had meant. If he admired her, this nobleman would want to add her to his collection. What price would he pay for her and what could she demand?

Shizuka bowed to the floor as they stepped past her and the young man appeared from the shadows. He was as fine boned and as delicate as a girl.

'Mamoru,' Fujiwara said, 'Lady Otori has kindly consented to look at my pathetic pieces. Come with us.'

As the young man bowed to her, Fujiwara said, 'You should learn from her. Study her. She is a perfect specimen.'

Kaede followed them into the centre of the house, where there was a courtyard and a stage area.

'Mamoru is an actor,' Fujiwara said. 'He plays

women's roles. I like to present dramas in this small space.'

Maybe it was not large, but it was exquisite. Plain wooden pillars supported the ornately carved roof, and on the backdrop a twisted pine tree was painted.

'You must come and watch a performance,' Fujiwara said. 'We are about to start rehearsing *Atsumori*. We are waiting for our flute player to arrive. But before that we will present *The Fulling Block*. Mamoru can learn a lot from you and I would like your opinion of his performance.'

When she said nothing he went on, 'You are familiar with drama?'

'I saw a few plays when I was at Lord Noguchi's,' she replied. 'But I know little about it.'

'Your father told me you were a hostage with the Noguchi.'

'From the age of seven.'

'What curious lives women lead,' he remarked, and a chill came over her.

They went from the theatre to another reception room that gave out onto a smaller garden. Sunlight streamed into it and Kaede was grateful for its warmth. But the sun was already low over the mountains. Soon their peaks would hide it and their jagged shadows would cover the valley. She could not help shivering.

'Bring a brazier,' Fujiwara ordered. 'Lady Otori is cold.'

Mamoru disappeared briefly and came back with a much older man who carried a small brazier, glowing with charcoal.

'Sit near it,' Fujiwara said. 'It is easy to take a chill at this time of year.'

Mamoru left the room again, never speaking, his movements graceful, deferential and soundless. When he returned he was carrying a small paulownia wood chest which he set down carefully on the floor. He left the room and returned three more times, each time bringing a chest or box. Each was of a different wood, zelkova, cypress, cherry, polished so that the colour and grain spoke of the long life of the tree, the slope it had grown on, the seasons of hot and cold, rain and wind that it had endured.

Fujiwara opened the chests one by one. Within lay bundles, objects wrapped in several layers of cloth. The wrapping cloths themselves were beautiful, although obviously very old: silks of the finest weave and the most subtle colours, but what lay within these cloths far surpassed anything Kaede had ever seen. He unwrapped each one, placed it on the floor in front of her and invited her to take it up, caress it with her fingers, touch it to her lips or to her brow, for often the feel and the scent of the object were as important as its look. He rewrapped and replaced each one before displaying the next.

'I look at them rarely,' he said, with love in his voice. 'Each time an unworthy gaze falls on them it diminishes them. Just to unwrap them is an erotic act for me. To share them with another whose gaze enhances rather than diminishes is one of my greatest, but rarest, pleasures.'

Kaede said nothing, knowing little of the value or tradition of the objects before her: the tea bowl of pink-brown pottery, at once fragile and sturdy, the jade figure of the Enlightened One, seated within the lotus, the gold lacquered box that was both simple and intricate. She simply gazed, and it seemed to her that the beautiful things had their own eyes and gazed back at her.

Mamoru did not stay to look at the objects, but after

what seemed a long time – for Kaede time had stopped – he returned with a large, flat box. Fujiwara took out a painting: a winter landscape with two crows, black against the snow, in the foreground.

'Ah, Sesshu,' she whispered, speaking for the first time.

'Not Sesshu, in fact, but one of his masters,' he corrected her. 'It's said that the child cannot teach the parent, but in Sesshu's case we must allow that the pupil surpassed the teacher.'

'Is there not a saying that the blue of the dye is deeper than the blue of the flower?' she replied.

'You approve of that, I expect.'

'If neither child nor pupil were ever wiser nothing would ever change.'

'And most people would be very satisfied!'

'Only those who have power,' Kaede said. 'They want to hold onto their power and position, while others see that same power and desire it. It's within all men to be ambitious and so they make change happen. The young overthrow the old.'

'And is it within women to be ambitious?'

'No one bothers to ask them.' Her eyes returned to the painting. 'Two crows, the drake and the duck, the stag and the hind – they are always painted together, always in pairs.'

'That is the way nature intends it,' Fujiwara said. 'It is one of K'ung Fu-Tzu's five relationships after all.'

'And the only one open to women. He only sees us as wives.'

'That is what women are.'

'But surely a woman could be a ruler or a friend?' Her eyes met his.

'You are very bold for a girl,' he replied, the nearest she had seen him come to laughing. She flushed and looked again at the painting.

'Terayama is famous for its Sesshus,' Fujiwara said. 'Did you see them there?'

'Yes, Lord Otori wanted Lord Takeo to see them and copy them.'

'A younger brother?'

'His adopted son.' The last thing Kaede wanted to do was to talk to Fujiwara about Takeo. She tried to think of something else to say, but all thoughts deserted her, except for the memory of the painting Takeo had given her of the little mountain bird.

'I presume he carried out the revenge? He must be very courageous. I doubt my son would do as much for me.'

'He was always very silent,' she said, longing to talk about him, yet fearing to. 'You would not think him particularly courageous. He liked drawing and painting. He turned out to be fearless.' She heard her own voice and stopped abruptly, sure she was transparent to him.

'Ah,' Fujiwara said, and looked at the painting again for a long time.

'I mustn't intrude on your affairs,' he said finally, his eyes returning to her face, 'but surely you will be married to Lord Shigeru's son?'

'There are other considerations,' she said, trying to speak lightly. 'I have land here and at Maruyama that I must lay claim to. If I go and skulk with the Otori in Hagi I may lose all that.'

'I feel you have many secrets for someone so young,' he murmured. 'I hope one day to hear them.'

The sun was slipping towards the mountains. The

shadows from the huge cedars began to stretch out towards the house.

'It is growing late,' he said. 'I am sorry to lose you but feel I must send you on your way. You will come again soon.' He wrapped up the painting and replaced it in its box. She could smell the faint fragrance of the wood and of the rue leaves placed inside to ward off insects.

'Thank you from my heart,' she said as they rose. Mamoru had returned silently to the room and now bowed deeply as she passed by him.

'Look at her, Mamoru,' Fujiwara said. 'Watch how she walks, how she returns your bow. If you can capture that you can call yourself an actor.'

They exchanged farewells, Lord Fujiwara himself coming out onto the veranda to see her into the palanquin and sending retainers to accompany her.

'You did well,' Shizuka told her when they were home. 'You intrigued him.'

'He despises me,' Kaede said. She felt exhausted from the encounter.

'He despises women, but he sees you as something different.'

'Something unnatural.'

'Maybe,' Shizuka said laughing. 'Or something unique and rare that no one else possesses.'

Five

The following day Fujiwara sent presents for her, with an invitation to attend a performance of a play at the full moon. Kaede unwrapped two robes, one old and restrained, beautifully embroidered with pheasants and autumn grasses in gold and green on ivory-coloured silk, the other new, it seemed, and more flamboyant, with deep purple and blue peonies on pale pink.

Hana and Ai came to admire them. Lord Fujiwara had also sent food, quail and sweet fish, persimmons and bean cakes. Hana, like all of them always on the edge of hunger, was deeply impressed.

'Don't touch,' Kaede scolded her. 'Your hands are dirty.'

Hana's hands were stained from gathering chestnuts, but she hated anyone to reprimand her. She pulled them behind her back and stared angrily at her older sister.

'Hana,' Kaede said, trying to be gentle. 'Let Ayame wash your hands, then you may look.'

Kaede's relationship with her younger sister was still uneasy. Privately she thought Hana had been spoiled by Ayame and Ai. She wished she could persuade her father to teach Hana too, feeling the girl needed discipline and challenges in her life. She wanted to instil them herself, but lacked the time and the patience to do so. It was something else she would have to think about during the long winter months. Now Hana ran off to the kitchen, crying.

'I'll go to her,' Ai said.

'She is so self-willed,' Kaede said to Shizuka. 'What is to become of her when she is so beautiful and so stubborn?'

Shizuka gave her a mocking look, but said nothing.

'What?' Kaede said. 'What do you mean?'

'She is like you, lady,' Shizuka murmured.

'So you said before. She is luckier than I am, though.' Kaede fell silent, thinking of the difference between them. When she was Hana's age she had been alone in Noguchi castle for over two years. Perhaps she was jealous of her sister and it was this that made her impatient with her. But Hana really was running wild beyond control.

She sighed, gazing on the beautiful robes, longing to feel the softness of the silk against her skin. She told Shizuka to bring a mirror and held the older robe up to her face to see the colours against her hair. She was more impressed than she revealed by the gifts. Lord Fujiwara's interest flattered her. He had said that she intrigued him; he intrigued her no less.

She wore the older robe, for it seemed more suitable for late autumn, when she and her father, Shizuka and Ai, went to visit Lord Fujiwara for the performance. They were to stay overnight since the drama would go on until late, under the full moon. Hana, desperate to be invited too, sulked when they left and would not come out to say goodbye. Kaede wished she could have left her father behind too. His unpredictable behaviour worried her, and she was afraid he might shame himself further in company. But he, immensely flattered by the invitation, would not be dissuaded.

104

Several actors, Mamoru among them, presented *The Fulling Block*. The play made disturbed Kaede deeply. During her brief visit, Mamoru had studied her more than she had realized. Now she saw herself portrayed before her eyes, saw her movements, heard her own voice sigh, *The autumn wind tells of love grown cold*, as the wife went slowly mad waiting for her husband's return.

Brilliance of the moon, touch of the wind. The words of the chorus pierced her like a needle in her flesh.

Frost gleaming in pale light, chill the heart as the block beats and night winds moan.

Her eyes filled with tears. All the loneliness and the longing of the woman on the stage, a woman modelled on her, seemed indeed to be hers. She had even that week helped Ayame beat their silken robes with the fulling block to soften and restore them. Her father had commented on it, saying the repetitive beat of the block was one of the most evocative sounds of autumn. The drama stripped her of her defences. She longed for Takeo, completely, achingly. If she could not have him she would die. Yet even while her heart cracked she remembered that she must live for the child's sake. And it seemed she felt the first tiny flutter of its watery movement within her.

Above the stage the brilliant moon of the tenth month shone coldly down. Smoke from the charcoal braziers drifted skywards. The soft beat of the drums fell into the silence. The small group watching were rapt, possessed by the beauty of the moon and the power of emotion displayed before them.

Afterwards Shizuka and Ai returned to their room but, to Kaede's surprise, Lord Fujiwara asked her to remain in the company of the men as they drank wine and ate a series of exotic dishes, mushrooms, land crabs, pickled chestnuts, and tiny squid transported in ice and straw from the coast. The actors joined them, their masks laid aside. Lord Fujiwara praised them, and gave them gifts. Later, when the wine had loosened tongues and raised the level of noise, he addressed Kaede quietly.

'I am glad your father came with you. I believe he has not been well?'

'You are very kind to him,' she replied. 'Your understanding and consideration mean a great deal to us.' She did not think it was seemly to discuss her father's state of mind with the nobleman but Fujiwara persisted.

'Does he fall into gloomy states often?'

'He is a little unstable, from time to time. My mother's death, the war . . .' Kaede looked at her father, who was talking excitedly with one of the older actors. His eyes glittered, and he did indeed look a little mad.

'I hope you will turn to me if you need help at any time.'

She bowed silently, aware of the great honour he was paying her and confused by his attention. She had never sat like this in a room full of men and felt that she should not be there, yet was unsure of how to leave. He changed the subject deftly.

'What was your opinion of Mamoru? He learned well from you, I think.'

She did not answer for a moment, turning her gaze from her father to the young man, who had divested himself of his female role yet still retained the vestiges of it, of her.

'What can I say?' she said finally. 'He seemed brilliant to me.'

'But . . .?' he questioned.

'You steal everything from us.' She had meant to

say it lightly, but her voice sounded bitter to her own ears.

'*You?*' he repeated, slightly surprised.

'Men. You take everything from women. Even our pain – the very pain that you cause us – you steal it and portray it as your own.'

His opaque eyes searched her face. 'I have never seen a more convincing or moving portrayal than Mamoru's.'

'Why are women's roles not played by women?'

'What a curious idea,' he replied. 'You think you would have more authenticity because you imagine these emotions are familiar to you. But it is the actor's artifice in creating emotions that he cannot know intimately that displays his genius.'

'You leave us nothing,' Kaede said.

'We give you our children. Isn't that a fair exchange?'

Again she felt his eyes could see right through her. *I dislike him,* she thought, *even though he is intriguing. I will have nothing more to do with him, no matter what Shizuka says.*

'I have offended you,' he said as though he could read her thoughts.

'I am too insignificant for Lord Fujiwara to concern himself with,' she replied. 'My feelings are of no importance.'

'I take great interest in your feelings: they are always so original and unexpected.'

Kaede made no response. After a second he went on, 'You must come and see our next play. It is to be *Atsumori*. We await only our flute player. He is a friend of Mamoru's who is expected any day now. You are familiar with the story?'

'Yes,' she said, her mind turning to the tragedy. She

was still thinking about it later when she lay in the guest room with Ai and Shizuka: the youth so beautiful and gifted at music, the rough warrior who slays him and takes his head, and then in remorse becomes a monk, seeking the peace of the Enlightened One. She thought about Atsumori's wraith, calling from the shadows, *Pray for me. Let my spirit be released.*

The unfamiliar excitement, the emotions aroused by the play, the lateness of the hour all made her restless. Thinking about Atsumori, the flute player, she drifted between sleeping and waking, and seemed to hear the notes of a flute coming from the garden. The sound reminded her of something. She was descending towards sleep, soothed by the music, when she remembered.

She woke instantly. It was the same music she had heard at Terayama. The young monk who had shown them the paintings – surely he had played the same notes, so laden with anguish and longing?

She pushed back the quilt and got up quietly, slid aside the paper screen and listened. She heard a quiet knock, the scrape of the wooden door opening, Mamoru's voice, the voice of the flute player. At the end of the passage a lamp in a servant's hand briefly lit their faces. She was not dreaming. It was him.

Shizuka whispered from behind her. 'Is everything all right?'

Kaede closed the screen and went to kneel beside her. 'It is one of the monks from Terayama.'

'Here?'

'He is the flute player they have been waiting for.'

'Makoto,' Shizuka said.

'I never knew his name. Will he remember me?'

'How can he forget?' Shizuka replied. 'We will leave

early. You must plead illness. He must not see you un-expectedly. Try and sleep for a while. I will wake you at daybreak.'

Kaede lay down, but sleep was slow to come. Finally she dozed a little and woke to see daylight behind the shutters and Shizuka kneeling beside her.

She wondered if it were possible to steal away. The household was already stirring. She could hear the shutters being opened. Her father always woke early. She could not leave without at least informing him.

'Go to my father and tell him I am unwell and must go home. Ask him to make my apologies to Lord Fujiwara.'

Shizuka came back after several minutes. 'Lord Shirakawa is most reluctant for you to leave. He wants to know if you are well enough to go to him.'

'Where is he?'

'He is in the room overlooking the garden. I have asked for tea to be brought to you, you look very pale.'

'Help me dress,' Kaede said. Indeed she felt faint and unwell. The tea revived her a little. Ai was awake now, lying under the quilt, her sweet-natured face pink cheeked and dark eyed from sleep, like a doll's.

'Kaede, what is it? What's the matter?'

'I am ill. I need to go home.'

'I'll come with you.' Ai pushed back the quilt.

'It would be better if you stayed with father,' Kaede told her. 'And apologize to Lord Fujiwara on my behalf.'

She knelt on an impulse and stroked her sister's hair. 'Stand in for me,' she begged.

'I don't think Lord Fujiwara has even noticed my existence,' Ai said. 'It is you who have entranced him.'

The caged birds in the garden were calling noisily. *He*

will find out my deception, and never want to see me again, Kaede thought, but it was not the nobleman's reaction that she feared. It was her father's.

'The servants told me Lord Fujiwara sleeps late,' Shizuka whispered. 'Go and speak to your father. I have asked for the palanquin.'

Kaede nodded, saying nothing. She stepped onto the polished wood of the veranda. How beautifully the boards were laid. As she walked towards the room where her father was, scenes from the garden unfolded before her eyes, a stone lantern, framed by the last red leaves of the maple, the sun glittering on the still water of a pool, the flash of yellow and black from the long-tailed birds on their perches.

Her father sat looking out onto the garden. She could not help feeling pity for him. Lord Fujiwara's friendship meant so much to him.

In the pool a heron waited, as still as a statue.

She dropped to her knees and waited for her father to speak.

'What's this nonsense, Kaede? Your rudeness is beyond belief!'

'Forgive me, I am not well,' she murmured. When he did not reply she raised her voice a little. 'Father, I am unwell. I am going home now.'

He still said nothing, as if ignoring her would make her go away. The heron rose with a sudden beat of wings. Two young men walked into the garden, to look at the caged birds.

Kaede looked around the room, seeking a screen or something that she might hide behind but there was nothing.

'Good morning!' her father called cheerfully.

110

The men turned to acknowledge him. Mamoru saw her. There was a moment when she thought he would leave the garden without approaching her, but Lord Fujiwara's treatment of her the previous night, when he had included her in the men's party, must have emboldened him. He led the other man forward and began the formal introductions to her father. She bowed deeply, hoping to hide her face. Mamoru gave the monk's name, Kubo Makoto, and the name of the temple at Terayama. Makoto bowed too.

'Lord Shirakawa,' Mamoru said, 'and his daughter, Lady Otori.'

The young monk could not prevent his reaction. He turned pale and his eyes went to her face. He recognized her and spoke in the same moment.

'Lady Otori? You married Lord Takeo after all? Is he here with you?'

There was a moment of silence. Then Kaede's father spoke. 'My daughter's husband was Lord Otori Shigeru.'

Makoto opened his mouth as if he would deny it, thought better of it, and bowed without speaking.

Kaede's father leaned forward. 'You are from Terayama? You did not know that the marriage took place there?'

Makoto said nothing. Her father spoke to her without turning his head. 'Leave us alone.'

She was proud of how steady her voice was when she spoke. 'I am going home. Please make my apologies to Lord Fujiwara.'

He made no response to her. *He will kill me*, she thought. She bowed to the two young men, saw their embarrassment and their discomfort. As she walked away, forcing herself not to hurry, not to move her head, a wave of emotion began to uncurl in her belly. She saw she would always be the object of those embarrassed looks, that scorn. She gasped at the intensity of the feeling, the sharpness of the despair that came with it. *Better to die*, she thought. *But what about my child, Takeo's child? Must it die with me?*

At the end of the veranda Shizuka was waiting for her. 'We can leave now, lady. Kondo will come with us.'

Kaede allowed the man to lift her into the palanquin. She was relieved to be inside, in the semi-darkness where no one could see her face. *Father will never look at my face again*, she thought. *He will turn his eyes away even when he kills me.*

When she reached her house she took off the robe that Fujiwara had given her and folded it carefully. She put on one of her mother's old robes, with a quilted garment underneath. She was cold to the bone and she did not want to tremble.

'You are back!' Hana came running into the room. 'Where is Ai?'

'She stayed at Lord Fujiwara's a little longer.'

'Why did you come back?' the child asked.

'I didn't feel well. I'm all right now.' On an impulse Kaede said, 'I'm going to give you the robe, the autumn one you liked so much. You must put it away and look after it, until you are old enough to wear it.'

'Don't you want it?'

'I want you to have it, and to think of me when you wear it and pray for me.'

Hana stared at her, her eyes sharp. 'Where are you going?' When Kaede did not reply she went on, 'Don't go away again, older sister.'

'You won't mind,' Kaede said, trying to tease her. 'You won't miss me.'

To her dismay Hana began to sob noisily, and then to scream. 'I will miss you! Don't leave me! Don't leave me!'

Ayame came running. 'Now what is it, Hana? You must not be naughty with your sister.'

Shizuka came into the room. 'Your father is at the ford,' she said. 'He has come alone, on horseback.'

'Ayame,' Kaede said, 'take Hana out for a while. Take her to the forest. All the servants must go with you. I want no one in the house.'

'But, Lady Kaede, it's so early and still so cold.'

'Please do as I say,' Kaede begged. Hana cried more wildly as Ayame led her away.

'It is grief that makes her so wild,' Shizuka said.

'I am afraid I must inflict still more on her,' Kaede exclaimed. 'But she must not be here.'

She stood and went to the small chest where she kept a few things. She took the knife from it, felt its weight in her forbidden left hand. Soon it would no longer matter to anyone which hand she had used.

'Which is best, in the throat or in the heart?'

'You don't have to do it,' Shizuka said quietly. 'We can flee. The Tribe will hide you. Think of the child.'

'I can't run away!' Kaede was surprised at the loudness of her own voice.

'Then let me give you poison. It will be swift and painless. You will simply fall asleep and never—'

Kaede cut her short. 'I am a warrior's daughter. I'm not afraid of dying. You know better than anyone how often I have thought of taking my own life. First I must ask Father's forgiveness, then I must use the knife on myself. My only question is, which is better?'

113

Shizuka came close to her. 'Place the point here, at the side of your neck. Thrust it sideways and upwards. That will slash the artery.' Her voice, matter of fact to start with, faltered, and Kaede saw there were tears in her eyes. 'Don't do it,' Shizuka whispered. 'Don't despair yet.'

Kaede transferred the knife to her right hand. She heard the shouts of the guard, the horse's hoof beats as her father rode through the gate. She heard Kondo greet him.

She gazed out onto the garden. A sudden flash of memory came to her of herself as a little child, running the length of the veranda from her father to her mother and back again. *I've never remembered that before,* she thought, and whispered soundlessly, *Mother, Mother!*

Her father stepped onto the veranda. As he came through the doorway both she and Shizuka dropped to their knees, foreheads to the ground.

'Daughter,' he said, his voice uncertain and thin. She looked up at him and saw his face streaked with tears, his mouth working. She had been afraid of his anger, but now she saw his madness and it frightened her more.

'Forgive me,' she whispered.

'I must kill myself now.' He sat heavily in front of her, taking his dagger from his belt. He looked at the blade for a long time.

'Send for Shoji,' he said finally. 'He must assist me. Tell your man to ride to his house and fetch him.'

When she made no response he shouted suddenly, 'Tell him!'

'I'll go,' Shizuka whispered. She crawled on her knees to the edge of the veranda; Kaede heard her speak to Kondo, but the man did not leave. Instead he stepped up onto the veranda and she knew he was waiting just out-side the doorway.

Her father made a sudden gesture towards her. She could not help flinching, thinking he was about to hit her. He said, 'There was no marriage!'

'Forgive me,' she said again. 'I have shamed you. I am ready to die.'

'But there is a child?' He was staring at her as though she were a viper that would strike at any moment.

'Yes, there is a child.'

'Who is the father? Or don't you know? Was he one of many?'

'It makes no difference now,' she replied. 'The child will die with me.'

She thought, *Thrust the knife sideways and upwards.* But she felt the child's tiny hands grip her muscles, pre-venting her.

'Yes, yes, you must take your own life.' His voice rose, taking on a shrill energy. 'Your sisters must also kill them-selves. This is my last command to you. Thus the Shirakawa family will disappear, not before time. And I will not wait for Shoji. I must do it myself. It will be my final act of honour.'

He loosened his sash and opened his robe, pushing aside his undergarment to expose his flesh. 'Don't turn away,' he said to Kaede. 'You must watch. It is you who have driven me to this.' He placed the point of the blade against the loose, wrinkled skin and drew a deep breath.

She could not believe it was happening. She saw his knuckles tighten around the handle, saw his face contort. He gave a harsh cry and the dagger fell from his hands. But there was no blood, no wound. Several more sharp cries issued from him, then gave way to racking sobs.

115

'I cannot do it,' he wailed. 'My courage has all gone. You have sapped me, unnatural woman that you are. You have taken my honour and my manhood. You are not my daughter; you are a demon! You bring death to all men; you are cursed.' He reached out and grabbed her, pulling at her garments. 'Let me see you,' he cried. 'Let me see what other men desire! Bring death to me as you have to others.'

'No,' she screamed, fighting against his hands, trying to push him away. 'Father, no!'

'You call me Father? I am not your father. My real children are the sons I never had; the sons you and your cursed sisters took the place of. Your demonic powers must have killed them in your mother's womb!' His madness gave him strength. She felt the robes pulled from her shoulders, his hands on her skin. She could not use the knife; she could not escape him. As she struggled against his grip the robe slipped to her waist, exposing her. Her hair came loose and fell around her bare shoulders.

'You are beautiful,' he shouted. 'I admit it. I have desired you. While I taught you I lusted after you. It was my punishment for going against nature. I am completely corrupted by you. Now bring me death!'

'Let me go, Father,' she cried, trying to stay calm, hoping to reason with him. 'You are not yourself. If we must die let us do it with dignity.' But all words seemed weak and meaningless in the face of his delusions.

His eyes were wet, his lips quivering. He seized her knife and threw it across the room, held both her wrists in his left hand and pulled her towards him. With his right hand he reached under her hair, drew it aside, bent over her and put his lips on the nape of her neck.

Horror and revulsion swept over her, followed by

116

fury. She had been prepared to die, in accordance with the harsh code of her class, to salvage her family's honour. But her father, who had instructed her so rigidly in that code, who had taught her assiduously about the superiority of his sex, had surrendered to madness, revealing what lay beneath the strict rules of conduct of the warrior class: the lust and selfishness of men. The fury brought to life the power that she knew lay within her and she remembered how she had slept in ice. She called to the White Goddess. *Help me!*

She heard her own voice – 'Help me! Help me!' – and even as she cried out her father's grip slackened. *He has come to his senses,* she thought, pushing him away. She scrambled to her feet, pulling her robe around her and retying the sash and, almost without thinking, stumbled to the furthest side of the room. She was sobbing with shock and rage.

She turned and saw Kondo kneeling in front of her father, who sat half-upright, supported, she thought at first, by Shizuka. Then she realized that her father's eyes saw nothing. Kondo plunged his hand, it seemed, into her father's belly and slashed crossways. The cut made a foul soft noise, and the blood hissed and bubbled as it foamed out.

Shizuka let go of the man's neck, and he fell forwards. Kondo placed the knife in his right hand.

The vomit rose in her throat then and she doubled up, retching. Shizuka came to her, her face expressionless. 'It's all over.'

'Lord Shirakawa lost his mind,' Kondo said. 'And took his own life. He has had many episodes of madness and often spoke of so doing. He died honourably and with great courage.' He stood and looked directly at her.

There was a moment when she could have called for the guards, denounced both of them and had them executed, but the moment passed and she did nothing. She knew she would never reveal the murder to anyone.

Kondo smiled very slightly and continued, 'Lady Otori, you must demand allegiance from the men. You must be strong. Otherwise any one of them will seize your domain and usurp you.'

'I was about to kill myself,' she said slowly. 'But it seems there is no need now.'

'No need,' he agreed. 'As long as you are strong.'

'You must live for the child's sake,' Shizuka urged her. 'No one will care who the father is, if only you are powerful enough. But you must act now. Kondo, summon the men as quickly as possible.'

Kaede let Shizuka lead her to the women's rooms, wash her, and change her clothes. Her mind was quivering with shock but she clung to the knowledge of her own power. Her father was dead and she was alive. He had wanted to die; it was no hardship for her to pretend that he had indeed taken his own life and had died with honour, a desire he had often expressed. Indeed, she thought bitterly, she was respecting his wishes and protecting his name. She would not, however, obey his last command to her. She would not kill herself and she would not allow her sisters to die either.

Kondo had summoned the guards, and boys were sent to the village to fetch the men who lived on farms. Within the hour most of her father's retainers were assembled. The women had brought out the mourning clothes so recently put away after her mother's death, and the priest had been sent for. The sun came up higher, melting the frost. The air smelled of smoke and pine needles. Now that the first shock was over Kaede was driven by a feeling she hardly understood, a fierce need to secure what was hers, to protect her sisters and her household, to ensure nothing of hers was lost or stolen. Any one of the men could take her estate from her; they would not hesitate if she showed the slightest sign of weakness. She had seen the utter ruthlessness that lay beneath Shizuka's light-hearted pose and Kondo's ironic exterior. That ruthlessness had saved her life and she would match it with her own.

She recalled the decisiveness that she had seen in Arai, which made men follow him, which had brought most of the Three Countries under his sway. She must now show the same resolution. Arai would respect their alliance, but if anyone else took her place would he hold back from war? She would not let her people be devastated, she would not let her sisters be taken away as hostages.

Death still beckoned her, but this new fierce spirit within her would not allow her to respond. *I am indeed possessed,* she thought, as she stepped onto the veranda to speak to the men assembled in the garden. *How few they are,* she thought, remembering the numbers her father used to command when she was a child. Ten were Arai's men, whom Kondo had selected, and there were twenty or so who still served the Shirakawa. She knew them all by name, had made it her business since she returned to get to know their position and something of their character.

Shoji had been one of the first to arrive, had prostrated himself before her father's body. His face still bore the traces of tears. He stood at her right hand, Kondo on her left. She was aware of Kondo's deference to the older man, and aware that it was a pretence, like most of what he did. *But he killed my father for me,* she thought. *He is bound to me now. But what price will he exact in return?*

The men knelt before her, heads lowered, then sat back on their heels as she spoke.

'Lord Shirakawa has taken his own life,' she said. 'It was his choice, and whatever my grief, I must respect and honour his deed. My father intended me to be his heir. It was for that purpose that he began instructing me as if I were his son. I mean to carry out his wishes.' She paused for a moment, hearing his final words to her, so different. *I am completely corrupted by you. Now bring me death.* But she did not flinch. To the watching men she seemed to radiate some deep power. It illuminated her eyes and made her voice irresistible. 'I ask my father's men to swear allegiance to me as you did to him. Since Lord Arai and I are in alliance, I expect those of you who serve him to continue to serve me. In return I offer you both protection and advancement. I plan to consolidate Shirakawa, and next year take up the lands willed to me at Maruyama. My father will be buried tomorrow.'

Shoji was the first to kneel before her. Kondo followed, though again his demeanour unnerved her. *He is play-acting,* she thought. *Allegiance means nothing to him. He is from the Tribe. What schemes do they have for me that I know nothing about? Can I trust them? If I find I cannot trust Shizuka what will I do?*

Her heart quailed within her, though none of the men filing before her would have guessed. She received their allegiance, noting each one, picking out their characteristics, their clothes, armour and weapons. They were mostly ill-equipped, the laces of their armour broken and frayed, their helmets dented and cracked, but they all had bows and swords, and she knew most of them had horses.

All knelt to her save two. One, a giant of a man, Hirogawa, called out in a loud voice, 'All respect to your ladyship, but I've never served a woman and I'm too old to start now.' He made a perfunctory bow and walked to the gate with a swagger that infuriated her. A smaller man, Nakao, followed him without a word, without even bowing.

Kondo looked at her. 'Lady Otori?'

'Kill them,' she said, knowing she had to be ruthless, and knowing she had to start now.

He moved faster than she would have thought possible, cutting down Nakao before the man realized what was happening. Hirogawa turned in the gateway and drew his sword.

'You have broken your allegiance and must die,' Kondo shouted at him.

The large man laughed. 'You are not even from Shirakawa. Who's going to take any notice of you?' He held his sword in both hands, ready to strike. Kondo took a quick step forward but as Hirogawa's blow fell, Kondo parried it with his own sword, thrusting the other man's blade aside with unexpected strength, wielding his own weapon like an axe. In the return motion he whipped it back into Hirogawa's unprotected belly. Now more like a razor than an axe, the sword slid through the flesh. As Hirogawa faltered forwards, Kondo stepped out to the right and behind him. Spinning round he struck downwards, opening the man's back from shoulder to hip.

Kondo did not look at the dying men but turned to face the others. He said, 'I serve Lady Otori Kaede, heir to Shirakawa and Maruyama. Is there anyone else here who will not serve her as faithfully as I?'

No one moved. Kaede thought she saw anger in

Shoji's face but he simply pressed his lips together, saying nothing.

In recognition of their past service to her father she allowed the families of the dead men to collect the bodies and bury them, but because the men had disobeyed her she told Kondo to turn their dependents out of their homes and take their land for herself.

'It was the only thing to do,' Shizuka told her, 'If you had allowed them to live they would have caused unrest here or joined your enemies.'

'Who are my enemies?' Kaede said. It was late in the evening. They sat in Kaede's favourite room. The shutters were closed but the braziers hardly warmed the chill night air. She pulled the quilted robes more closely around her. From the main room came the chanting of priests, keeping vigil with the dead man.

'Lady Maruyama's stepdaughter is married to a cousin of Lord Iida, Nariaki. They will be your main rivals in claiming the domain.'

'But most of the Seishuu hate the Tohan,' Kaede replied. 'I believe I will be welcomed by them. I am the rightful heir, after all, the closest blood relative to Lady Maruyama.'

'No one's questioning your legal right,' Shizuka replied. 'But you will have to fight to obtain your inheritance. Would you not be content with your own domain here at Shirakawa?'

'The men I have are so few, and pitifully equipped,' Kaede said thoughtfully. 'Just to hold Shirakawa I will need a small army. I cannot afford one with the resources we have here. I will need the wealth of Maruyama. When the mourning period is over, you must send someone to Lady Naomi's chief retainer, Sugita Haruki. You know who he is; we met him on our journey to Tsuwano. Let's hope he is still in charge of the domain.'

'I must send someone?'

'You or Kondo. One of your spies.'

'You want to employ the Tribe?' Shizuka said in surprise.

'I already employ you,' Kaede replied. 'Now I want to make use of your skills.' She wanted to question Shizuka closely about many things, but she was exhausted, with an oppressive feeling in her belly and womb. *In the next day or so I will talk to her,* she promised herself, *but now I must lie down.*

Her back ached; when she was finally in bed she could not get comfortable and sleep would not come. She had gone through the whole terrible day and she was still alive, but now that the house was quiet, the weeping and chanting stilled, a deep sense of dread came over her. Her father's words rang in her ears. His face and the faces of the dead men loomed before her eyes. She feared their ghosts would try to snatch Takeo's child from her. Finally she slept, her arms wrapped around her belly.

She dreamed her father was attacking her. He drew the dagger from his belt but instead of plunging it into his own belly he came close to her, put his hand on the back of her neck and drove the dagger deep into her. An agonizing pain swept through her, making her wake with a cry. The pain surged again rhythmically. Her legs were already awash with blood.

Her father's funeral took place without her. The child slipped from her womb like an eel, and her life's blood followed. Then fever came, turning her vision red, setting her tongue babbling, tormenting her with hideous visions.

Shizuka and Ayame brewed all the herbs known to

them, then in despair burned incense and struck gongs to banish the evil spirits that possessed her, called for priests and a spirit girl to drive them away.

After three days it seemed nothing would save her. Ai never left her side. Even Hana was beyond tears. Around the hour of the Goat Shizuka had stepped outside to fetch fresh water, when one of the men at the guardhouse called to her.

'Visitors are coming. Men on horses and two palanquins. Lord Fujiwara, I think.'

'He must not come in,' she said. 'There is pollution by blood as well as by death.'

The bearers set the palanquins down outside the gate, and she dropped to her knees as Fujiwara looked out.

'Lord Fujiwara, forgive me. It is impossible for you to come in.'

'I was told Lady Otori is gravely ill,' he replied. 'Let me talk to you in the garden.'

She remained kneeling as he walked past her, then rose and followed him to the pavilion by the stream. He waved his servants away, and turned to Shizuka.

'How serious is it?'

'I do not think she will live beyond tonight,' Shizuka replied in a low voice. 'We have tried everything.'

'I have brought my physician,' Fujiwara said. 'Show him where to go and then come back to me.'

She bowed to him, and went back to the gate where the physician, a small, middle-aged man with a kind, intelligent look about him, was emerging from the second palanquin. She took him to the room where Kaede lay, her heart sinking at the sight of her pale skin and unfocussed eyes. Kaede's breathing was rapid and shallow, and every now and then she gave a sharp cry, whether of fear or pain it was impossible to tell.

When she came back Lord Fujiwara was standing gazing towards the end of the garden, where the stream fell away over rocks. The air was beginning to chill and the sound of the waterfall was bleak and lonely. Shizuka knelt again and waited for him to speak.

'Ishida is very skilled,' he said. 'Don't give up hope yet.'

'Lord Fujiwara's kindness is extreme,' she murmured. She could only think of Kaede's pale face and wild eyes. She longed to return to her, but she could not leave without the nobleman's permission.

'I am not a kind man,' he replied. 'I am motivated mainly by my own desires, by selfishness. It is my nature to be cruel.' He glanced briefly at her and said, 'How long have you served Lady Shirakawa? You are not from this part of the country?'

'I was sent to her in the spring while she was still at Noguchi castle.'

'Sent by whom?'

'By Lord Arai.'

'Indeed? And do you report back to him?'

'What can Lord Fujiwara mean?' Shizuka said.

'There is something about you that is unusual in a servant. I wondered if you might be a spy.'

'Lord Fujiwara has too high an opinion of my abilities,' Shizuka replied.

'I hope you never have cause to incite my cruelty.'

She heard the threat behind his words and said nothing.

He went on as if talking to himself. 'Her person, her life touch me in a way I have never felt before. I thought myself long past experiencing any new emotion. I will not let anyone or anything – even death – take her away from me.

'Everyone who sees her is bewitched by her,' Shizuka whispered, 'but fate has been unusually harsh to her.'

'I wish I knew her true life,' he said. 'I know she has many secrets. The recent tragedy of her father's death is another, I suppose. I hope you will tell me one day, if she cannot.' His voice broke. 'The idea that such beauty might perish pierces my soul,' he said. Shizuka thought she heard artificiality in his voice, but his eyes were filled with tears. 'If she lives I will marry her,' he said. 'That way I will have her with me always. You may go now. But will you tell her that?'

'Lord Fujiwara.' Shizuka touched her forehead to the ground and crept away backwards.

If she lives . . .

Six

*M*atsue was a northern town, cold and austere.
We arrived in the middle of autumn when the
wind from the mainland howled across a sea as
dark as iron. Once the snows began, like Hagi, Matsue
would be cut off from the rest of the country for three
months. It was as good a place as any to learn what I had
to learn.

For a week we had walked all day, following the coast
road. It did not rain, but the sky was often overcast and
each day was shorter and colder than the last. We stopped
at many villages and showed the children juggling, spinning tops and games with string that Yuki and Keiko
knew. At night we always found shelter with merchants
who were part of the Tribe network. I lay awake till late
listening to whispered conversations, my nostrils filled
with the smells of the brewery or of soybean foodstuff. I
dreamed of Kaede, and longed for her, and sometimes
when I was alone I would take out Shigeru's letter and
read his last words, in which he had charged me to avenge
his death and to take care of Lady Shirakawa.
Consciously I had made the decision to go to the Tribe
but, even in those early days, just before sleep, unbidden
images came to me of his uncles, unpunished in Hagi, and
of his sword, Jato, sleeping at Terayama.

By the time we arrived at Matsue Yuki and I were

lovers. It happened with inevitability, yet not through my will. I was always aware of her on the road, my senses tuned to her voice, her scent. But I was too unsure of my future, my position in the group, too guarded and wary to make any move towards her. It was obvious that Akio also found her attractive. He was at ease with her as with no one else, seeking out her company, walking beside her on the road, sitting next to her at meals. I did not want to antagonize him further.

Yuki's position in the group was unclear. She deferred to Akio and always treated him with respect, yet she seemed equal to him in status and, as I had reason to know, her skills were greater. Keiko was obviously lower down in the order, perhaps from a lesser family or a collateral branch. She continued to ignore me, but showed blind loyalty to Akio. As for the older man, Kazuo, everyone treated him as a mixture between a servant and an uncle. He had many practical skills, including thievery.

Akio was Kikuta through both father and mother. He was a second cousin to me and had the same shaped hands. His physical skills were astounding; he had the fastest reflexes of anyone I've ever met and could leap so high he seemed to be flying, but apart from his ability to perceive the use of invisibility and the second self, and his dexterity in juggling, none of the more unusual Kikuta gifts had come to him. Yuki told me this one day when we were walking some way ahead of the others.

'The masters fear the gifts are dying out. Every generation seems to have fewer.' She gave me a sideways look and added, 'That's why it's so important to us to keep you.'

Her mother had said the same thing and I would have liked to have heard more but Akio shouted at me that it was my turn to push the cart. I saw the jealousy in his face as I walked towards him. I understood it, and his hostility to me, all too well. He was fanatically loyal to the Tribe, having been raised in their teachings and way of life; I could not help but realize that my sudden appearance was likely to usurp many of his ambitions and hopes. But understanding his antipathy did not make it any easier to bear, nor did it make me like him.

I said nothing as I took the handles of the cart from him. He ran forward to walk beside Yuki, whispering to her, forgetting, as he often did, that I could hear every word. He'd taken to calling me the Dog, and the nickname had enough truth in it to stick. As I've said before, I have an affinity with dogs, I can hear the things they hear and I've known what it's like to be speechless.

'What were you saying to the Dog?' he asked her.

'Teaching, teaching,' she replied, off-hand. 'There's so much he needs to learn.'

But what she turned out to be best at teaching was the art of love.

Both Yuki and Keiko took on the role of prostitutes on the road if they needed to. So did many of the Tribe, men and women, no one thinking any the worse of them for it. It was simply another role to assume, then discard. Of course, the clans had quite different ideas about the virginity of their brides and the fidelity of their wives. Men could do what they liked; women were expected to be chaste. The teachings I had grown up with were somewhere between the two: the Hidden are supposed to be pure in matters of physical desire, but in practice are forgiving of each other's lapses, as they are in all things.

On our fourth night we stayed in a large village with a wealthy family. Despite the scarcity in the whole area following the storms, they had stockpiles of supplies and they were generous hosts. The merchant offered us women, maids from his household, and Akio and Kazuo accepted. I made an excuse of some sort, which brought a storm of teasing, but the matter was not forced. Later, when the girls came to the room and lay down with the other men, I moved my mattress outside onto the veranda, and shivered under the brittle ice points of the stars. Desire, longing for Kaede, to be honest, at that moment for any woman, tormented me. The door slid open, and one of the girls from the household, I thought, came out onto the veranda. As she closed the door behind her, I caught her fragrance, and recognized her tread.

Yuki knelt beside me. I reached out for her and pulled her down next to me. Her girdle was already undone, her robe loose. I remember feeling the most immense gratitude to her. She loosened my clothes, making it all so easy for me – too easy: I was too quick. She scolded me for my impatience, promising to teach me. And so she did.

The next morning Akio looked at me searchingly. 'You changed your mind last night?'

I wondered how he knew, if he had heard us through the flimsy screens or if he was just guessing.

'One of the girls came to me. It seemed impolite to turn her away,' I replied.

He grunted and did not pursue the matter, but he watched Yuki and me carefully, even though we said nothing to each other, as though he knew something had changed between us. I thought about her constantly, swinging between elation and despair, elation because the act of love with her was indescribably wonderful, despair because she was not Kaede, and because what we did together bound me ever more closely to the Tribe.

I couldn't help remembering Kenji's comment as he left: *it's a good thing Yuki's going to be around to keep an eye on you.* He had known this would happen. Had he planned it with her, instructed her? Did Akio of course know, because he had been told? I was filled with misgivings, and I did not trust Yuki, but it didn't stop me going to her every time I had the chance. She, so much wiser in these matters, made sure the chance arose often. And Akio's jealousy grew more apparent every day.

So our little group came to Matsue, outwardly united and in harmony, but in fact torn by intense emotions that, being true members of the Tribe, we concealed from outsiders and from each other.

We stayed at the Kikuta house, another merchant's place smelling of fermenting soybeans, paste and sauce. The owner, Gosaburo, was Kotaro's youngest brother, also first cousin to my father. There was little need for secrecy. We were now well beyond the Three Countries and Arai's reach and, in Matsue, the local clan, the Yoshida, had no quarrel with the Tribe, finding them equally useful for moneylending, spying and assassination. Here we had news of Arai, who was busy subduing the East and the Middle Country, making alliances, fighting border skirmishes and setting up his administration. We heard the first rumours of his campaign against the Tribe and his intention to clear his lands of them, rumours that were the source of much mirth and derision.

I will not set down the details of my training. Its aim was to harden my heart and instil in me ruthlessness. But even now, years on, the memory of its harshness and cruelty makes me flinch and want to turn my eyes away. They were cruel times: maybe Heaven was angry, maybe men were taken over by devils, maybe when the powers

131

of good weaken, the brutal, with its nose for rot, storms in. The Tribe, cruellest of the cruel, flourished.

I was not the only Tribe member in training. There were several other boys, most of them much younger, all of them born Kikuta and raised in the family. The one closest to me in age was a solidly built, cheerful-faced young man with whom I was often paired. His name was Hajime, and though he did not exactly deflect Akio's rage towards me – to do so openly would be unthinkably disobedient – he often managed to draw some of it away. There was something about him I liked, though I would not go as far as to say I trusted him. His fighting skills were far greater than mine. He was a wrestler, and also strong enough to pull the huge bows of the master archers, but in the skills that are given rather than learned, neither he nor any of the others came near what I could do. It was only now that I began to realize how exceptional these skills were. I could go invisible for minutes on end, even in the bare white-walled hall; sometimes not even Akio could see me. I could split myself while fighting, and watch my opponent grapple with my second self from the other side of the room. I could move without sound, while my own hearing became ever more acute, and the younger boys quickly learned never to look me directly in the eye. I had put all of them to sleep at one time or another. I was learning slowly to control this skill as I practised on them. When I looked into their eyes I saw the weaknesses and fears that made them vulnerable to my gaze: sometimes their own inner fears, sometimes fear of me and the uncanny powers that had been given to me.

Every morning I did exercises with Akio to build up strength and speed. I was slower and weaker than he was in almost all areas and he had gained nothing in patience.

But to give him his due he was determined to teach me some of his skills in leaping and flying and he succeeded. Part of those skills were in me already – my stepfather after all used to call me a wild monkey – and his brutal but skilful teaching drew them to the surface and forced me to control them. After only a few weeks I was aware of the difference in me, of how much I had hardened in mind and body.

We always finished with bare-hand fighting – not that the Tribe used this art much, preferring assassination to actual combat – but we were all trained in it. Then we sat in silent meditation, a robe slung across our cooling bodies, keeping our body temperature up by force of will. My head was usually ringing from some blow or fall, and I did not empty my mind as I was supposed to, but instead dwelt savagely on how I would like to see Akio suffer. I gave to him all of Jo-An's torment that he'd once described to me.

My training was designed to encourage cruelty and I embraced it at the time wholeheartedly, glad for the skills it was giving me, delighted at how they enhanced those I had learned with the Otori warriors' sons back when Shigeru was still alive. My father's Kikuta blood came to life in me. My mother's compassion drained away, along with all the teachings of my childhood. I no longer prayed; neither the secret god, nor the Enlightened One, nor the old spirits meant anything to me. I did not believe in their existence and I saw no evidence that they favoured those who did. Sometimes in the night I would wake suddenly and catch an unprotected glimpse of myself, and shudder at what I was becoming, and then I would rise silently and, if I could, go and find Yuki, lie down with her and lose myself in her.

We never spent the whole night together. Our encounters were always short and usually silent. But one afternoon we found ourselves alone in the house, apart from the servants who were occupied in the shop. Akio and Hajime had taken the younger boys to the shrine for some dedication ceremony, and I had been told to copy some documents for Gosaburo. I was grateful for the task. I rarely held a brush in my hands and because I had learned to write so late I was always afraid the characters would desert me. The merchant had a few books and, as Shigeru had instructed me, I read whenever I could, but I had lost my ink stone and brushes at Inuyama and had hardly written since.

I diligently copied the documents, records from the shop, accounts of the amounts of soybeans and rice purchased from local farmers, but my fingers were itching to draw. I was reminded of my first visit to Terayama, the brilliance of the summer day, the beauty of the paintings, the little mountain bird I had drawn and given to Kaede.

As always when I was thinking of the past, my heart unguarded, she came to me and took possession of me all over again. I could feel her presence, smell the fragrance of her hair, hear her voice. So strongly was she with me, I had a moment of fear, as if her ghost had slipped into the room. Her ghost would be angry with me, filled with resentment and rage for abandoning her. Her words rang in my ears: *I'm afraid of myself. I only feel safe with you.*

It was cold in the room and already growing dark, with all the threat of the winter to come. I shivered, full of remorse and regret. My hands were numb with cold.

I could hear Yuki's footsteps approaching from the back of the building. I started writing again. She crossed the courtyard and stepped out of her sandals onto the veranda of the records room. I could smell burning char-coal. She had brought a small brazier which she placed on the floor next to me.

'You look cold,' she said. 'Shall I bring tea?'

'Later, maybe.' I laid down the brush and held my hands out to the warmth. She took them and rubbed them between her own.

'I'll close the shutters,' she said.

'Then you'll have to bring a lamp. I can't see to write.'

She laughed quietly. The wooden shutters slid into place, one after another. The room went dim, lit only by the faint glow of the charcoal. When Yuki came back to me she had already loosened her robe. Soon we were both warm. But after the act of love, as wonderful as ever, my unease returned. Kaede's spirit had been in the room with me. Was I causing her anguish and arousing her jealousy and spite?

Curled against me, the heat radiating from her, Yuki said, 'A message came from your cousin.'

'Which cousin?' I had dozens of them now.

'Muto Shizuka.'

I eased myself away from Yuki so she would not hear the quickened beating of my heart. 'What did she say?'

'Lady Shirakawa is dying. Shizuka said she feared the end was very near.' Yuki added in her indolent, sated voice, 'Poor thing.'

She was glowing with life and pleasure. But the only thing I was aware of in the room was Kaede, her frailty, her intensity, her supernatural beauty. I called out to her in my soul, *You cannot die. I must see you again. I will come for you. Don't die before I see you again!*

Her spirit gazed on me, her eyes dark with reproach and sorrow.

Yuki turned and looked up at me, surprised by my silence. 'Shizuka thought you should know – was there something between you? My father hinted as much, but he said it was just green love. He said everyone who saw her became infatuated with her.'

I did not answer. Yuki sat up, pulling her robe around her. 'It was more than that, wasn't it? You loved her.' She seized my hands and turned me to face her. 'You loved her,' she repeated, the jealousy beginning to show in her voice. 'Is it over?'

'It will never be over,' I said. 'Even if she dies I can never stop loving her.' Now that it was too late to tell Kaede, I knew that it was true.

'That part of your life is finished,' Yuki said quietly but fiercely. 'All of it. Forget her! You will never see her again.' I could hear the anger and frustration in her voice.

'I would never have told you if you had not mentioned her.' I pulled my hands away from her and dressed again. The warmth had gone from me as swiftly as it had come. The brazier was cooling.

'Bring some more charcoal,' I told Yuki. 'And lamps. I must finish the work.'

'Takeo,' she began, and then broke off abruptly. 'I'll send the maid,' she said, getting to her feet. She touched the back of my neck as she left, but I made no response. Physically we had been deeply involved: her hands had massaged me, and struck me in punishment. We had killed side by side, we had made love. But she had barely brushed the surface of my heart, and at that moment we both knew it.

I made no sign of my grief, but I wept inwardly for Kaede and for the life that we might have had together. No further word came from Shizuka, though I never

136

stopped listening for messengers. Yuki did not mention the subject again. I could not believe Kaede was dead, and in the daytime I clung to that belief, but the nights were different.

The last of the colour faded as leaves fell from maple and willow. Strings of wild geese flew southwards across the sullen sky. Messengers became less frequent as the town began to close down for winter. But they still came from time to time, bringing news of Tribe activities, of the fighting in the Three Countries and, always, bringing new orders for our trade.

For that was how we described our work of spying and killing. Trade, with human lives measured out as so many units. I copied records of these too, often sitting till late into the night with Gosaburo, the merchant, moving from the soybean harvest to the other deadlier one. Both showed a fine profit, though the soybeans had been affected by the storms while the murders had not, though one candidate for assassination had drowned before the Tribe could get to him and there was an ongoing dispute about payment.

The Kikuta, being more ruthless, were supposed to be more skilled at assassination than the Muto, who were traditionally the most effective spies. These two families were the aristocracy of the Tribe; the other three, the Kuroda, Kudo and Imai, worked at more menial and hum-drum tasks, being servants, petty thieves, informants and so on. Because the traditional skills were so valued there were many marriages between Muto and Kikuta, fewer between them and the other families, though the exceptions often threw up geniuses like the assassin Shintaro.

After dealing with the accounts Kikuta Gosaburo would give me lessons in genealogy, explaining the intricate relationships of the Tribe that spread like an autumn spider's web across the Three Countries, into the north and beyond. He was a fat man with a double chin like a woman's and a smooth, plump face, deceptively gentle-looking. The smell of fermentation clung to his clothes and skin. If he was in a good mood he would call for wine and move from genealogy into history – the Tribe history of my ancestors. Little had changed in hundreds of years. Warlords might rise and fall, clans flourish and disappear, but the trade of the Tribe in all the essentials of life went on for ever. Except now Arai wanted to bring about change. All other powerful warlords worked with the Tribe. Only Arai wanted to destroy them.

Gosaburo's chins wobbled with laughter at the idea.

At first I was called on only as a spy, sent to overhear conversations in taverns and teahouses, ordered to climb over walls and roofs at night and listen to men confiding in their sons or their wives. I heard the townspeople's secrets and fears, the Yoshida clan's strategies for spring, the concerns at the castle about Arai's intentions beyond the borders and about peasant uprisings close to home. I went into the mountain villages, listened to those peasants and identified the ring leaders.

One night Gosaburo clicked his tongue in disapproval at a long overdue account. Not only had no payments been made, but more goods had been ordered. The man's name was Furoda, a low-rank warrior who had turned to farming to support his large family and his liking for the good things in life. Beneath his name I read the symbols that indicated the rising level of intimidation already used against him: a barn had been set alight, one of his daughters abducted, a son beaten up, dogs and horses killed. Yet he still sank ever more deeply into the Kikuta's debt.

'This could be one for the Dog,' the merchant said to Akio, who had joined us for a glass of wine. Like everyone except Yuki, he used Akio's nickname for me.

Akio took the scroll and ran his eyes over Furoda's sad history. 'He's had a lot of leeway.'

'Well, he's a likeable fellow. I've known him since we were boys. I can't go on making allowances for him though.'

'Uncle, if you don't deal with him, isn't everyone going to expect the same leniency?' Akio said.

'That's the trouble. No one's paying on time at the moment. They all think they can get away with it because Furoda has.' Gosaburo sighed deeply, his eyes almost disappearing in the folds of his cheeks. 'I'm too soft-hearted. That's my problem. My brothers are always telling me.'

'The Dog is soft-hearted,' Akio said, 'but we're training him not to be. He can take care of Furoda for you. It will be good for him.'

'If you kill him he can never pay his debts,' I said.

'But everyone else will.' Akio spoke as if pointing out an obvious truth to a simpleton.

'It's often easier to claim from a dead man than a live one,' Gosaburo added, apologetically.

I did not know this easy-going, pleasure-loving, irresponsible man, and I did not want to kill him. But I did. A few days later I went at night to his house on the outskirts of town, silenced the dogs, went invisible and slipped past the guards. The house was well barred but I waited for him outside the privy. I had been watching the house and I knew he always rose in the early hours to relieve himself. He was a large, fleshy man who'd long since given up any training and who had handed over the heavy work on the land to his sons. He'd grown soft. He died with hardly a sound.

When I untwisted the garrotte, rain had started to fall. The tiles of the walls were slippery. The night was at its darkest. The rain could almost be sleet. I returned to the Kikuta house silenced by the darkness and the cold as if they had crept inside me and left a shadow on my soul.

Furoda's sons paid his debts, and Gosaburo was pleased with me. I let no one see how much the murder had disturbed me but the next one was worse. It was on the orders of the Yoshida family. Determined to put a stop to the unrest among the villagers before winter, they put in a request for the leader to be eradicated. I knew the man, knew his secret fields, though I had not yet revealed them to anyone. Now I told Gosaburo and Akio where he could be found alone every evening and they sent me to meet him there.

He had rice and sweet potatoes concealed in a small cave cut into the side of the mountain and covered with stones and brushwood. He was working on the banks of the field when I came silently up the slope. I'd misjudged him: he was stronger than I thought, and he fought back with his hoe. As we struggled together, my hood slipped back and he saw my face. Recognition came into his eyes, mixed with a sort of horror. In that moment I used the second self, came behind him and cut his throat, but I'd heard him call out to my image.

'Lord Shigeru!'

I was covered with blood, his and mine, and dizzy from the blow I'd not quite avoided. The hoe had glanced against my scalp and the scrape was bleeding freely. His words disturbed me deeply. Had he been calling to Shigeru's spirit for help, or had he seen my likeness and mistaken me for him? I wanted to question him, but his eyes stared blankly up at the twilight sky. He was gone beyond speech for ever.

I went invisible and stayed so until I was nearly back at the Kikuta house, the longest period I had ever used it for. I would have stayed like that for ever if I could. I could not forget the man's last words, and then I remembered what Shigeru had said, so long ago, in Hagi. *I have never killed an unarmed man, nor killed for pleasure.*

The clan lords were highly satisfied. The man's death had taken the heart out of the unrest. The villagers promptly became docile and obedient. Many of them would die of starvation before the end of winter. It was an excellent result, Gosaburo said.

But I began to dream of Shigeru every night. He entered the room and stood before me, as if he had just come out of the river; blood and water streaming from him, saying nothing, his eyes fixed on me, as if he were waiting for me, the same way he had waited with the patience of the heron for me to speak again.

Slowly it began to dawn on me that I could not bear the life I was living, but I did not know how to escape it. I had made a bargain with the Kikuta that I was now finding impossible to keep. I'd made the bargain in the heat of passion, not expecting to live beyond that night, and with no understanding of my own self. I'd thought the Kikuta master, who seemed to know me, would help me resolve the deep divisions and contradictions of my nature, but he had sent me away to Matsue with Akio, where my life with the Tribe might be teaching me how to hide these contradictions but was doing nothing to solve them; they were merely being driven deeper inside me.

My black mood worsened when Yuki went away. She

said nothing to me about it, just vanished one day. In the morning I heard her voice and her tread while we were at training. I heard her go to the front door and leave without bidding anyone farewell. I listened all day for her return, but she did not come back. I tried asking casually where she was; the replies were evasive and I did not want to question Akio or Gosaburo directly. I missed her deeply but was also relieved that I no longer had to face the question of whether to sleep with her or not. Every day since she had told me about Kaede I'd resolved I would not, and every night I did.

Two days later, while I was thinking about her during the meditation period at the end of the morning exercises, I heard one of the servants come to the door and call softly to Akio. He opened his eyes slowly and with the air of calm composure that he always assumed after meditating (and which I was convinced was only assumed) he rose and went to the door.

'The master is here,' the girl said, 'He is waiting for you.'

'Hey, Dog,' Akio called to me. The others sat without moving a muscle, without looking up, as I stood. Akio jerked his head, and I followed him to the main room of the house where Kikuta Kotaro was drinking tea with Gosaburo.

We entered the room and bowed to the floor before him.

'Sit up,' he said, and studied me for a few moments. Then he addressed Akio. 'Have there been any problems?'

'Not really,' Akio said, implying there had been quite a few.

'What about attitude? You have no complaints?'

Akio shook his head slowly.

'Yet before you left Yamagata . . .?'

I felt that Kotaro was letting me know he knew everything about me.

'It was dealt with,' Akio replied briefly.

'He's been quite useful to me,' Gosaburo put in.

'I'm glad to hear it,' Kotaro said dryly.

His brother got to his feet and excused himself – the pressures of business, the need to be in the shop. When he had left the master said, 'I spoke to Yuki last night.'

'Where is she?'

'That doesn't matter. But she told me something that disturbs me a little. We did not know that Shigeru went to Mino expressly to find you. He let Muto Kenji believe the encounter happened by chance.'

He paused, but I said nothing. I remembered the day Yuki had found this out, while she was cutting my hair. She had thought it important information, important enough to pass on to the master. No doubt she had told him everything else about me.

'It makes me suspect Shigeru had a greater knowledge of the Tribe than we realized,' Kotaro said. 'Is that true?'

'It's true that he knew who I was,' I replied. 'He had been friends with the Muto master for many years. That's all I know of his relationship with the Tribe.'

'He never spoke to you of anything more?'

'No.' I was lying. In fact Shigeru had told me more, the night we had talked in Tsuwano – that he had made it his business to find out about the Tribe and that he probably knew more about them than any other outsider. I had never shared this information with Kenji and I saw no reason to pass it on to Kotaro. Shigeru was dead and I was now bound to the Tribe, but I was not going to betray his secrets.

I tried to make my voice and face guileless and said, 'Yuki asked me the same thing. What does it matter now?'

'We thought we knew Shigeru, knew his life,' Kotaro answered. 'He keeps surprising us, even after his death. He kept things hidden even from Kenji – the affair with Maruyama Naomi for example. What else was he hiding?'

I shrugged slightly. I thought of Shigeru, nicknamed the Farmer, with his open-hearted smile, his seeming frankness and simplicity. Everyone had misjudged him, especially the Tribe. He had been so much more than any of them had suspected.

'Is it possible that he kept records of what he knew about the Tribe?'

'He kept many records of all sorts of things,' I said, sounding puzzled. 'The seasons, his farming experiments, the land and crops, his retainers. Ichiro, his former teacher, helped him with them but he often wrote himself.'

I could see him, writing late into the night, the lamp flickering, the cold penetrating, his face alert and intelligent, quite different from its usual bland expression.

'The journeys he made, did you go with him?'

'No, apart from our flight from Mino.'

'How often did he travel?'

'I'm not sure; while I was in Hagi he did not leave the city.'

Kotaro grunted. Silence crept into the room. I could barely hear the others' breathing. From beyond came the noon sounds of shop and house: the click of the abacus, the voices of customers, peddlers crying in the street outside. The wind was rising, whistling under the eaves,

144

shaking the screens. Already its breath held the hint of snow.

The master spoke finally. 'It seems most likely that he did keep records. In which case they must be recovered. If they should fall into Arai's hands at this moment it would be a disaster. You will have to go to Hagi. Find out if the records exist and bring them back here.'

I could hardly believe it. I had thought I would never go there again. Now I was to be sent back to the house I loved so much.

'It's a matter of the nightingale floor,' Kotaro said. 'I believe Shigeru had one built around his house and you mastered it.'

It seemed I was back there: I felt the heavy night air of the sixth month, saw myself run as silently as a ghost, heard Shigeru's voice: *Can you do it again?*

I tried to keep my face under control, but I felt the flicker in the smile muscles.

'You must leave at once,' Kotaro went on, 'You have to get there and back before the snows begin. It's nearly the end of the year. By the middle of the first month both Hagi and Matsue will be closed by snow.'

He had not sounded angry before, but now I realized he was, profoundly. Perhaps he had sensed my smile.

'Why did you never tell anyone this?' he demanded. 'Why did you keep it from Kenji?'

I felt my own anger rise in response. 'Lord Shigeru did so and I followed his lead. My first allegiance was to him. I would never have revealed something he wanted kept secret. I was one of the Otori then, after all.'

'And still thinks he is,' Akio put in. 'It's a question of loyalties. It always will be with him.' He added under his breath, 'A dog only knows one master.'

I turned my gaze on him, willing him to look at me so I could shut him up, put him to sleep, but after one swift, contemptuous glance, he stared at the floor again.

'Well, that will be proved one way or the other,' Kotaro replied. 'I think this mission will test your loyalties to the full. If this Ichiro knows of the existence and contents of the records, he'll have to be removed, of course.'

I bowed, without saying anything, wondering if my heart had been hardened to the extent where I could kill Ichiro, the old man who had been Shigeru's teacher and then mine: I'd thought I wanted to often enough when he was chastizing me and forcing me to learn, but he was one of the Otori, one of Shigeru's household. I was bound to him by duty and loyalty as well as by my own grudging respect and, I realized now, affection.

At the same time I was exploring the master's anger, feeling its taste in my mouth. It had a quality to it that was like Akio's more or less permanent state of rage against me, as if they both hated and feared me. *The Kikuta were delighted to discover Isamu had left a son,* Kenji's wife had said. If they were so delighted why were they so angry with me? But hadn't she also said, *we all were*? And then Yuki had told me of her mother's old feelings for Shintaro. Could his death really have delighted her?

She had seemed at that moment like a garrulous old woman, and I had taken her words at face value. But moments later she'd allowed me a glimpse of her skills. She'd been flattering me, stroking my vanity in the same way as she'd stroked my temples with her phantom hands. The reaction of the Kikuta to my sudden appearance was darker and more complex than they would have me believe: maybe they were delighted with my skills but there was also something about me that alarmed them, and I still did not understand what it was.

The anger that should have cowed me into obedience instead made me more stubborn, indeed struck fire on that stubbornness and gave me energy. I felt it coiled inside me, as I wondered at the fate that was sending me back to Hagi.

'We are entering a dangerous time,' the master said, studying me, as if he could read my thoughts. 'The Muto house in Yamagata was searched and ransacked. Someone suspected you had been there. However, Arai has returned to Inuyama now, and Hagi is a long way from there. It's a risk for you to return, but the risk of records coming into anyone else's hands is far greater.'

'What if they aren't in Lord Shigeru's house? They could be hidden anywhere.'

'Presumably Ichiro will know. Question him, and bring them back from wherever they are.'

'Am I to leave immediately?'

'The sooner the better.'

'As an actor?'

'No actors travel at this time of year,' Akio said scornfully. 'Besides, we will go alone.'

I'd been offering a silent prayer that he would not be coming with me. The master said, 'Akio will accompany you. His grandfather – your grandfather – has died and you are returning to Hagi for the memorial service.'

'I would prefer not to travel with Akio,' I said.

Akio drew his breath in sharply. Kotaro said, 'There are no preferences for you. Only obedience.'

I felt the stubbornness spark, and looked directly at him. He was staring into my eyes as he had once before:

he had put me to sleep immediately then. But this time I could meet his gaze without giving into it. There was something behind his eyes that made him flinch slightly from me. I searched his look and the suspicion leaped into my mind.

This is the man who killed my father.

I felt a moment of terror at what I was doing, then my own gaze steadied and held. My teeth bared though I was far from smiling. I saw the master's look of astonishment and saw his vision cloud. Then Akio was on his feet, striking me in the face, almost knocking me to the ground.

'How dare you do that to the master? You have no respect, you scum.'

Kotaro said, 'Sit down, Akio.'

My eyes snapped back to him, but he was not looking at me.

'I'm sorry, master,' I said softly. 'Forgive me.'

We both knew my apology was hollow. He stood swiftly and covered the moment with anger.

'Ever since we located you we have been trying to protect you from yourself.' He did not raise his voice but there was no mistaking his fury. 'Not only for your own sake, of course. You know what your talents are and how useful they could be to us. But your upbringing, your mixed blood, your own character all work against you. I thought training here would help, but we don't have time to continue it. Akio will go with you to Hagi and you will continue to obey him in all things. He is far more experienced than you; he knows where the safe houses are, whom to contact and who can be trusted.'

He paused while I bowed in acceptance, and then went on, 'You and I made a bargain at Inuyama. You chose to disobey my orders then and return to the castle.

148

The results of Iida's death have not been good for us. We were far better off under him than under Arai. Apart from our own laws of obedience that any child learns before they turn seven, your life is already forfeit to me by your own promise.'

I did not reply. I felt he was close to giving up on me, that his patience with me, the understanding of my nature that had calmed and soothed me, was running dry. As was my trust in him. The terrible suspicion lay in my mind; once it had arisen there was no eradicating it – my father had died at the hands of the Tribe, had maybe even been killed by Kotaro himself, because he had tried to leave them. Later I would realize that this explained many things about the Kikuta's dealings with me, their insistence on my obedience, their ambivalent attitude to my skills, their contempt for my loyalty to Shigeru, but at that time it only increased my depression. Akio hated me, I had insulted and offended the Kikuta master, Yuki had left me, Kaede was probably dead . . . I did not want to go on with the list. I gazed with unseeing eyes at the floor while Kikuta and Akio discussed details of the journey.

We left the following morning. There were many travellers on the road, taking advantage of the last weeks before the snow fell, going home for the New Year Festival. We mingled with them, two brothers returning to our home town for a funeral. It was no hardship to pretend to be overcome by grief. It seemed to have become my natural state. The only thing that lightened the blackness that enveloped me was the thought of seeing the house in Hagi, and hearing for one last time its winter song.

My training partner, Hajime, travelled with us for the

149

first day; he was on his way to join a wrestling stable for the winter to prepare for the spring tournaments. We stayed that night with the wrestlers, and ate the evening meal with them. They consumed huge stews of vegetables and chicken, a meat they considered lucky because the chicken's hands never touch the ground, with noodles made of rice and buckwheat, more for each one than most families would eat in a week. Hajime, with his large bulk and calm face, resembled them already. He had been connected with this stable, which was run by the Kikuta, since he was a child, and the wrestlers treated him with teasing affection.

Before the meal we bathed with them in the vast steamy bathhouse, built across a scalding, sulphurous spring. Masseurs and trainers mingled among them, rubbing and scrubbing the massive limbs and torsos. It was like being among a race of giants. They all knew Akio, of course, and treated him with ironic deference because he was part of the boss's family, mixed with kindly scorn because he was not a wrestler. Nothing was said about me, and nobody paid me any attention. They were absorbed in their own world. I obviously had only the slightest connection to it and therefore was of no interest to them.

So I said nothing, but listened. I overheard plans for the spring tournament, the hopes and desires of the wrestlers, the jokes whispered by the masseurs, the propositions made, spurned or accepted. And much later, when Akio had ordered me to bed and I was already lying on a mat in the communal hall, I heard him and Hajime in the room below. They had decided to sit up for a while and drink together, before they parted the next day.

I tuned out the snores of the wrestlers and concentrated on the voices below. I could hear them clearly through the floor. It always amazed me that Akio seemed to forget how acute my hearing was. I supposed he did not want to acknowledge my gifts and this made him underestimate me. At first I thought it was a weakness in him, almost the only one; later it occurred to me that there were some things he might have wanted me to hear.

The conversation was commonplace – the training Hajime would undergo, the friends they'd caught up with – until the wine began to loosen their tongues.

'You'll go to Yamagata, presumably?' Hajime asked.

'Probably not. The Muto master is still in the mountains, and the house is empty.'

'I assumed Yuki had gone back to her family.'

'No, she's gone to the Kikuta village, north of Matsue. She'll stay there until the child is born.'

'The child?' Hajime sounded as dumbfounded as I was.

There was a long silence. I heard Akio drink and swallow. When he spoke again his voice was much quieter. 'She is carrying the Dog's child.'

Hajime hissed through his teeth. 'Sorry, cousin, I don't want to upset you but was that part of the plan?'

'Why should it not have been?'

'I always thought, you and she . . . that you would marry eventually.'

'We have been promised to each other since we were children,' Akio said. 'We may still marry. The masters wanted her to sleep with him, to keep him quiet, to distract him, to get a child if possible.'

If he felt pain he was not showing it. 'I was to pretend suspicion and jealousy,' he said flatly. 'If the Dog knew he was being manipulated, he might never have gone with her. Well, I did not have to pretend it – I did not realize she would enjoy it so much. I could not believe how she was with him, seeking him out day and night like a bitch in heat . . .' His voice broke off. I heard him gulp down a cup of wine and heard the clink and gurgle of the flask as more was poured.

'Good must come of it though,' Hajime suggested, his voice regaining some of its cheerfulness. 'The child will inherit a rare combination of talents.'

'So the Kikuta master thinks. And this child will be with us from birth. It will be raised properly, with none of the Dog's deficiencies.'

'It's astonishing news,' Hajime said. 'No wonder you've been preoccupied.'

'Most of the time I'm thinking about how I'll kill him,' Akio confessed, drinking deeply again.

'You've been ordered to?' Hajime said bleakly.

'It all depends on what happens at Hagi. You might say he's on his last chance.'

'Does he know that? That he's being tested?'

'If he doesn't, he'll soon find out,' Akio said. After another long pause he said, 'If the Kikuta had known of his existence they would have claimed him as a child and brought him up. But he was ruined first by his upbringing and then by his association with the Otori.'

'His father died before he was born. Do you know who killed him?'

'They drew lots,' Akio whispered. 'No one knows who actually did it, but it was decided by the whole family. The master told me this in Inuyama.'

'Sad,' Hajime murmured, 'So much talent wasted.'

'It comes from mixing the blood,' Akio said. 'It's true that it sometimes throws up rare talents but they seem to come with stupidity. And the only cure for stupidity is death.'

Shortly afterwards they came to bed. I lay still, feigning sleep, until daybreak, my mind gnawing uselessly at the news. I was sure that no matter what I did or failed to do in Hagi Akio would seize on any excuse to kill me there.

As we bade farewell to Hajime the next morning he would not look me in the eye. His voice held a false cheerfulness, and he stared after us, his expression glum. I imagine he thought he would never see me again.

We travelled for three days, barely speaking to each other, until we came to the barrier that marked the beginning of the Otori lands. It presented no problem to us, Akio having been supplied with the necessary tablets of identification. He made all the decisions on our journey: where we should eat, where we should stop for the night, which road we should take. I followed passively. I knew he would not kill me before we got to Hagi; he needed me to get into Shigeru's house, across the nightingale floor. After a while I began to feel a sort of regret that we weren't good friends, travelling together. It seemed a waste of a journey. I longed for a companion, someone like Makoto or my old friend from Hagi, Fumio, with whom I could talk on the road and share the confusion of my thoughts.

Once we were in Otori land I expected the countryside to look as prosperous as it had when I had first travelled through it with Shigeru, but everywhere bore signs of the ravages of the storms and the famine that followed them. Many villages seemed to be deserted, damaged houses stood unrepaired, starving people begged at the sides of the road. I overheard snatches of conversation, how the Otori lords were now demanding 60 per cent of the rice harvest, instead of the 40 per cent they had taken previously, to pay for the army they were raising to fight Arai, and how men might as well kill themselves and their children rather than starve slowly to death when winter came.

Earlier in the year we might have made the journey more swiftly by boat, but the winter gales were already lashing the coast, driving foaming grey waves onto the black shore. The fishermen's boats were moored in such shelter as they could find, or pulled high onto the shingle, lived in by families until spring. Throughout winter the fishing families burned fires to get salt from the sea water. Once or twice we stopped to warm ourselves and eat with them, Akio paying them a few small coins. The food was meagre: salt fish, soup made from kelp, sea urchins and small shell fish.

One man begged us to buy his daughter, take her with us to Hagi, use her ourselves or sell her to a brothel. She could not have been more than thirteen years old, barely into womanhood. She was not pretty, but I can still recall her face, her eyes both frightened and pleading, her tears, the look of relief when Akio politely declined, the despair in her father's attitude as he turned away.

That night Akio grumbled about the cold, regretting his decision. 'She'd have kept me warm,' he said more than once.

I thought of her, sleeping next to her mother, faced with the choice between starvation and what would have been no more than slavery. I thought about Furoda's family, turned out of their shabby, comfortable house, and I thought of the man I'd killed in his secret field, and the village that would die because of me.

These things did not bother anyone else – it was the way the world was – but they haunted me. And of course, as I did every night, I took out the thoughts that had lain within me all day and examined them.

Yuki was carrying my child. It was to be raised by the Tribe. I would probably never even set eyes on it.

The Kikuta had killed my father because he had broken the rules of the Tribe, and they would not hesitate to kill me.

I made no decisions and came to no conclusions. I simply lay awake for long hours of the night, holding the thoughts as I would hold black pebbles in my hand, and looking at them.

The mountains fell directly to the sea around Hagi, and we had to turn inland and climb steeply before we crossed the last pass and began the descent towards the town.

My heart was full of emotion, though I said nothing and gave nothing away. The town lay as it always had in the cradle of the bay, encircled by its twin rivers and the sea. It was late afternoon on the day of the winter solstice, and a pale sun was struggling through grey clouds. The trees were bare, fallen leaves thick underfoot. Smoke from the burning of the last rice stalks spread a blue haze that hung above the rivers, level with the stone bridge.

Preparations were already being made for the New Year Festival: sacred ropes of straw hung everywhere and dark-leaved pine trees had been placed by doorways; the shrines were filling with visitors. The river was swollen with the tide that was just past the turn and ebbing. It sang its wild song to me and beneath its churning waters I seemed to hear the voice of the stonemason, walled up inside his creation, carrying on his endless conversation with the river. A heron rose from the shallows at our approach.

When we crossed the bridge I read again the inscription that Shigeru had read to me: *The Otori clan welcomes the just and the loyal. Let the unjust and the disloyal beware.*

Unjust and disloyal. I was both. Disloyal to Shigeru, who had entrusted his lands to me, and unjust as the Tribe are, unjust and pitiless.

I walked through the streets, head down and eyes lowered, changing the set of my features in the way Kenji had taught me. I did not think anyone would recognize me. I had grown a little and had become both leaner and more muscular during the past months. My hair was cut short, my clothes were those of an artisan. My body language, my speech, my gait – everything about me had changed since the days when I'd walked through these streets as a young lord of the Otori clan.

We went to a brewery on the edge of town. I'd walked by it dozens of times in the past, knowing nothing of its real trade. *But,* I thought, *Shigeru would have known.* The idea pleased me, that he had kept track of the Tribe's activities, had known things that they were ignorant of, had known of my existence.

The place was busy with preparations for the winter's work. Huge amounts of wood were being gathered to heat the vats and the air was thick with the smell of fermenting rice. We were met by a small, distracted man, who resembled Kenji. He was from the Muto family; Yuzuru was his given name. He had not been expecting visitors so late in the year, and my presence and what we told him of our mission unnerved him. He took us hastily inside to another concealed room.

'These are terrible times,' he said. 'The Otori are

156

certain to start preparing for war with Arai in the spring. It's only winter that protects us now.'

'You've heard of Arai's campaign against the Tribe?'

'Everyone's talking about it,' Yuzuru replied. 'We've been told we should support the Otori against him as much as we can for that reason.' He shot a look at me and said resentfully, 'Things were much better under Iida. And surely it's a grave mistake to bring him here. If anyone should recognize him . . .'

'We'll be gone tomorrow,' Akio replied. 'He just has to retrieve something from his former home.'

'From Lord Shigeru's? It's madness. He'll be caught.'

'I don't think so. He's quite talented.' I thought I heard mockery beneath the compliment and took it as one more indication that he meant to kill me.

Yuzuru stuck out his bottom lip. 'Even monkeys fall from trees. What can be so important?'

'We think Otori might have kept extensive records on the Tribe's affairs.'

'Shigeru? The Farmer? Impossible!'

Akio's eyes hardened. 'Why do you think that?'

'Everyone knows . . . well, Shigeru was a good man. Everyone loved him. His death was a terrible tragedy. But he died because he was . . .' Yuzuru blinked furiously and looked apologetically at me. 'He was too trusting. Innocent almost. He was never a conspirator. He knew nothing about the Tribe.'

'We have reasons to think otherwise,' Akio said. 'We'll know who's right before tomorrow's dawn.'

'You're going there tonight?'

'We must be back in Matsue before the snows come.'

'Well, they'll be early this year. Possibly before the year's end.' Yuzuru sounded relieved to be talking about something as mundane as the weather. 'All the signs are for a long, hard winter. And if spring's going to bring war, I wish it may never come.'

It was already freezing within the small dark room, the third such that I had been concealed in. Yuzuru himself brought us food, tea, already cooling by the time we tasted it, and wine. Akio drank the wine, but I did not, feeling I needed my senses to remain acute. We sat without speaking as night fell.

The brewery quietened around us, though its smell did not diminish. I listened to the sounds of the town, each one so familiar to me that I felt I could pinpoint the exact street, the exact house, it came from. The familiarity relaxed me, and my depression began to lift a little. The bell sounded from Daishoin, the nearest temple, for the evening prayers. I could picture the weathered building, the deep green darkness of its grove, the stone lanterns that marked the graves of the Otori lords and their retainers. I fell into a sort of waking dream in which I was walking among them.

Then Shigeru came to me again, as if from out of a white mist, dripping with water and blood, his eyes burning black, holding an unmistakable message for me. I snapped awake, shivering with cold.

Akio said, 'Drink some wine, it'll steady your nerves.'

I shook my head, stood and went through the limbering up exercises the Tribe use until I was warm. Then I sat in meditation, trying to retain the heat, focussing my mind on the night's work, drawing together all my powers, knowing now how to do at will what I had once done by instinct.

From Daishoin the bell sounded. Midnight.

I heard Yuzuru approaching, and the door slid open.

He beckoned to us and led us through the house to the outer gates. Here he alerted the guards, and we went over the wall. One dog barked briefly, but was silenced with a cuff.

It was pitch dark, the air icy, a raw wind blowing off the sea. On such a foul night no one was on the streets. We went silently to the river bank and walked south-east towards the place where the rivers joined. The fish weir where I had often crossed to the other side lay exposed by the low tide. Just beyond it was Shigeru's house. On the near bank boats were moored. We used to cross the river in them to his lands on the opposite side, the rice fields and farms where he had tried to teach me about agriculture and irrigation, crops and coppices. And boats had brought the wood for the tea room and the nightingale floor, listing low in the water with the sweet-smelling planks, fresh cut from the forests beyond the farms. Tonight it was too dark even to make out the mountain slopes where the trees had grown.

We crouched by the side of the narrow road and looked at the house. There were no lights visible, just the dim glow of a brazier from the guardroom at the gate. I could hear men and dogs breathing deeply in sleep. The thought crossed my mind: they would not have slept so had Shigeru been alive. I was angry on his behalf, not least with myself.

Akio whispered, 'You know what you have to do?'

I nodded.

'Go then.'

We made no other plans. He simply sent me off as if I were a falcon or a hunting dog. I had a fair idea what his own plan was: when I returned with the records he would take them – and I would be reported unfortunately killed by the guards, my body thrown into the river.

I crossed the street, went invisible, leaped the wall and dropped into the garden. Immediately the muffled song of the house enveloped me: the sighing of the wind in the trees, the murmur of the stream, the splash of the waterfall, the surge of the river as the tide began to flow. Sorrow swept over me. What was I doing returning here in the night like a thief? Almost unconsciously I let my face change, let my Otori look return.

The nightingale floor extended around the whole house, but it held no threat to me. Even in the dark I could still cross it without making it sing. On the further side I climbed the wall to the window of the upper room – the same route the Tribe assassin, Shintaro, had taken over a year ago. At the top I listened. The room seemed empty.

The shutters were closed against the freezing night air, but they were not bolted, and it was easy to slide them apart enough to creep through. Inside it was barely any warmer and even darker. The room smelled musty and sour as if it had been closed for a long time, as if no one sat there any more save ghosts.

I could hear the household breathing and recognized the sleep of each one. But I could not place the one I needed to find: Ichiro. I stepped down the narrow staircase, knowing its favourite creaks as I knew my own hands. Once below I realized the house was not completely dark as it had appeared from the street. In the furthest room, the one Ichiro favoured, a lamp was burning. I went quietly towards it. The paper screen was closed but the lamp threw the shadow of the old man onto it. I slid open the door.

He raised his head and looked at me without surprise. He smiled sorrowfully and made a slight movement with his hand. 'What can I do for you? You know I would do anything to bring you peace but I am old. I have used the pen more than the sword.'

'Teacher,' I whispered. 'It's me. Takeo.' I stepped into the room, slid the door closed behind me and dropped to my knees before him.

He gave a shudder as if he had been asleep and just woken, or as if he had been in the world of the dead and been called back by the living. He grabbed my shoulders and pulled me towards him, into the lamplight. 'Takeo? Can it really be you?' He ran his hands over my head, my limbs, as though fearing I were an apparition, tears trickling down his cheeks. Then he embraced me, cradling my head against his shoulder, as if I were his long-lost son. I could feel his thin chest heaving.

He pulled back a little and gazed into my face. 'I thought you were Shigeru. He often visits me at night. He stands there in the doorway. I know what he wants, but what can I do?' He wiped away the tears with his sleeve. 'You've grown like him. It's quite uncanny. Where have you been all this time? We thought you too must have been murdered, except that every few weeks someone comes to the house looking for you, so we assumed you were still alive.'

'I was hidden by the Tribe,' I said, wondering how much he knew of my background. 'First in Yamagata, for the last two months in Matsue. I made a bargain with them. They kidnapped me at Inuyama but released me to go into the castle and bring Lord Shigeru out. In return I agreed to enter their service. You may not know that I am bound to them by blood.'

'Well, I'd assumed it,' Ichiro said. 'Why else would Muto Kenji have turned up here?' He took my hand and pressed it with emotion. 'Everyone knows the story of how you rescued Shigeru and slew Iida in revenge. I don't mind telling you, I always thought he was making a grave mistake adopting you, but you silenced all my misgivings and paid all your debts to him that night.'

'Not quite all. The Otori lords betrayed him to Iida and they are still unpunished.'

'Is that what you have come for? That would bring rest to his spirit.'

'No, I was sent by the Tribe. They believe Lord Shigeru kept records on them and they want to retrieve them.'

Ichiro smiled wryly. 'He kept records of many things. I go through them every night. The Otori lords claim your adoption was not legal and that anyway you are probably dead, therefore Shigeru has no heirs and his lands must revert to the castle. I've been looking for more proof so that you may keep what is yours.' His voice became stronger and more urgent. 'You must come back, Takeo. Half the clan will support you for what you did in Inuyama. Many suspect that Shigeru's uncles planned his death and are outraged by it. Come back and finish your revenge!'

Shigeru's presence was all around us. I expected him at any moment to walk into the room with his energetic step, his open-hearted smile, and the dark eyes that looked so frank yet hid so much.

'I feel I must,' I said slowly. 'I will have no peace unless I do. But the Tribe will certainly try to kill me if I desert them – more than try, they will not rest until they have succeeded.'

Ichiro took a deep breath. 'I don't believe I have mis-judged you,' he said. 'If I have, you came prepared to kill me anyway. I am old, I am ready to move on. But I would like to see Shigeru's work finished. It's true, he did keep records on the Tribe. He believed no one could bring peace to the Middle Country while the Tribe were so strong, so he devoted himself to finding out all he could about them and wrote it all down. He made sure no one knew what was in his records, not even me. He was extremely secretive, far more than anyone ever realized. He had to be: for ten years both Iida and his uncles had tried to get rid of him.'

'Can you give them to me?'

'I will not give them back to the Tribe,' he said. The lamp flickered, suddenly sending a crafty look across his face that I had never seen before. 'I must get more oil or we'll be sitting in darkness. Let me wake Chiyo.'

'Better not,' I said, even though I would have loved to have seen the old woman who ran the house and treated me like a son. 'I can't stay.'

'Did you come alone?'

I shook my head. 'Kikuta Akio is waiting for me outside.'

'Is he dangerous?'

'He's almost certainly going to try to kill me. Especially if I return to him empty-handed.' I was wondering what hour it was, what Akio was doing. The house's winter song was all around me. I did not want to leave it. My choices seemed to be narrowing. Ichiro would never hand over the records to the Tribe; I would never be able to kill him to get them. I took my knife from my sash, felt its familiar weight in my hand. 'I should take my own life now.'

'Well, it would be one answer,' Ichiro said, and sniffed. 'But not a very satisfactory one. I would then have two unquiet ghosts visiting me in the night. And Shigeru's murderers would go unpunished.'

The lamp spluttered. Ichiro stood. 'I'll get more oil,' he muttered. I listened to him shuffling through the house and thought about Shigeru. How many nights would he have sat until late in this very room? Boxes of scrolls stood around me. As I gazed idly at them I suddenly remembered with complete clarity the wooden chest that I had carried up the slope as a gift for the abbot on the day we had visited the temple to see the Sesshu paintings. I thought I saw Shigeru smile at me.

When Ichiro had returned and fixed the lamp he said, 'Anyway, the records aren't here.'

'I know,' I said. 'They are at Terayama.'

Ichiro grinned. 'If you want my advice, even though you never took any notice of it in the past, go there. Go now, tonight. I'll give you money for the journey. They'll hide you for the winter. And from there you can plan your revenge on the Otori lords. That's what Shigeru wants.'

'It's what I want too. But I made a bargain with the Kikuta master. I am bound to the Tribe now by my word.'

'I think you swore allegiance to the Otori first,' Ichiro said. 'Didn't Shigeru save your life before the Tribe had even heard of you?'

I nodded.

'And you said Akio would kill you? They have already broken faith with you. Can you get past him? Where is he?'

'I left him in the road outside. He could be anywhere now.'

'Well, you can hear him first, can't you? And what about those tricks you used to play on me? Always some-where else when I thought you were studying.'

164

'Teacher,' I began. I was going to apologize but he waved me silent.

'I forgive you everything. It was not my teaching that enabled you to bring Shigeru out of Inuyama.'

He left the room again and came back with a small string of coins and some rice cakes wrapped in kelp. I had no carrying cloth or box to put them in and anyway I was going to need both hands free. I tied the money into my loin cloth beneath my clothes, and put the rice cakes in my belt.

'Can you find the way?' he said, starting to fuss as he used to in the past over a shrine visit or some other outing.

'I think so.'

'I'll write you a letter to get you through the barrier. You're a servant of this household – it's what you look like – making arrangements for my visit to the temple next year. I'll meet you in Terayama when the snows melt. Wait for me there. Shigeru was in alliance with Arai. I don't know how things stand between you, but you should seek Arai's protection. He will be grateful for any information he can use against the Tribe.'

He took up the brush and wrote swiftly. 'Can you still write?' he asked, without looking up.

'Not very skilfully.'

'You'll have all winter to practise.' He sealed the letter and stood. 'By the way, what happened to Jato?'

'It came into my hands. It's being kept for me at Terayama.'

'Time to go back for it.' He smiled again and grumbled, 'Chiyo's going to kill me for not waking her.'

I slipped the letter inside my clothes and we embraced.

'Some strange fate ties you to this house,' he said. 'I

believe it is a bond you cannot escape.' His voice broke and I saw he was close to tears again.

'I know it,' I whispered. 'I will do everything you suggest.' I knew I could not give up this house and inheritance. They were mine. I would reclaim them. Everything Ichiro said made perfect sense. I had to escape from the Tribe. Shigeru's records would protect me from them, and give me bargaining power with Arai. If I could only get to Terayama . . .

Seven

I left the house the same way I had come, out through the upstairs window, down the wall and across the nightingale floor. It slept under my feet but I vowed next time I walked on it I would make it sing. I did not scale the wall back into the street. Instead I ran silently through the garden, went invisible and, clinging like a spider to the stones, climbed through the opening where the stream flowed into the river. I dropped into the nearest boat, untied it, took up the oar that lay in the stern, and pushed off into the river.

The boat groaned slightly under my weight, and the current lapped more strongly at it. To my dismay the sky had cleared. It was much colder and, under the three-quarters moon, much brighter. I heard the thud of feet from the bank, sent my image back to the wall, and crouched low in the boat. But Akio was not deceived by my second self. He leaped from the wall as if he were flying. I went invisible again, even though I knew it was probably useless against him, bounded from my boat and flew low across the surface of the water into another of the boats that lay against the river wall. I scrabbled to undo its rope, and pushed off with its oar. I saw Akio land and steady himself against the rocking of the craft; then he sprang and flew again as I split myself, left the second self in one boat and leaped for the other. I felt the air shift as we passed each other. Controlling my fall I dropped into my first boat, took up the oar and began to scull faster than I ever had in my life. My second self faded as Akio grasped it and I saw him prepare to leap again. There was no escape unless I went into the river. I drew my knife and as he landed stabbed at him with one hand. He moved with his usual speed and ducked easily under the knife. I had anticipated his move and caught him on the side of the head with the oar. He fell, stunned for a moment, while I, thrown off balance by the violent rocking of the boat, narrowly escaped tumbling overboard. I dropped the oar and clung to the wooden side. I did not want to go into the freezing water unless I took him with me and drowned him. As I slid to the other side of the boat Akio recovered. He leaped straight upwards and came down on top of me. We fell together and he seized me by the throat.

I was still invisible, but helpless, pinned under him like a carp on the cook's slab. I felt my vision blacken; then he loosened his grip slightly.

'You traitor,' he said. 'Kenji warned us you would go back to the Otori in the end. I'm glad you did, because I've wanted you dead since the first time we met. You're going to pay now. For your insolence to the Kikuta, for my hand. And for Yuki.'

'Kill me,' I said, 'as your family killed my father. You will never escape our ghosts. You will be cursed and haunted till the day you die. You murdered your own kin.'

The boat moved beneath us, drifting with the tide. If Akio had used his hands or knife then, I would not be telling this story. But he couldn't resist one last taunt. 'Your child will be mine. I'll bring him up properly as a real Kikuta.' He shook me violently. 'Show me your face,' he snarled. 'I want to see your look when I tell you how I'll teach him to hate your memory. I want to watch you die.'

He leaned closer, his eyes searching for my face. The boat drifted into the path of the moon. As I saw its brightness I let visibility return and looked straight into his eyes. I saw what I wanted to find: the jealous hatred of me that clouded his judgment and weakened him.

He realized in a split second, and tried to wrench his gaze away, but the blow from the oar must have slowed his usual quickness and it was too late. He was already made dizzy by the encroaching Kikuta sleep. He slumped sideways, his eyelids flickering erratically as he fought it. The boat tipped and rocked. His own weight took him headfirst into the river.

The boat drifted on, faster now, carried by the swelling tide. In the moonlit road across the water I saw the body surface. It floated gently. I was not going to go back and finish him off. I hoped he'd drown or freeze to death but I left it to fate. I took up the oar and sculled the boat to the further shore.

By the time I got there I was shivering with cold. The first roosters were crowing and the moon was low in the sky. The grass on the bank was stiff with frost and stones and twigs gleamed white. I disturbed a sleeping heron and wondered if it was the one that came to fish in Shigeru's garden. It flew off from the highest branches of the willow with the familiar clack of wings.

I was exhausted but far too wrought up to think of sleep and anyway I had to keep moving to warm myself. I forced myself to a quick pace, following the narrow mountain road towards the south-east. The moon was bright and I knew the track. By daybreak I was over the first pass and on my way down to a small village. Hardly anyone was stirring but an old woman was blowing up the embers in her hearth and she heated some soup for me in return for one of the coins. I complained to her about my senile old master sending me off on a wild-goose chase through the mountains to a remote temple. The winter would undoubtedly finish him off and I'd be stranded there.

She cackled and said, 'You'll have to become a monk then!'

'Not me. I like women too much.'

This pleased her and she found some freshly pickled plums to add to my breakfast. When she saw my string of coins she wanted to give me lodging as well as food. Eating had brought the sleep demon closer and I longed to lie down but I was too afraid of being recognized and I already regretted I had said as much as I had to her. I might have left Akio in the river but I knew how the river gives up its victims, both the living and the dead, and I feared his pursuit. I was not proud of my defection from the Tribe after I had sworn to obey them, and in the cold light of morning I was beginning to realize what the rest of my life would be like. I had made my choice to return to the Otori, but now I would never be free from the dread of assassination. An entire secret organization would be drawn up against me to punish me for my disloyalty. To slip through their web I had to move faster than any of their messengers would. And I had to get to Terayama before it began to snow.

The sky had turned the colour of lead when I reached Tsuwano on the afternoon of the second day. My thoughts were all of my meeting there with Kaede and the sword-training session when I had fallen in love with her. Was her name already entered in the ledgers of the dead? Would I have to light candles for her now every year at the Festival of the Dead until I died? Would we be joined in the afterworld or were we condemned never to meet again either in life or in death. Grief and shame gnawed at me. She had said, *I only feel safe with you*, and I had abandoned her. If fate were to be kind and she were to come into my hands again I would never let her go.

I regretted bitterly my decision to go with the Tribe and I went over the reasons behind my choice many times. I believed I had made a bargain with them and my life was forfeit to them – that was one thing. But beyond that I blamed my own vanity. I had wanted to know and develop the side of my character that came from my father, from the Kikuta, from the Tribe: the dark inheritance that gave me skills I was proud of. I had responded eagerly and willingly to their seduction, the mixture of flattery, understanding and brutality with which they had used and manipulated me. I wondered how much chance I had to get away from them.

My thoughts went round and round in circles. I was walking in a kind of daze. I'd slept a little in the middle of the day in a hollow off the side of the road but the cold woke me. The only way to stay warm was to keep walking. I skirted the town and, descending through the pass, picked up the road again near the river. The current had subsided from the full flood caused by the storms that had delayed us in Tsuwano and the banks had been mended, but the bridge here, a wooden one, was still in ruins. I paid a boatman to take me across. No one else was travelling so late; I was his last customer. I felt he was eyeing me curiously but he did not speak to me. I could not place him as Tribe but he made me uneasy. He dropped me on the other side and I walked quickly away. When I turned at the corner of the road he was still watching me. I made a movement with my head but he did not acknowledge it.

It was colder than ever, the air dank and icy. I was already regretting that I had not found shelter for the night. If I was caught by a blizzard before the next town I stood little chance of surviving. Yamagata was still several days away. There would be a post station at the fief border but, despite Ichiro's letter and my disguise as a servant, I did not want to spend the night there – too many curious people, too many guards. I didn't know what to do so I kept walking.

Night fell. Even with my Tribe-trained eyes it was hard to see the road. Twice I wandered off it and had to retrace my steps. Once I stumbled into some sort of hole or ditch, with water at the bottom, soaking my legs up to the knees. The wind howled and strange sounds came from the woods, reminding me of legends of monsters and goblins and making me think the dead walked behind me.

By the time the sky began to pale in the east I was frozen to the bone and shivering uncontrollably. I was glad to see the dawn but it gave no relief from the bitter cold. Instead it just brought home to me how alone I was. For the first time the idea crept insidiously into my head that if the fief border was manned by Arai's men I would give myself up to them. They would take me to Arai, but first they would surely give me something hot to drink. They would sit me down inside by the fire and make tea for me. I became obsessed by the thought of that tea. I could feel the heat of the steam on my face, the warmth of the bowl in my hands. I was so obsessed by it that I did not notice someone walking behind me.

I was aware suddenly of a presence at my back. I turned, astonished that I had not heard the footfall on the road, had not even heard breathing. I was amazed, even frightened, at my apparent loss of hearing. It was as though this traveller had fallen from the sky or walked above the ground as the dead do. Then I knew that either exhaustion had unhinged my mind or I was indeed seeing a ghost, for the man walking just behind me was the out-caste, Jo-An, who I thought had been tortured to death by Arai's men in Yamagata.

So great was the shock I thought I would faint. The blood rushed from my head, making me stagger. Jo-An grabbed me as I fell, his hands seeming real enough, strong and solid, smelling of the tannery. Earth and sky turned around me and black spots darkened my sight. He lowered me to the ground and pushed my head between my knees. Something was roaring in my ears, deafening me. I crouched like that, his hands holding my head, until the roaring lessened and the dark receded from my vision. I stared at the ground. The grass was rimed by frost and tiny particles of black ice lay between each stone. The wind howled in the cedars. Apart from that the only sound was my teeth chattering.

Jo-An spoke. There was no doubt; it was his voice. 'Forgive me, lord. I startled you. I didn't mean to alarm you.'

'They told me you were dead. I didn't know if you were a living being or a ghost.'

'Well, I might have died for a while,' he whispered. 'Arai's men thought so and threw my body out in the marshland. But the Secret God had other plans for me and sent me back to this world. My work here is not yet done.'

I lifted my head carefully and looked at him. He had a new scar, not long healed, from nose to ear, and several teeth missing. I took his wrist and brought his hand round so I could see it. The nails were gone, the fingers clubbed and twisted.

'I should be asking your forgiveness,' I said, sickened.

'Nothing happens to us that is not planned by God,' he replied.

I wondered why any god's plans had to include torture but I did not say this to Jo-An. Instead I asked, 'How did you find me?'

'The boatman came to me and told me he had ferried someone he thought was you across the river. I've been waiting for word of you. I knew you would come back.' He took up the bundle he'd placed by the side of the road and began to untie it. 'The prophecy has to be fulfilled, after all.'

'What prophecy?' I remembered that Kenji's wife had called him the lunatic.

He didn't answer. He took two small millet cakes from the cloth, prayed over them, and gave one to me.

'You are always feeding me,' I said. 'I don't think I can eat.'

'Drink then,' Jo-An said, and handed me a rough bamboo flask. I wasn't sure about drinking either but I thought it might warm me. As soon as the liquor hit my stomach the darkness came roaring back and I vomited several times so hard I was racked by violent shuddering.

Jo-An clicked his tongue as you would to a horse or an ox. He had the patient touch of a man used to dealing with animals, though of course he dealt with them at the moment of their death and then, afterwards, flayed their

174

corpses. When I could speak again I said through chattering teeth, 'I must keep moving.'

'Where are you heading?' he asked.

'Terayama. I'll spend the winter there.'

'Well,' he said, and fell into one of his familiar silences. He was praying, listening to some inner voice that would tell him what to do. 'It's good,' he said finally. 'We'll go over the mountain. If you go by road they'll stop you at the barrier and anyway it will take too long; it will snow before you get to Yamagata.'

'Over the mountain?' I looked up at the jagged peaks that stretched away to the north-east. The road from Tsuwano to Yamagata skirted around their foot, but Terayama itself lay directly behind them. Around the range the clouds hung low and grey, with the dull damp sheen that presages snow.

'It's a steep climb,' Jo-An said. 'You must rest a little before you attempt it.'

I began to think about getting to my feet. 'I don't have time. I must get to the temple before it snows.'

Jo-An looked up at the sky and sniffed the wind. 'It will be too cold to snow tonight, but it could well start tomorrow. We'll ask the Secret One to hold it back.'

He stood and helped me up. 'Can you walk now? It's not far back to the place I live. You can rest there, then I'll take you to the men who will show you the way over the mountain.'

I felt faint, as though my body had lost its substance, almost as though I'd split myself and somehow gone with my image. I was thankful for the Tribe training that had taught me to find those reserves of strength of which most men are unaware. Slowly, as I concentrated my breathing, I felt some energy and toughness return. Jo-An no doubt attributed my recovery to the power of his prayers. He regarded me for a moment with his deep-sunk eyes, then turned with a flicker of a smile and began to walk back the way we had come.

I hesitated for a moment, partly because I hated the thought of retracing my steps, losing the ground it had cost me so much to cover, but also because I recoiled from going with the outcaste. It was one thing to talk with him at night, alone, quite another to walk close to him, to be seen in his company. I reminded myself that I was not yet an Otori lord, and no longer one of the Tribe, that Jo-An was offering me help and shelter, but my skin crawled as I followed him.

After walking for less than an hour we turned off the road onto a smaller path that followed the banks of a narrow river, through a couple of miserable villages. Children ran out to beg for food, but they backed away when they recognized the outcaste. In the second village two older boys were bold enough to throw stones. One of them nearly struck me on the back – I heard it coming in time to step aside – and I was going to go back and punish the brat, but Jo-An restrained me.

Long before we reached it I could smell the tannery. The river widened and eventually flowed into the main channel. At the confluence stood the rows of wooden frames, skins stretched on them. Here in this damp sheltered spot they were protected from frost, but as winter's bite strengthened they would be taken down and stored till spring. Men were already at work, all outcastes of course, half-naked despite the cold, all as skeletally thin as Jo-An and with the same beaten look like mistreated dogs. Mist hung on the river, mingled with smoke from charcoal fires. A floating bridge made of reeds and bamboo lashed together with cords had been constructed across the river. I remembered Jo-An telling me to come to the outcastes' bridge if I ever needed help. Now some fate had brought me here – he would say the power of the secret god, no doubt.

On the far side of the frames a few small wooden huts had been erected. They looked as if one strong wind would flatten them. As I followed Jo-An to the threshold of the nearest one, the men continued their work but I was aware of their gaze. Each one looked at me with a kind of intense entreaty, as though I meant something to them and could help them in some way.

Trying to mask my reluctance I stepped inside, not needing to remove my shoes as the floor was earthen. A small fire burned in the hearth. The air was thick with smoke, making my eyes sting. There was one other person inside, huddled in the corner, under a pile of hides. I thought it was Jo-An's wife until he came forward on his knees and bowed his head to the dirt before me. It was the man who had ferried me across the river.

'He walked most of the night to tell me he'd seen you,' Jo-An said apologetically. 'He needed to rest a little before returning.'

I was aware of the sacrifice it entailed, not only the lonely walk through the goblin-haunted darkness, but the danger from robbers and patrols and the loss of a day's fees.

'Why did he do this for me?'

The boatman sat up then, raising his eyes and looking briefly at me. He said nothing, but the look he gave me was the same one I'd seen in the gaze of the tannery workers, a look of passion and hunger. I had seen it before, months earlier, on the faces of people as we rode back from

Terayama to Yamagata, the look they threw out like an appeal to Shigeru. They had found in Shigeru the promise of something – justice, compassion – and now these men looked for the same thing in me. Whatever Jo-An had told them about me had transformed me into their hope.

And something in me responded to this, just as it had to the villagers, to the farmers with their hidden fields. They were treated like dogs, beaten and starved, but I saw them as men, with the brains and hearts of men, no less than any warrior or merchant. I had been brought up among people like them, and been taught that the secret god saw them all with equal eyes. No matter what I became, no matter what other teaching I received from the Otori or the Tribe, despite my own reluctance even, it was impossible for me to forget this.

Jo-An said, 'He is your man now. As I am, as we all are. You only have to call on us.' He grinned, his broken teeth flashing in the dim light. He had made tea and handed me a small wooden bowl. I felt the steam rise against my face. The tea was made from twigs, such as we used to drink in Mino.

'Why should I call on you? What I'm going to need is an army!' I drank, and felt the warmth begin to spread through me.

'Yes, an army,' Jo-An replied. 'Many battles lie ahead of you. The prophecy says it.'

'How can you help me then? It's forbidden for you to kill.'

'Warriors will kill,' Jo-An replied, 'but there are many things they won't do which are equally necessary. Things they consider beneath them. Building, slaughtering, bury-ing. You'll realize it when you need us.'

The tea settled my stomach. Jo-An brought out two

more small millet balls, but I had no appetite and made the boatman eat my share. Jo-An did not eat either, but put the second ball away again. I saw the other man's eyes follow it and gave him some coins before he left. He did not want to take them but I pressed them into his hand.

Jo-An mumbled the blessing of departure over him and then pulled aside the hides so I could take his place under them. The warmth of the tea stayed with me. The hides stank, but they kept out the cold and muffled sound. I thought briefly how any one of those starving men might betray me for a bowl of soup but I had no alternative now; I had to trust Jo-An. I let the darkness fall over me and take me down into sleep.

He woke me a few hours later. It was well after noon. He gave me tea, hardly more than hot water, and apologized for having no food to offer me.

'We should leave now,' he said 'If we are to get to the charcoal burners before dark.'

'The charcoal burners?' I usually woke swiftly but this day I was groggy with sleep.

'They are still on the mountain. They have paths they use through the forest that will take you over the border. But they will leave with the first snow.' He paused for a moment and then said, 'We have to speak to someone on the way.'

'Who?'

'It won't take long.' He gave me one of his slight smiles. We went outside and I knelt by the river bank and splashed water on my face. It was icy; as Jo-An had predicted the temperature had dropped and the air was drier. It was too cold and too dry to snow.

I shook the water from my hands while he spoke to the men. Their eyes flickered towards me. When we left, they stopped work, and knelt with bowed heads as I walked past.

'They know who I am?' I asked Jo-An in a low voice. Again, I feared betrayal from these men who had so little.

'They know you are Otori Takeo,' he replied, 'the Angel of Yamagata who will bring justice and peace. That's what the prophecy says.'

'What prophecy?' I asked again.

He said, 'You will hear it for yourself.'

I was filled with misgivings. What was I doing entrusting my life to this lunatic? I felt every extra moment wasted would keep me from reaching Terayama before either the snow or the Tribe caught up with me. But I realized now that my only hope was to go over the mountain. I had to follow Jo-An.

We crossed the smaller river a little way upstream by a fish weir. We passed few people, a couple of fishermen, and some girls taking food to the men who were burning rice stalks and spreading dung on the empty fields. The girls climbed up the bank rather than cross our path and one of the fishermen spat at us. The other cursed Jo-An for blighting the water. I kept my head low and my face averted, but they paid no attention to me. In fact they avoided looking at us directly, as though even that contact would bring pollution and bad luck.

Jo-An seemed to take no notice of the hostility, retreating into himself as if into a dark cloak, but when we had passed them he said, 'They would not allow us to use the wooden bridge to take the hides across. That's why we had to learn to build our own. Now the other bridge is destroyed but they still refuse to use ours.' He shook his head and whispered, 'If only they knew the Secret One.'

On the further bank we followed the river for another mile and then turned off towards the north-east, and began to climb. The bare-branched maples and beeches gave way to pines and cedars. As the forest deepened the path darkened and grew steeper and steeper until we were clambering over rocks and boulders, going as often on all fours as upright. The sleep had refreshed me and I could feel strength returning. Jo-An climbed tirelessly, hardly even panting. It was hard to guess his age. Poverty and suffering had hollowed him out, so he looked like an old man, but he might have been no more than thirty. There was something unearthly about him as though he had indeed returned from the dead.

We finally came over a crest and stood on a small plateau. A huge rock lay across it, fallen from the crag above. Below us I could see the glint of the river, almost as far as Tsuwano. Smoke and mist drifted across the valley. The clouds were low, hiding the mountain range on the opposite side. The climb had warmed us, even made us sweat, but when we stopped our breath came white on the raw air. A few late berries still glowed red on leafless bushes; otherwise there was no colour anywhere. Even the evergreen trees were muted almost to black. I could hear water trickling, and two crows were calling to each other from the crag. When they fell silent I heard someone breathing.

The sound came, slow and measured, from the rock itself. I slowed my own breathing, touched Jo-An on the arm and made a gesture with my head towards it.

He gave me a smile and spoke quietly. 'It's all right. This is who we have come to see.'

The crows cawed again, their voices harsh and ominous. I began to shiver. The cold was creeping up on me, surrounding me. The fears of the previous night threatened to surface again. I wanted to keep moving. I did not want to meet whoever was concealed behind the rock, breathing so slowly they could hardly be human.

'Come,' Jo-An said, and I followed him around the edge of the rock, keeping my eyes away from the drop below. Behind, a cave was hollowed out of the side of the mountain. Water dripped from its roof. Over the centuries it had formed spears and columns and worn out a channel on the ground that led to a small deep pool, its sides as regular as a cistern and limestone white. The water itself was black.

The roof of the cave sloped, following the shape of the mountain, and in the upper, drier side sat a figure that I would have thought was a statue if I had not heard its breathing. It was greyish white, like the limestone, as though it had sat there so long it had started to calcify. It was hard to tell if it was male or female: I recognized it as one of those ancient people, a hermit, monk or nun, who had gone beyond sex and gender and grown so close to the next world he or she was almost pure spirit. The hair fell like a white shawl, the face and hands were grey like old paper.

The figure sat in meditation on the floor of the cave with no sign of strain or discomfort. In front of it was a kind of stone altar, bearing fading flowers, the last of the autumn lilies, and other offerings: two bitter oranges, their skins wrinkling, a small piece of fabric and some coins of little value. It was like any other shrine to the god of the mountain, except carved into the stone was the sign the Hidden use, the one Lady Maruyama had traced on my hand in Chigawa so long ago.

Jo-An untied his cloth and took out the last millet

cake. He knelt and placed it carefully on the altar, then bowed his head to the ground. The figure opened its eyes and gazed on us, gazed but did not see. The eyes were clouded with blindness. An expression came over the face that made me drop to my knees and bow before it – a look of profound tenderness and compassion, blended with complete knowledge. I had no doubt I was in the presence of a holy being.

'Tomasu,' it said, and I thought its voice a woman's rather than a man's. It was so long since anyone had called me by the water name my mother had given me that the hair on the back of my neck stood up and when I shivered it was not only from cold.

'Sit up,' she said. 'I have words to say that you are to hear. You are Tomasu of Mino, but you have become both Otori and Kikuta. Three bloods are mixed in you. You were born into the Hidden, but your life has been brought into the open and is no longer your own. Earth will deliver what Heaven desires.'

She fell silent. The minutes passed. The cold entered my bones. I wondered if she would say anything else. At first I was amazed that she knew who I was; then I thought Jo-An must have told her about me. If this was the prophecy it was so obscure that it meant nothing to me. If I knelt there much longer I thought I would freeze to death, but I was held by the force of the blind woman's eyes.

I listened to the breath of the three of us and to the sounds of the mountain, the crows still cawing in their harsh voices, the cedars restless in the north-east wind, the trickle and drip of water, the groaning of the mountain itself as the temperature dropped and the rocks shrank.

'Your lands will stretch from sea to sea,' she said finally. 'But peace comes at the price of bloodshed. Five battles will buy you peace, four to win and one to lose. Many must die, but you yourself are safe from death, except at the hands of your own son.'

Another long silence followed. With every second the light darkened towards evening and the air chilled. My gaze wandered round the cave. At the holy woman's side stood a prayer wheel on a small wooden block carved with lotus leaves around its edge. I was puzzled. I knew many mountain shrines were forbidden to women and none I had ever seen had contained such a mixture of symbols, as though the secret god, the Enlightened One and the spirits of the mountain all dwelt here together.

She spoke as if she saw my thoughts; her voice held a kind of laughter mixed with wonder. 'It is all one. Keep this in your heart. It is all one.'

She touched the prayer wheel and set it turning. Its rhythm seemed to steal into my veins to join my blood. She began to chant softly, words I had never heard before and did not understand. They flowed over and around us, eventually fading into the wind. When we heard them again they had become the farewell blessing of the Hidden. She handed us a bowl and told us to drink from the pool before we left.

A thin layer of ice was already forming on the surface and the water was so cold it bit into my teeth. Jo-An wasted no time but led me quickly away, glancing anxiously towards the north. Before we went back over the crest I took one last look at the holy woman. She sat motionless; from this distance she seemed like part of the rock. I could not believe she would stay out here alone all night.

'How does she survive?' I questioned Jo-An. 'She'll die of cold.'

He frowned. 'She is sustained by God. It does not matter to her if she dies.'

'She is like you, then?'

'She is a holy person. Once I thought she was an angel, but she is a human being, transformed by the power of God.'

He did not want to talk more. He seemed to have caught my urgency. We descended at a rapid pace until we came to a small rock fall which we clambered over. On the other side was a narrow path, made by men walking single file into the dark forest. Once on the path we began to climb again.

Fallen leaves and pine needles muffled our footsteps. Beneath the trees it was almost night. Jo-An went faster still. The pace warmed me a little, but my feet and legs seemed to be slowly turning to stone, as if the limey water I'd drunk were calcifying me. And my heart was chilled too by the old woman's baffling words and all that they implied for my future. I had never fought in a battle: was I really to wage five of them? If bloodshed was the price of peace, in five battles it would be a heavy cost indeed. And the idea that my own son, not yet even born, would be the one to kill me filled me with unbearable sadness.

I caught up with Jo-An and touched him on the arm. 'What does it mean?'

'It means what it says,' he replied, slowing a little to catch his breath.

'Did she say the same words to you, earlier?'

'The same.'

'When was it?'

'After I died and came back to life. I wanted to live

like her, a hermit on the mountain. I thought I might be her servant, her disciple. But she said my work in the world was not yet finished, and she spoke the words about you.'

'You told her who I was, my past life and everything?'

'No,' he said patiently. 'There was no need to tell her for she already knew. She said I must serve you, because only you will bring peace.'

'Peace?' I repeated. Was this what she meant by Heaven's desire? I wasn't even sure what the word signified. The very idea of peace seemed like one of the fantasies of the Hidden, the stories of the kingdom that my mother would whisper to me at night. Would it ever be possible to stop the clans from fighting? The whole warrior class fought: it was what they were bred and trained and lived for. Apart from their traditions and personal sense of honour, there was the constant need for land to maintain armies to gain more land, the military codes and shifting webs of alliances, the overweening ambition of warlords like Iida Sadamu, and now, more than likely, Arai Daiichi. 'Peace through war?'

'Is there any other way?' Jo-An replied. 'There will be battles.'

Four to win, one to lose.

'That is why we are preparing now. You noticed the men at the tannery, saw their eyes. Ever since your merciful actions at Yamagata castle when you put an end to the suffering of the tortured Hidden, you have been a hero to these people. Then your service to Lord Shigeru at Inuyama . . . even without the prophecy they would have been ready to fight for you. Now they know God is with you.'

'She sits in a mountain shrine and uses a prayer

wheel,' I said. 'Yet she blessed us after the fashion of your people.'

'Our people,' he corrected me.

I shook my head. 'I no longer follow those teachings. I have killed many times. Do you really believe she speaks the words of your god?'

For the Hidden teach that the secret god is the only true one, and the spirits that everyone else worships are delusions.

'I don't know why God tells me to listen to her,' he admitted. 'But he does, and so I do.'

He is mad, I thought, *the torture and the fear have driven him out of his mind.* 'She said, it is all one. But you don't believe that, surely?'

He whispered, 'I believe all the teachings of the Secret One. I have followed them since childhood. I know them to be true. But it seems to me there is a place beyond the teachings, a place beyond words, where that could be the truth. Where all the beliefs are seen to issue from the one source. My brother was a priest; he would have said this was heresy. I have not been to this place yet, but it is where she dwells.'

I was silent, thinking about how his words applied to myself. I could feel the three elements that made up my nature, coiled within me like three separate snakes, each one deadly to the others if it were allowed to strike. I could never live one life without denying two-thirds of myself. My only way was to go forwards, to transcend the divisions, and find a means of uniting them.

'And you also,' Jo-An added, reading my thoughts.

'It is what I would like to believe,' I said finally. 'But whereas for her it is a place of deepest spirituality, I am perhaps more practical. To me it just seems to make sense.'

'So you are the one who will bring peace.'

I did not want to believe this prophecy. It was both far more and far less than I wanted for my own life. But the old woman's words had fallen into my inner being and I could not get rid of them.

'The men at the tannery, your men, they won't fight, will they?'

'Some will,' Jo-An said.

'Do they know how to?'

'They can be taught. And there are many other things they can do, building, transport, guiding you over secret paths.'

'Like this one?'

'Yes, the charcoal burners made this one. They conceal the entrances with rock piles. They have ways over the whole mountain.'

Farmers, outcastes, charcoal burners – none of them was supposed to carry weapons or join in the wars of the clans. I wondered how many others were like the farmer I had killed at Matsue, or Jo-An. What a waste of their courage and intelligence not to use men like that. If I were to train and arm them, I would have all the men I needed. But would warriors fight alongside them? Or would they just consider me an outcaste too?

I was occupied with these thoughts when I caught the whiff of burning and a few moments later heard the distant sound of voices, and other noises of human activity, the thud of an axe, the crackle of fire. Jo-An noticed as I swung my head.

'You hear them already?'

I nodded, listening, counting how many there were. Four from the voices, I thought, maybe another who did not speak, but who moved with a distinctive tread, no dogs, which seemed unusual. 'You know I am half-Kikuta, from the Tribe. I have many of their talents.'

He couldn't help flinching slightly. These talents seem like witchcraft to the Hidden. My own father had renounced all his Tribe skills when he had been converted to the beliefs of the Hidden: he had died because he had taken their vow never to kill again.

'I know it,' Jo-An replied.

'I'll need all of them if I'm to do what you expect of me.'

'The Tribe are children of the devil,' he muttered, adding quickly as he had once before, 'but your case is different, lord.'

It made me realize the risks he was taking for me, not only from human forces, but from supernatural ones. My Tribe blood must have made me as dangerous in his mind as a goblin or a river spirit. I was amazed again at the strength of the convictions that drove him and at how completely he had placed himself in my hands.

The smell of burning grew stronger. Flecks of ash were settling on our clothes and skin, reminding me ominously of snow. The ground took on a greyish look. The path led into a clearing between the trees where there were several charcoal ovens banked over with damp soil and turf. Only one still burned, patches of red glowing from its crevices. Three men were engaged in dismantling the cold ovens and bundling the charcoal. Another knelt by a cooking fire where a kettle hung steaming from a three-legged stand. Four, yet I still felt there had been five. I heard a heavy footfall behind me, and the involuntary intake of breath that precedes an attack. I pushed Jo-An aside and leaped around to face whoever it was trying to ambush us.

He was the largest man I had ever seen, arms already stretched out to seize us. One huge hand, one stump. Because of the stump I hesitated to wound him more. Leaving my image on the path I slipped behind him, and called to him to turn around, holding the knife where he could see the blade clearly and threatening to cut his throat.

Jo-An was shouting, 'It's me, you blockhead! It's Jo-An!'

The man by the fire let out a great shout of laughter and the charcoal burners came running.

'Don't hurt him, sir,' they called to me. 'He doesn't mean any harm. You surprised him, that's all.'

The giant had lowered his arms and stood with his one hand held out in a gesture of submission.

'He's mute,' Jo-An told me. 'But even with one hand he's as strong as two oxen, and he's a hard worker.'

The charcoal burners were clearly worried I was going to punish one of their greatest assets. They threw themselves at my feet, begging for mercy. I told them to get up and keep their giant under control.

'I could have killed him!'

They all got up, said the words of welcome, clapped Jo-An on the shoulder, bowed again to me, and made me sit down by the fire. One of them poured tea from the kettle. I had no idea what it was made from; it tasted unlike anything I'd ever had before but it was hot. Jo-An took them to one side and they had a huddled whispered conversation of which I could hear every word.

Jo-An told them who I was, which produced gasps and more bowing, and that I had to get to Terayama as soon as possible. The group argued a little about the safest route and whether to start right away or wait till morning, then they came back to the fire, sat in a circle and stared at me, their eyes glowing in their dark faces. They were covered in soot and ash, barely clothed, yet not noticing the cold. They spoke as a group, and seemed to think and feel as one. I imagined that here in the forest they followed their own rules, living like wild men, almost like animals.

'They've never spoken to a lord before,' Jo-An said. 'One of them wants to know if you are the hero Yoshitsune, returned from the mainland. I told them that though you wander the mountains like Yoshitsune and are pursued by all men, you will be an even greater hero for he failed, but you are promised success by God.'

'Will the lord allow us to cut wood where we please?' one of the older men asked. They did not speak to me directly but addressed all their remarks to Jo-An. 'There are many parts of the forest where we are no longer allowed to go. If we cut a tree there . . .' He made a graphic gesture of slicing his own neck.

'A head for a tree, a hand for a branch,' said another. He reached over to the giant, and held up the mutilated arm. The stump had healed over with a puckered, livid scar, traces of grey running back up the limb where it had been cauterized. 'Tohan clan officials did this to him a couple of years ago. He didn't understand, but they still took his hand.'

The giant held it out to me, nodding several times, his face bewildered and sorrowful.

I knew the Otori clan also had laws forbidding indiscriminate felling of trees: it was to protect the forests for ever, but I did not think they enforced such harsh penalties. I wondered what was the point of half-crippling a man; was a human life really worth less than a tree's?

'Lord Otori will reclaim all these lands,' Jo-An said. 'He will rule from sea to sea. He will bring justice.'

They bowed again, swearing that they would serve me, and I promised I would do all I could for them, when that day came. Then they fed us – meat: small birds they had caught and a hare. I ate meat so rarely I could not remember when I had last tasted it, apart from the wrestlers' chicken stew. That flesh, however, had been bland compared with the hare. They'd trapped it a week ago, saving it for their final night on the mountain, burying it out of the sight of any clan official who might come prying round the camp. It tasted of the earth and of blood.

While we ate they discussed their plans for the following day. They decided that one of them would show me the way to the border. They did not dare cross it themselves but the way down the mountain to Terayama was plain enough, they thought. We would leave at first light and it should take me no more than twelve hours, if the snow held off.

The wind had shifted slightly to the north, and it held a threatening rawness. They had already planned to dismantle the last oven that evening and begin the trek down the mountain the following day. Jo-An could help them if he stayed overnight, standing in for the man who would be my guide.

'They don't object to working with you?' I said to Jo-An later. I was puzzled by the charcoal burners. They ate meat so they did not follow the teachings of the Enlightened One, they did not pray over their food in the manner of the Hidden, and they accepted the outcaste to eat and work alongside, quite unlike the villagers.

'They are also outcaste,' he replied. 'They burn

corpses as well as wood. But they are not of the Hidden. They worship the spirits of the forest, in particular the god of fire. They believe he will travel down the mountain with them tomorrow and dwell with them all winter, keeping their houses warm. In the spring they accompany him back to the mountain.' Jo-An's voice held a note of disapproval. 'I try to tell them about the secret god,' he said. 'But they say they cannot leave their ancestors' god for who then would light the fire for the ovens?'

'Maybe it's all one,' I said, teasing him a little, for the meat and the warmth that the fire god had provided had raised my spirits.

He gave me one of his slight smiles, but said no more on the subject. He looked suddenly exhausted. The light was almost gone and the charcoal burners invited us into their shelter. It was roughly built from branches and covered with hides which I guessed they had swapped for charcoal with the tanners. We crawled in with them, all huddled together against the cold. My head, closest to the oven, was warm enough, but my back was icy, and when I turned over I thought my eyelids would freeze shut.

I did not sleep much, but lay listening to the deep breathing of the men around me, thinking about my future. I had thought I had placed myself under the death sentence of the Tribe, each day hardly expecting to be still alive at nightfall, but the prophetess had given me back my life. My own skills had developed relatively late: some of the boys I had trained with in Matsue were already showing signs of talent as young as eight or nine. How old would my son be? How long would it be before he was skilled enough to confront me? Maybe as much as sixteen years; it was nearly my entire lifetime. This bald calculation gave me a great deal of hope.

Sometimes I believed in the prophecy and sometimes I did not, and so it has been all my life.

Tomorrow I would be at Terayama. I would have Shigeru's records of the Tribe, I would hold Jato in my hands again. In the spring I would approach Arai. Armed with my secret information on the Tribe, I would seek his support against Shigeru's uncles. For it was obvious to me that my first encounter must be with them. Avenging Shigeru's death and taking up my inheritance would give me what I most needed, a power base in impregnable Hagi.

Jo-An slept restlessly, twitching and whimpering. I realized he was probably always in pain, yet awake he gave no sign of it. Towards dawn the cold eased a little and I slept deeply for about an hour, only to wake with a soft feathery sound filling my ears, the sound I dreaded. I crawled to the entrance of the shelter. In the firelight I could see the flakes beginning to fall, could hear the tiny hiss as they melted on the embers. I shook Jo-An and woke the charcoal burners.

'It's snowing!'

They leaped up, lit branches for torches, and began to pack up their camp. They had no more desire to be trapped on the mountain than I did. The precious charcoal from the last oven was wrapped in the damp hides off the shelter. They prayed quickly over the embers of the fire, and placed them in an iron pot to be carried with them down the mountain.

The snow was still fine and powdery, mostly not settling, but melting as soon as it touched the ground. However, as dawn came we could see that the sky was grey and ominous, the clouds full of more snow to come. The wind was picking up too; when the heavier snow did start to fall it would be as a blizzard.

There was no time to eat, no time even for tea. Once all the charcoal was ready the men were eager to get away. Jo-An dropped to his knees before me but I raised him up and embraced him. His frame in my arms was as bony and frail as an old man's.

'We will meet again in the spring,' I said. 'I will send word to you at the outcastes' bridge.'

He nodded, suddenly overcome with emotion as though he could not bear to let me out of his sight. One of the men raised a bundle and placed it across his shoulders. The others were already filing down the slope. Jo-An made a clumsy gesture to me, a cross between a farewell and a blessing. Then he turned and, stumbling a little under the weight of the burden, walked away.

I watched him for a moment, finding myself repeating under my breath the familiar words the Hidden use when they part.

'Come, lord,' my guide called to me anxiously, and I turned and followed him up the slope.

We climbed for what must have been nearly three hours. My guide paused only to bend twigs now and then to mark the path back. The snow stayed the same, light and dry, but the higher we climbed the more it settled until ground and trees all had a thin powdering of white. The rapid climb warmed me, but my stomach was growling with hunger. The meat the night before had given it false expectations. It was impossible to guess the hour. The sky was a uniform brownish grey, and the ground was beginning to give off the strange disorientating light of a snowy landscape.

When my guide stopped we were halfway up the main peak of the mountain range. The path we'd been following now twisted away downwards. I could see the valley below through the veil of falling flakes, the massive branches of the beeches and cedars already turning white.

'Can't go any further with you,' he said. 'Want my advice you turn back with me now. Blizzard's coming. Best part of a day's walk to the temple, even in fair weather. You go on, you perish in the snow.'

'It's impossible for me to go back,' I replied. 'Come a little further with me. I'll pay you well for it.' But I could not persuade him, nor did I really want to. He seemed uneasy and lonely without his fellows. I gave him half the coins I had left anyway and in return he gave me a leg bone from the hare, with a fair bit of meat still attached to it.

He described the path I had to take, pointing out the landmarks across the valley as best he could in the dim light. A river ran through it, he told me, not knowing I'd already heard it long before. This marked the fief boundary. There was no bridge but at one point it was narrow enough to jump across. The pools beneath held water spirits and the current was swift, so I must be careful not to fall in. Also, as this was the easiest place to cross, sometimes it was patrolled, though he did not think that was likely on such a day as this.

Once into the next fief I was to continue in an easterly direction, descending towards a small shrine. Here the paths forked. I must take the right-hand, lower path. I had to keep going east, otherwise I would find myself climbing the mountain range. The wind was from the north-east now, so I had to keep it against my left shoulder. He touched my shoulder twice to emphasize this, peering into my face with his narrow eyes.

'You don't look like a lord,' he said, his features twisting in a sort of smile. 'But good luck to you anyway.'

I thanked him, and set off down the slope, gnawing the bone as I went, cracking it open with my teeth and sucking out the marrow. The snow became slightly wetter and denser, melting more slowly on my head and clothes. The man was right, I did not look like a lord. My hair, which had not been cut since Yuki had clipped it in the style of an actor, hung shaggy round my ears and I had not shaved for days. My clothes were soaked and filthy. I certainly did not smell like a lord. I tried to remember when I'd last had a bath – and suddenly recalled the wrestlers' stable, our first night out from Matsue: the vast bathhouse, the conversation I'd overheard between Akio and Hajime.

I wondered where Yuki was now, if she had heard of my defection. I could hardly bear to think about the child. In the light of the prophecy, the idea of my son being kept from me and taught to hate me had become even more painful. I remembered Akio's taunt; it seemed the Kikuta knew my character better than I knew it myself.

The noise of the river grew louder, almost the only sound in the snow-filled landscape. Even the crows were silent. The snow was starting to cap the boulders along the water's edge, as I came within sight of the river. It fell from the mountain some distance upstream in a waterfall, then spread wide between steep crags, tumbling over rocks in a series of rapids before being forced into a narrow channel between two flat outcrops. Ancient, twisted pines clung to the sides of the crags and the whole landscape, whitened out by the snow, looked as if it were waiting for Sesshu to come and paint it.

I crouched down behind a boulder where a small pine clung precariously to the thin soil. It was more of a bush than a tree and it gave me a little shelter. The snow was covering the path but it was easy enough to see where it led and where to jump across the river. I looked at the crossing for a while, listening intently.

The pattern of the water over the rocks was not quite constant. Every now and then a lull appeared, bringing an uncanny silence as though I were not the only creature listening. It was easy to imagine spirits dwelling beneath the water, stopping and starting the flow, teasing and provoking humans, luring them to the edge.

I thought I could even hear them breathing. Then, just as I'd isolated the sound, the ripple and babble of the river started up again. It was infuriating. I knew I was wasting time, crouched in a bush being gradually covered by snow, listening to spirits, but slowly the conviction grew that there was someone breathing, not all that far from me.

Just beyond the narrow crossing the river dropped another ten feet or so into a series of deep pools. I caught a sudden movement and realized a heron, almost completely white, was fishing in one of them, oblivious to the snow. It was like a sign – the Otori emblem on the boundary of the Otori fief – perhaps a message from Shigeru that I had made the right choice at last.

The heron was on the same side of the river as I was, working its way along the pool towards me. I wondered what it found to eat in midwinter when frogs and toads were hidden away in the mud. It seemed tranquil and unafraid, certain that nothing threatened it in this lonely place. As I watched it, feeling just as safe, thinking that at any moment I would walk to the river and jump across, something startled it. It swung its long head towards the shore and instantly launched itself into flight. The clack of its wings sounded once above the water and then it disappeared silently downstream.

What had it seen? I strained my eyes, staring at the same spot. The river fell silent for a moment, and I heard breathing. I flared my nostrils, and on the north-easterly wind caught a faint, human scent. I could see no one, yet I knew someone was there, lying invisible in the snow.

He was so placed that if I went directly to the crossing he could easily cut me off. If he could maintain invisibility for as long as he had, he had to be from the Tribe, and so might be able to see me as soon as I approached the river. My only hope was to take him by surprise and jump further upstream, where the crossing was wider.

There was no point in waiting any longer. I took a deep, silent breath and ran out from the cover of the pine tree and down the slope. I kept to the path as long as I could, not sure of the footing beneath the snow. As I broke away from it towards the river I looked sideways and saw my enemy rise up out of the snow. He was dressed entirely in white. I felt a moment of relief that he had not been invisible, merely camouflaged – maybe he was not from the Tribe, maybe he was just a border guard – then the dark chasm loomed beneath me and I jumped.

The river roared and fell silent, and in the silence I heard something come spinning through the air behind me. As I landed I threw myself to the ground, scrabbling on the icy rock, almost losing my grip. The flying object whistled over my head. If I'd been standing it would have caught me in the back of the neck. Before me lay the star-shaped hole it made in the snow. Only the Tribe use such throwing knives, and they usually use several, one after the other.

I rolled, pulled myself to safety, still keeping low, and went invisible at once. I knew I could maintain invisibility until I reached the shelter of the forest, but I did not know if he could see me or not and I forgot about the tracks I would leave in the snow. Luckily for me he also slipped as he leaped across the river and while he looked bigger and heavier than me and could probably run faster, I had a head start on him.

Under the cover of the trees I split myself and sent the image sideways up the slope, while I ran on down the path, knowing that I could not outrun him for long, that my only hope was to ambush him somehow. Ahead the path curved round a large rocky outcrop; a tree branch hung above it. I ran around the corner, stepped back in my own footprints and sprang for the branch. I pulled myself up on it and took out my knife, wishing I had Jato. The other weapons I carried were those with which I'd been meant to kill Ichiro: garrotte and neck spike. But the Tribe are hard to kill with their own weapons, just as they are hard to outwit with their own tricks. My best hope was the knife. I stilled my breathing, went invisible, listened to him falter as he saw my second self, then heard him run again.

I knew I would only have one chance. I dropped on him from above. My weight unbalanced him and as he stumbled I found a gap in his neck protection and drove the knife into the main artery of the throat, pulling it crossways through the windpipe as Kenji had taught me. He made a grunt of amazement – one I've often heard from Tribe members who don't expect to have to play the part of the victim – and the stumble turned into a fall. I slipped from him. His hands went up to his throat where the breath was whistling noisily and the blood was spurting. Then he went down for good, on his face, the blood turning the snow red.

I went through his clothes and took the rest of the

knives and his short sword, which was a particularly fine one. He had a selection of poisons, which I also took, having none of my own at that time. I had no idea who he was. I removed his gloves and looked at his palms, but they did not bear the distinctive straight line of the Kikuta, and as far as I could see he had no tattoos.

I left his body for the crows and foxes, thinking it would be a welcome winter meal for them, and hurried on as quickly and as silently as possible, fearing he might be one of a band, watching the river, waiting for me. The blood was racing through me; I was warmed by my flight and the brief struggle, and I was deeply, primitively glad it was not me lying dead in the snow.

I was slightly alarmed that the Tribe had caught up with me so quickly and had known where I would be going. Had Akio's body been discovered, and messages sent already, by horse, from Hagi to Yamagata? Or was Akio still alive? I cursed myself for not taking the time to finish him off. Maybe the encounter should have frightened me more, should have made me realize what it would be like to be hunted by the Tribe for the rest of my life. I did realize it, but I was enraged that they should try to kill me like a dog in the forest and cheered by the fact that their first attempt had failed. The Tribe might have managed to kill my father, but Kenji himself had said no one would have been able to get near him if he had not taken a vow never to kill again. I knew I had all his talents, maybe even more. I would not let the Tribe near me. I would carry on Shigeru's work and break their power.

All these thoughts whirled through my mind as I slogged on through the snow. They gave me energy and sharpened my resolve to survive. After I'd finished with the Tribe, I turned my rage against the Otori lords, whose treachery seemed even greater to me. Warriors pretended that honour and loyalty were all important to them, yet their deceptions and betrayals were as deep and as self-serving as the Tribe's. Shigeru's uncles had sent him to his death and were now trying to dispossess me. They did not know what lay in store for them.

If they could've seen me, knee-deep in drifts of snow, ill-clad, ill-equipped, with no men, money or land, they would certainly have lost no sleep over any threat I posed them.

I could not stop and rest. I had no alternative but to keep walking until I reached Terayama or dropped in my tracks from exhaustion, but every now and then I stepped off the path and listened for any sound of pursuit. I heard nothing except the moan of the wind and the soft hiss of the flakes as they fell, until, late in the day when the light was beginning to fade, I thought I could hear snatches of sound from below.

It was the last thing I would have expected to hear out on the mountain as the forest filled with snow. It sounded like flute music, as lonely as the wind in the pines, as fleeting as the flakes. It sent shivers down my spine, not only from the usual effect music has on me but from a deeper fear. I believed I had come too close to the edge of the world and was hearing spirits. I thought of the mountain goblins who lure humans and keep them captive below the ground for thousands of years. I wished I could form the prayers my mother taught me but my lips were frozen and anyway I no longer believed in their power.

The music grew louder. I was approaching its source, but I could not stop walking, as though it had enchanted me and was drawing me towards itself. I rounded the corner and saw the path fork. Immediately I remembered what my guide had told me and, indeed, there was the little shrine, just visible, three oranges placed before it glowing bright beneath their caps of snow. Behind the shrine was a small hut with wooden walls and a thatched roof. My fears subsided at once and I almost laughed aloud. It was no goblin I'd heard but some monk or hermit who had retreated to the mountain to seek enlightenment.

Now I could smell smoke. The warmth drew me irresistibly. I could imagine the coals drying my soaked feet, bringing them back from the blocks of ice they'd turned into. I could almost feel the heat on my face. The door of the hut was open to let light in and smoke out. The flute player had neither heard nor seen me. He was lost in the sorrowful, unearthly music.

Even before I saw him, I knew who he was. I had heard the same music before, night after night as I grieved at Shigeru's grave. It was Makoto, the young monk who had comforted me. He sat cross-legged, his eyes closed. He was playing the long bamboo flute, but a smaller transverse flute lay on the cushion beside him. A brazier burned smokily near the entrance. At the back of the hut was a raised sleeping area. A wooden fighting pole leaned against the wall but no other weapons were visible. I stepped in – even with the brazier it was only slightly warmer than outside – and said quietly, 'Makoto?'

He did not open his eyes or stop playing.

I said his name again. The music faltered and he took the flute from his lips. He spoke in a whisper, wearily. 'Leave me alone. Stop tormenting me. I am sorry. I am sorry.' He still did not look up.

As he took up the flute again I knelt before him and

touched him on the shoulder. He opened his eyes, looked at me and, taking me completely by surprise, leaped to his feet, throwing the flute aside. He backed away from me, seized the pole and held it out threateningly. His eyes were filled with suffering, his face gaunt as though he had been fasting. 'Stay away from me,' he said, his voice low and hoarse.

I stood too. 'Makoto,' I said gently. 'It's no enemy. It's me. Otori Takeo.'

I took a step towards him and he immediately swung the pole at my shoulder. I saw it coming and deflected it a little and luckily in the small space he could not swing it hard or he would have broken my collarbone. As it was he knocked me to the ground. The shock must have reverberated up to his hands for he dropped the pole and looked at them in astonishment and then at me on the floor.

'Takeo?' he said. 'You're real? It's not your ghost?'

'Real enough to half knock out,' I said, getting up and flexing my arm. Once I was sure nothing was broken I reached inside my clothes for my knife. I felt safer with it in my hand.

'Forgive me,' he said. 'I would never hurt you. It's just that I have seen your apparition so often.' He looked as if he would reach out to touch me, then drew back. 'I can't believe it's you? What strange fate brings you here at this hour?'

'I am going to Terayama. Twice I've been offered refuge there. Now I need to accept that offer, until spring.'

'I can't believe it's you,' he repeated. 'You're soaked. You must be freezing.' He looked round the tiny hut. 'I have so little to offer you.' He turned towards the sleeping area, tripped over the pole and bent to retrieve it.

Placing it back against the wall, he took one of the thin hempen quilts from the bed. 'Take off your clothes. We'll dry them. Wrap yourself in this.'

'I must keep going,' I said. 'I'll just sit by the fire for a while.'

'You'll never get to Terayama tonight. It will be dark in an hour and it's still five hours walk. Spend the night here, we'll go together in the morning.'

'The blizzard will have closed the path by then,' I said. 'I want to be snowed in at the temple, not snowed out.'

'This is the first fall of the year,' he replied. 'It's heavy on the mountain, but from here downwards it is more sleet than snow.' He smiled and quoted the old poem, '"*On nights when, rain mixing in, the snow falls . . .*" unfortunately I am as poor as the poet and his family!'

It was one of the first pieces Ichiro had taught me to write and it brought him to my mind with piercing clarity. I was beginning to shiver violently. Now I was no longer moving I was indeed freezing. I began to peel off the wet clothes. Makoto took them and stretched them before the brazier, adding a little wood and blowing up the embers.

'This looks like blood,' he said. 'Are you hurt?'

'No, someone tried to kill me at the border.'

'This blood is his, then?'

I nodded, not sure how much to tell him, for his safety as well as my own.

'Is anyone following you?' he said.

'Either following me or lying in wait for me. That's how it will be for the rest of my life.'

'Will you tell me why?' He lit a taper from the fire and held it to the wick of an oil lamp. The lamp spluttered reluctantly into life. 'There's not much oil,' he apologized, and went to close the outer shutters.

Night stretched before us. 'Can I trust you?' I said.

The question made him laugh. 'I have no idea what you've been through since we last met or what brings you to this place now. And you know nothing about me. If you did you would not need to ask. I'll tell you everything later. In the meantime, yes, you can trust me. If you trust no one else, trust me.'

A note of deep emotion had crept into his voice. He turned away. 'I'll warm some soup,' he said. 'I'm sorry, I have neither wine nor tea.'

I remembered how he had comforted me in my terrible grief after Shigeru's death. He had reassured me while I was racked by remorse and had held me until grief had given way to desire, and both had been assuaged.

'I cannot stay with the Tribe,' I said. 'I've left them, and they will pursue me until they execute me.'

Makoto took a pot from the corner of the room and placed it carefully over the embers. He looked towards me again.

'They wanted me to find the records Shigeru kept of them,' I said. 'They sent me to Hagi. I was supposed to kill Ichiro, my teacher, and give the records to them. But of course they weren't there.'

Makoto smiled, but still said nothing.

'That is one of the reasons why I have to reach Terayama. Because that's where they are. You knew, didn't you?'

'We would have told you if you had not already chosen to go with the Tribe,' he said. 'But our duty to Lord Shigeru meant we could not take the risk. He entrusted the records to us for he knew our temple is one of the few in the Three Countries that has not been infiltrated by Tribe members.'

He poured the soup into a bowl and handed it to me. 'I only have one bowl. I didn't expect visitors. And the last person I expected was you!'

'Why are you here?' I asked him. 'Are you going to spend the winter here?' I didn't voice the thought, but I doubted he would survive. Maybe he didn't want to. I drank a mouthful of soup. It was hot and salty, but that was about all you could say for it. And this seemed to be the only food he had. What had happened to the energetic young man I'd first met at Terayama? What had driven him to this state of resignation, almost despair?

I pulled the quilt around me and edged a little closer to the fire. As always I listened. The wind had strengthened and was whistling through the thatch. Every now and then a gust made the lamp flicker, throwing grotesque shadows onto the opposite wall. The noise of whatever was falling outside was not the soft breath-like touch of snow, but harder and more sleety.

Now that the doors were closed the hut was warming up. My clothes were beginning to steam. I drained the bowl and passed it back to him. He filled it, took a sip, and placed it on the floor.

'The winter, the rest of my life, whichever turns out to be the longer,' he said, looked at me, looked down. 'It's hard for me to talk to you, Takeo, since so much of it concerns you, but the Enlightened One has seen fit to bring you here, so I have to try. Your presence changes everything. I told you, your apparition has been constantly with me, you visit me at night in dreams. I have been striving to overcome this obsession.'

He smiled self-mockingly. 'Since I was a child I have

tried to practise detachment from the world of the senses. My only desire was enlightenment. I craved holiness. I'm not saying I've never had attachments – you know what it's like when men live together without women. Terayama is no exception. But I never fell in love with anyone. I never became obsessed as I did with you.' Again the smile curved his lips. 'I won't go into why. It's not important and, anyway, I'm not sure I even know. However, after Lord Shigeru's death, you were out of your mind with grief. I was moved by your suffering. I wanted to comfort you.'

'You did comfort me,' I said, in a low voice.

'For me it went beyond comfort! I didn't realize it would be so powerful. I loved the way I felt and was grateful for experiencing what I'd never felt before, and I loathed it. It made all my spiritual strivings seem like a hollow sham. I went to our abbot and told him I thought I should leave the temple and return to the world. He suggested I go away for a while to think about my decision. I have a boyhood friend in the West, Mamoru, who had been pleading with me to visit him. You know, I play the flute a little. I was invited to join Mamoru and others in presenting a drama, *Atsumori*.'

He fell silent. The wind threw a flurry of sleet against the wall. The lamp guttered so violently it almost went out. I had no idea what Makoto was going to say next but my heart had picked up speed and I could feel the pulse quickening in my throat. Not with desire, though the memory of desire was there, more a fear of hearing what I did not want to hear.

Makoto said, 'My friend lives in the household of Lord Fujiwara.'

I shook my head. I'd never heard of him.

'He is a nobleman living in exile from the capital. His lands run alongside the Shirakawa.'

Just to hear her name spoken was like being hit in the belly. 'Did you see Lady Shirakawa?'

He nodded.

'I was told she was dying.' My heart was hammering so hard I thought it would leap from my throat.

'She was gravely ill but she recovered. Lord Fujiwara's physician saved her life.'

'She's alive?' The dim lamp seemed to brighten until the hut was full of light. 'Kaede is alive?'

He studied my face, his own filled with pain. 'Yes, and I am profoundly thankful, for if she had died it would have been me who dealt the fatal blow.'

I was frowning, trying to puzzle out his words. 'What happened?'

'The Fujiwara household knew her as Lady Otori. It was believed that Lord Shigeru married her secretly at Terayama, on the day he came to his brother's grave, the day we met. I had not expected to see her in Lord Fujiwara's house, I had not been told of her marriage. I was completely taken aback when she was introduced to me. I assumed you had married her, that you were there yourself. I blurted out as much. Not only did I reveal to myself the strength and nature of my obsession with you, which I'd fooled myself I was recovering from, I destroyed her pretence in an instant, in the presence of her father.'

'But why would she claim such a thing?'

'Why does any woman claim to be married when she is not? She nearly died because she miscarried a child.'

I could not speak.

Makoto said, 'Her father questioned me about the marriage. I knew it had not taken place at Terayama. I tried to avoid answering him directly but he already had his own suspicions and I had said enough to confirm them. I did not know it then, but his mind was very unstable and he had often spoken of taking his own life. He slit his belly in her presence and the shock must have caused the miscarriage.'

I said, 'The child was mine. She should have been my wife. She will be.'

But as I heard my own words my betrayal of Kaede seemed all the more enormous. Would she ever forgive me?

'So I assumed,' he said. 'But when? What were you thinking of? A woman of her rank and family?'

'We were thinking of death. It was the night Shigeru died and Inuyama fell. We did not want to die without . . .' I was unable to continue.

After a few moments Makoto went on, 'I could not live with myself. My passion had led me deeply back into the world of suffering I thought I could escape. I felt I had done irreparable harm to another sentient being, even though only a woman, but at the same time some jealous part of me wanted her to die, because I knew that you loved her and that she must have loved you. You see, I am hiding nothing from you. I must tell you the worst about myself.'

'I would be the last to condemn you. My own conduct has been far more cruel in its effects.'

'But you belong to this world, Takeo, you live in the midst of it. I wanted to be different. Even that was revealed to me as the most hideous pride. I returned to Terayama and sought our abbot's permission to retire to this small hut where I would devote my flute playing and any passion that remained in me to serving the

Enlightened One, though I no longer even hope for his enlightenment, for I am completely unworthy of it.'

'We all live in the midst of the world,' I said. 'Where else is there to live?' As I spoke I thought I heard Shigeru's voice, *Just as the river is always at the door, so is the world always outside. And it is in the world that we have to live.*

Makoto was staring at me, his face suddenly open, his eyes brighter. 'Is that the message I am to hear? Is that why you were sent to me?'

'I hardly know my plans for my own life,' I replied. 'How can I fathom yours? But this was one of the first things I learned from Shigeru. It is in the world that we have to live.'

'Then let's take it as a command from him,' Makoto said, and I could see the energy beginning to flow back into him. He seemed to have been resigned to death, but now he was coming back to life before my eyes. 'You intend now to carry out his wishes?'

'Ichiro told me I must take revenge on Shigeru's uncles and claim my inheritance, and so I mean to. But as to how I achieve it, I have no idea. And I must marry Lady Shirakawa. That was also Shigeru's desire.'

'Lord Fujiwara wishes to marry her,' Makoto said carefully.

I wanted to brush this aside. I could not believe Kaede would marry anyone else. Her last words to me had been *I will never love anyone but you.* And before that she had said, *I am only safe with you.* I knew the reputation she had acquired, that any man who touched her died. I had lain with her and lived. I had given her a child. And I had abandoned her, she had nearly died, she had lost our child – would she ever forgive me?

Makoto went on, 'Fujiwara prefers men to women. But he seems to have become obsessed with Lady Shirakawa. He proposes a marriage in name only, to give her his protection. Presumably he is also not indifferent to her inheritance. Shirakawa is pitifully run down but there is always Maruyama.'

When I made no comment he murmured, 'He is a collector. She will become one of his possessions. His collection never sees the light of day. It is shown only to a few privileged friends.'

'That cannot happen to her!'

'What other choices does she have? She is lucky not to be completely disgraced. To have survived the deaths of so many men connected with her is shameful enough. But there is also something unnatural about her. They say she had two of her father's retainers put to death when they would not serve her. She reads and writes like a man. And apparently she is raising an army to claim Maruyama for herself in the spring.'

'Maybe she will be her own protection,' I said.

'A woman?' Makoto replied, scornful. 'It's impossible.'

I felt my heart swell with admiration for Kaede. What an ally she would make! If we were to marry we would hold half the Seishuu territory. Maruyama would give me all the resources I needed to fight the Otori lords. Once they were dealt with, only the former Tohan heartland, which was now Arai's, would prevent our lands stretching from sea to sea as the prophecy promised.

Now that the snow had begun everything had to wait till spring. I was exhausted, yet I burned with impatience. I dreaded Kaede making an irrevocable decision before I saw her again.

'You said you would go with me to the temple?'

Makoto nodded. 'We'll leave as soon as it's light.'

'But you would have stayed here all winter if I had not stumbled in on you?'

'I have no illusions,' he replied. 'I would probably have died here. Maybe you have saved my life.'

We talked until late into the night; at least, he talked, as if the presence of another human being had unlocked weeks of silence. He told me something of his background; he was four years older than I was and had been born into a low-ranking warrior family who had served the Otori until Yaegahara, and after that defeat had been forced to transfer their allegiance to the Tohan. He had been brought up as a warrior, but was the fifth son in a large family which became steadily more impoverished. From an early age his love of learning and his interest in religion had been encouraged, and when the family began its decline he had been sent to Terayama. He was eleven years old. His brother, then thirteen, had also been intended as a novice, but after the first winter had run away and had not been heard of since. The oldest brother had been killed at Yaegahara, and their father had died not long after. His two sisters were married to Tohan warriors and he had heard nothing from them for years. His mother still lived on the family farm, such as it was, with his two surviving brothers and their families. They hardly considered themselves as part of the warrior class any more. He saw his mother once or twice a year.

We talked easily, like old friends, and I remembered how I had longed for such a companion when I was on the road with Akio. A little older and much better educated than I was, Makoto had a gravity and thoughtfulness that contrasted with my reckless nature. Yet, as I was to find out later, he was both strong and courageous, still a warrior as well as a monk and a scholar.

He went on to tell me about the horror and outrage that had swept through Yamagata and Terayama after Shigeru's death.

'We were armed and prepared for an uprising. Iida had been threatening the destruction of our temple for some time, aware that we were growing richer and more powerful every year. He knew what strong resentment there was about being ceded to the Tohan and he hoped to nip any rebellion in the bud. You saw how the people regarded Lord Shigeru. Their sense of loss and grief at his death was terrible. I'd never seen anything like it. The riots in the town that the Tohan had feared while he lived erupted with even more violence at the news of his death. There was a spontaneous uprising; former Otori warriors, townspeople armed with stakes, even farmers with scythes and stones, advanced on the castle. We were poised to join the attack when news came of Iida's death and Arai's victory at Inuyama. The Tohan forces fell back, and we began to chase them towards Kushimoto.

'We met you on the road, with Iida's head. By then everyone was beginning to know the story about your rescue of Lord Shigeru. And they began to guess the identity of the one they called the Angel of Yamagata.'

He sighed and blew on the last of the embers. The lamp had long since gone out. 'When we returned to Terayama, you did not seem like a hero at all. You were as lost and grief-stricken as anyone I'd ever seen and still faced with heart-rending decisions. You interested me when we first met but I thought you strange – talented maybe but weak; your sense of hearing seemed freakish, like an animal's. Usually I consider myself a good judge of men. I was surprised when you were given an invitation to come back again and puzzled by Shigeru's confidence in you. I realized you were not what you seemed, saw what courage you must have had and glimpsed the strength of your emotions. I fell in love with you. As I said, it had never happened to me before. And I said I wasn't going to tell you why, but now I have.'

After a moment he added, 'I won't speak of it again.'

'There's no harm,' I replied. 'The opposite, rather. I need friendship more than anything else in the world.'

'Apart from an army?'

'That has to wait till spring.'

'I'll do anything in my power to help you.'

'What about your calling, your search for enlightenment?'

'Your cause is my calling,' he said. 'Why else would the Enlightened One bring you here to remind me that we live in the midst of the world? A bond of great strength exists between us. And I see now that I don't have to struggle against it.'

The fire was almost out. I could no longer see Makoto's face. Beneath the thin quilt I was shivering. I wondered if I could sleep, would ever sleep again, would ever stop listening for the assassin's breath. In a world that seemed almost entirely hostile Makoto's devotion touched me deeply. I could think of nothing to say. I took his hand and clasped it briefly in thanks.

'Will you keep watch while I sleep for a couple of hours?'

'Of course I will.'

'Wake me, and then you can sleep before we go.'

He nodded. I wrapped myself in the second quilt and

lay down. The faintest glow came from the fire. I could hear its dying susurration. Outside the wind had dropped a little. The eaves dripped; some small creature was rustling in the thatch. An owl hooted and the mouse went still. I drifted into an uneasy sleep and dreamed of children drowning. I plunged again and again into icy black water but was unable to save them.

The cold woke me. Dawn was just beginning to lighten the hut. Makoto sat in the position of meditation. His breathing was so slow I could hardly hear it, yet I knew he was completely alert. I watched him for a few moments. When he opened his eyes I looked away.

'You should have woken me.'

'I feel rested. I need very little sleep.' He said curiously, 'Why don't you ever look at me?'

'I might send you to sleep. It's one of the Tribe skills I inherited. I should be able to control it but I've put people to sleep without meaning to. So I don't look them in the eye.'

'You mean there's more than just the hearing? What else?'

'I can make myself invisible – for long enough to confuse an opponent or slip past a guard. And I can seem to remain in a place after I've left it or to be in two places at once. We call it using the second self.' I watched him without appearing to as I said this, for I was interested in his reaction.

He could not help recoiling slightly. 'Sounds more like a demon than an angel,' he muttered. 'Can all these people, the Tribe, do this?'

'Different people have different skills. I seem to have inherited many more than my share.'

'I knew nothing about the Tribe, did not even know

216

they existed, until our abbot spoke of you and your connection with them, after your visit in the summer.'

'Many think the skills are sorcery,' I said.

'Are they?'

'I don't know, because I don't know how I do them. The skills came to me. I did not seek them. But training enhances them.'

'I suppose like any skills they can be used for good or evil,' he said quietly.

'Well, the Tribe want only to use them for their own purposes,' I said. 'Which is why they will not let me live. If you come with me, you will be in the same danger. Are you prepared for that?'

He nodded. 'Yes, I'm prepared. Doesn't it alarm you though? It would make most men weak with fear.'

I did not know how to answer. I have often been described as fearless, but that seems too fine a word for a state that is more like invisibility, a gift I was born with. And fearlessness only comes on me from time to time and then takes energy to maintain. I know fear as well as any man. I didn't want to think about it then. I stood and took up my clothes. They were not really dry, and they felt clammy against my skin as I put them on. I went outside to piss. The air was raw and damp, but the snow had stopped and what lay on the ground was slushy. There were no footprints around the hut and shrine save my own, already half-covered. The track disappeared downhill. It was passable. The mountain and the forest were silent apart from the wind. Far in the distance I could hear crows, and a little closer some smaller bird piped in a mournful way. I could hear no sound of human existence, no axe on trunk, no temple bell, no village dog. The shrine spring made a low, welling sound. I washed my face and hands in the icy black water and drank deeply.

That was all the breakfast we had. Makoto packed his few possessions, tucked the flutes into his belt, and picked up the fighting pole. It was his only weapon. I gave him the short sword I'd taken from my assailant the day before, and he placed it next to the flutes in his belt.

As we set out a few flakes of snow were drifting down and they continued to fall all morning. The path, however, was not too thickly covered and Makoto of course knew the way well. Every now and then I slipped on an icy patch or stepped in a hole up to my knees. Soon my clothes were as wet as they'd been the night before. The path was narrow; we went in single file at a fair pace, hardly speaking. Makoto seemed to have no words left, and I was too busy listening – for the breath, the broken stick, the thrum of bowstring, the whistle of throwing knife. I felt like a wild animal, always in danger, always hunted.

The light paled to pearl grey, stayed like that for three hours or so, then began to darken. The flakes fell more heavily, beginning to swirl and settle. Around noon we stopped to drink from a small stream, but as soon as we stopped walking the cold attacked us, so we did not linger.

'This is the north river, which flows past the temple,' Makoto said. 'We follow its course all the way. It's less than two hours now.'

It seemed so much easier than my journey since I'd left Hagi. I almost began to relax. Terayama was only two hours away. I had a companion. We were going to get to the temple, and I would be safe for the winter. But the babbling of the river drowned out all other sound and so I had no warning of the men who were waiting for us.

There were two of them and they came at us out of the forest, like wolves. But they were anticipating one man – me – and Makoto's presence surprised them. They saw what they thought was a harmless monk and they went for him first, expecting him to run away. He dropped the first man with a blow to the head that must have cracked the skull. The second man had a long sword, which surprised me as the Tribe do not usually carry them. I went invisible as he swung at me, came up under his reach and slashed at his sword hand, trying to disable him. The knife glanced off his glove; I stabbed again and let my image appear at his feet. The second stab went home and blood began to drip from his right wrist as he swung again. My second self faded and I, still invisible, leaped on him, trying to slash him in the throat, wishing I had Jato and could fight him properly. He could not see me, but he grabbed at my arms and cried out in horror. I felt myself becoming visible and he realized it at the same time. He stared into my face as if he saw a ghost, his eyes widening in terror and then beginning to waver, as Makoto struck him from behind, cracking the pole against his neck. He went down like an ox, taking me down with him.

I scrambled out from beneath him, and pulled Makoto into the shelter of the rocks, in case there were more of them on the hillside. What I feared most were bowmen who could pick us off from afar. But the forest grew too thickly here to be able to use a bow from any distance. There was no sign of anyone else.

Makoto was breathing hard, his eyes bright. 'I realize now what you meant about your skills.'

'You're pretty skilful yourself! Thanks.'

'Who are they?'

I went to the two bodies. The first man was Kikuta – I could tell from his hands – but the second wore the Otori crest under his armour.

'This one is a warrior,' I said, gazing at the heron. 'That explains the sword. The other is from the Tribe – Kikuta.'

I did not know the man but we had to be relatives, linked by the lines on our palms.

The Otori warrior made me nervous. Had he come from Hagi? What was he doing with one of the Tribe's assassins? It seemed to be common knowledge that I was heading for Terayama. My thoughts flew to Ichiro. I prayed they had not extracted the information from him. Or was it Jo-An or one of the impoverished men I'd feared would betray me? Maybe these men had already been to the temple and there would be more of them waiting for us there.

'You completely disappeared,' Makoto said. 'I could only see your prints in the snow. It's extraordinary.' He grinned at me, his face transformed. It was hard to believe he was the same person as the despairing flute player of the previous night. 'It's been a while since I've had a decent fight. It's amazing how a brush with death makes life so beautiful.'

The snow seemed whiter and the cold more piercing. I was terribly hungry, yearning for the comforts of the senses: a scalding bath, food, wine, a lover's body naked against mine.

We went on with renewed energy. We needed it; in the last hour or so the wind increased and the snow began to fall heavily again. I had reason to become even more grateful to Makoto for by the end we were walking blind, yet he knew the path and never faltered. Since I had last been to the temple a wooden wall had been erected around the main buildings and at the gate guards challenged us. Makoto replied and they welcomed him excitedly. They had been anxious about him and were relieved that he had decided to return.

After they had barred the gate again and we were inside the guardroom they looked searchingly at me, not sure if they knew me or not. Makoto said, 'Lord Otori Takeo is seeking refuge here for the winter. Will you inform our abbot that he is here?'

One of them hurried away across the courtyard, his figure, bowed against the wind, turning white before he reached the cloister. The great roofs of the main halls were already capped with snow, the bare branches of the cherry and plum trees heavy with the blossom of winter.

The guards beckoned us to sit by the fire. Like Makoto they were young monks, their weapons bows, spears and poles. They poured us tea. Nothing had ever tasted quite as good to me. The tea and our clothes steamed together, creating a comforting warmth. I tried to fight it; I did not want to relax yet.

'Has anyone come here looking for me?'

'Strangers were noticed on the mountain early this morning. They skirted the temple and went on up into the forest. We had no idea they were looking for you. We were a little concerned for Makoto – we thought they might be bandits – but the weather was too bad to send anyone out. Lord Otori has arrived at a good time. The way you came down is already impassable. The temple will be closed now till spring.'

'It is an honour for us that you have returned,' one of them said shyly, and the glances they exchanged told me they had a fair idea of the significance of my appearance.

After ten minutes or so the monk came hurrying back. 'Our abbot welcomes Lord Otori,' he said, 'and asks that you will bathe and eat. He would like to speak with you when the evening prayers are finished.'

Makoto finished his tea, bowed formally to me and said he must get ready for evening prayers, as though he had spent the whole day in the temple with the other monks, not slogging through a blizzard and killing two men. His manner was cool and formal. I knew beneath it lay the heart of a true friend but here he was one of the monks, while I had to relearn how to be a lord. The wind howled around the gables, the snow drifted relentlessly down. I had come in safety to Terayama. The winter was mine to reshape my life.

I was taken to one of the temple guest rooms by the young man who'd brought the abbot's message. In spring and summer these rooms would have been full of visitors and pilgrims but now they were deserted. Even though the outer shutters were closed against the storm, it was bitterly cold. The wind moaned through the chinks in the wall, and through some of the larger ones snow drifted. The same monk showed me the way to the small bathhouse built above the hot spring. I took off my wet, filthy clothes and scrubbed myself all over. Then I eased my body into the hot water. It was even better than I'd imagined it would be. I thought of the men who had tried to kill me in the last two days and was fiercely glad I was alive. The water steamed and bubbled around me. I felt a rush of gratitude for it, that it should well up out of the mountain, bathe my aching body and unthaw my frozen limbs. I thought about mountains which were just as likely to spit out ash and fire or shake their sides and throw buildings around like kindling, and make men feel as helpless as the insects that crawl from burning logs. This mountain could have gripped me and frozen me to death but instead it had given me this scalding water.

My arms were bruised from the warrior's grip and there was a long, shallow cut on my neck where his sword must have grazed me. My right wrist, which had bothered me on and off ever since Akio had bent it backwards in Inuyama, tearing the tendons, now felt stronger. My body seemed more spare than ever but otherwise I was in good shape after the journey. And now I was clean too.

I heard footsteps in the room beyond and the monk called out that he had brought dry clothes and some food. I emerged from the water, my skin bright red from the heat, rubbed myself dry on the rags left there for that purpose and ran back along the boardwalk through the snow to the room.

It was empty; the clothes lay on the floor: clean loincloth, quilted undergarments, a silken outer robe, also quilted, and a sash. The robe was a dark plum colour, woven with a deeper pattern of purple, the Otori crest in silver on the back. I put it on slowly, relishing the touch of the silk. It had been a long time since I had worn anything of this quality. I wondered why it was at the temple and who had left it here. Had it been Shigeru's? I felt his presence envelop me. The first thing I would do in the morning would be to visit his grave. He would tell me how to achieve revenge.

The smell of the food made me realize how famished I was. The meal was more substantial than anything I'd had for days and it took me just two minutes to devour it. Then, not wanting to lose the heat from the bath, or to fall asleep, I went through some exercises, ending with meditation.

Beyond the wind and the snow I could hear the monks chanting from the main hall of the temple. The snowy night, the deserted room with its memories and ghosts, the serene words of the ancient sutras all combined to produce an exquisite bitter-sweet sensation. My spine chilled. I wished I could express it, wished I had paid more attention when Ichiro had tried to teach me poetry. I longed to hold the brush in my hand: if I could not express my feelings in words, perhaps I could paint them.

Come back to us, the old priest had said, *when all this is over* . . . Part of me wished I could do that and spend the rest of my days in this tranquil place. But I remembered how even here I had overheard plans of war; the monks were armed and the temple fortified now. It was far from over – indeed it was only just begun.

The chanting came to an end and I heard the soft pad of feet as the monks filed away to eat, then sleep for a few hours until the bell roused them at midnight. Footsteps approached the room from the cloister and the same monk came to the door and slid it open. He bowed to me and said, 'Lord Otori, our abbot wishes to see you now.'

I stood and followed him along the cloister. 'What's your name?'

'Norio, sir,' he replied and added in a whisper, 'I was born in Hagi.'

He did not say more, the rule of the temple being that no one spoke unnecessarily. We walked around the central courtyard, already filled with snow, past the eating hall where the monks knelt in silent rows, each with a bowl of food in front of him, past the main hall which smelled of incense and candle wax, where the golden figure sat gleaming in the dimness, to the third side of the square. Here lay a series of small rooms, used as offices and studies. From the furthest I could hear the click of prayer beads, the whisper of a sutra. We stopped outside the first room and Norio called in a low voice, 'Lord Abbot, your visitor is here.'

I was ashamed when I saw him, for it was the old priest himself, in the same worn clothes I had seen him in when I had last been at Terayama. I had thought him one of the old men of the temple, not its head. I had been so wrapped up in my own concerns I had not even known who he was. I dropped to my knees and touched my fore-head to the matting. As informal as ever, he came towards me, told me to sit up and embraced me. Then he sat back and studied me, his face illuminated by his smile. I smiled back, sensing his genuine pleasure and responding to it.

'Lord Otori,' he said. 'I am very glad you have returned to us safely. You have been much on my mind. You have been through dark times.'

'They are not over. But I seek your hospitality for the winter. I seem to be hunted by everyone and I need a place of safety while I prepare myself.'

'Makoto has told me a little of your situation. You are always welcome here.'

'I must tell you my purpose right away. I mean to claim my inheritance from the Otori and punish those responsible for Lord Shigeru's death. It may place the temple in some danger.'

'We are prepared for that,' he replied serenely.

'You are doing me a great kindness that I don't deserve.'

'I think you will find that those of us who have long-standing connections with the Otori consider ourselves in your debt,' he replied. 'And of course we have faith in your future.'

More than I have, I thought silently. I felt the colour come to my face. It was unthinkable that he should praise me, after all the mistakes I had made. I felt like an impostor, dressed in the Otori robe, with my hair cropped, no money, no possessions, no men, no sword.

'All endeavours start with a single action,' he said, as though he could read my mind. 'Your first action was to come here.'

'My teacher, Ichiro, sent me. He will meet me here in the spring. He advised me to seek Lord Arai's protection. I should have done that from the start.'

The abbot's eyes crinkled as he smiled. 'No, the Tribe would not have let you live. You were far more vulnerable then. You did not know your enemy. Now you have some inkling of their power.'

'How much do you know about them?'

'Shigeru confided in me and sought my advice often. On his last visit we spoke at length about you.'

'I didn't hear that.'

'No, he was careful to speak by the waterfall so you would not hear. Later we moved into this room.'

'Where you spoke of war.'

'He needed my assurance that the temple and the town would rise once Iida was dead. He was still in two minds about the assassination attempt, fearing he would simply be sending you to certain death. As it turned out it was his own death that sparked the uprising, and we could not have prevented it even if we had wanted to. However, Arai was in alliance with Shigeru, not with the Otori clan. If he can take this territory for himself he will. They will be at war by the summer.'

He was silent for a moment, then went on, 'The Otori intend to claim Shigeru's land and declare your adoption illegal. Not content with conspiring in his death they insult his memory. That's why I'm glad you intend to take up your inheritance.'

'Will the Otori ever accept me, though?' I held out my hands, palms upwards. 'I am marked as Kikuta.'

'We'll talk about that later. You'll be surprised how many are awaiting your return. You'll see in the spring. Your men will find you.'

'An Otori warrior already tried to kill me,' I said, unconvinced.

'Makoto told me. The clan will be split but Shigeru knew this and accepted it. The rift was not of his making – the seeds were sown when he was usurped after his father's death.'

'I hold Shigeru's uncles responsible for his death,' I said, 'But the more I learn the more it surprises me that they let him live so long.'

'Fate decrees the length of all our lives,' he replied. 'The Otori lords fear their own people. Their farmers are volatile by nature and tradition. They have never been completely cowed, like the peasants under the Tohan. Shigeru knew them and respected them and in turn won their respect and affection. That protected him against his uncles. Their loyalty will be transferred to you.'

'Maybe,' I said, 'but there is a more serious problem. I am now sentenced to death by the Tribe.'

His face was calm, ivory coloured in the lamplight. 'Which I imagine is another reason you are here.'

I thought he would go on but he fell silent. He was watching me with an expectant look on his face.

'Lord Shigeru kept records,' I said, speaking carefully

into the hushed room. 'Records of the Tribe and their activities. I am hoping you will make them available to me.'

'They have been kept here for you,' he replied. 'I will send for them now. And of course there is something else I have been keeping for you.'

'Jato,' I said.

He nodded. 'You are going to need it.'

He called to Norio and asked him to go to the storehouse and fetch the chest and the sword.

'Shigeru did not want to influence any decision you might make,' he said, as I listened to Norio's footsteps echoing away around the cloister. 'He was aware that your inheritance would cause divisions in your loyalty. He was quite prepared for you to choose your Kikuta side. In that case no one would ever have access to the records except myself. But since you have chosen your Otori side, the records are yours.'

'I have bought myself a few months of life,' I said, with a trace of self-contempt. 'There's no nobility in my choice unless it is that I am finally doing what Lord Shigeru wanted. It's hardly even a choice since my life with the Tribe was approaching an end. As for my Otori side, it is only by adoption and will be questioned by everyone.'

Again the smile lit his face, his eyes bright with understanding and wisdom. 'Shigeru's will is as good a reason as any.'

I felt he had some other knowledge that he would share with me later, but even as that thought came I heard footsteps returning. I could not help tensing before I recognized them as Norio's, slightly heavier this time – he was carrying the chest and the sword. He slid open the door and stepped inside, dropping to his knees. He placed the chest and the sword on the matting. I did not turn my head but I heard the soft sound they made. My pulse quickened, with a mixture of joy and fear, at the prospect of holding Jato again.

Norio closed the door behind him and, kneeling again, placed the precious objects in front of the abbot where I too could see them. They were both wrapped in pieces of old cloth, their power disguised. The abbot took Jato from its covering and held it out towards me in both hands. I took it in the same fashion, raised it above my head, and bowed to him, feeling the cool familiar weight of the scabbard. I longed to draw the sword and wake its steel song, but I would not do so in the presence of the abbot. I placed it reverently on the floor next to me while he unwrapped the chest.

A smell of rue rose from it. I recognized it at once. It was indeed the one I had carried under Kenji's eyes up the mountain path, thinking it some gift for the temple. Had Kenji no idea then of what it contained?

The old man opened the lid – it was not locked – and the smell of rue intensified. He lifted one of the scrolls and held it out to me.

'You were to read this one first. That was Shigeru's instruction to me.' As I took it, he said with sudden profound emotion, 'I did not think this moment would come.'

I looked into his eyes. Deep-set in his old face, they were as bright and as lively as a twenty-year-old's. He held my gaze and I knew he would never succumb to the Kikuta sleep. In the distance one of the smaller bells rang three times. In my mind's eye I could see the monks at prayer, in meditation. I felt the spiritual power of this holy place, concentrated and reflected in the person of the old man before me now. Again I felt a rush of gratitude, to him, to the belief that sustained him, to Heaven and to the different gods who, despite my own disbelief, seemed to have taken my life into their charge and care.

'Read it,' he prompted me. 'The rest you can study later, but read this one now.'

I unrolled the scroll, frowning at the script. I recognized Shigeru's hand and I knew the characters, my own name among them, but the words made no sense to me. My eyes darted up and down the columns; I unrolled a little more and found myself in a sea of names. It seemed to be a genealogy like the ones Gosaburo had explained to me in Matsue. Once I'd grasped that, I began to work it out. I went back to the introductory writing and read it carefully again. Then I read it a third time. I looked up at the abbot.

'Is it true?'

He chuckled softly. 'It seems it is. You do not see your own face, so you don't see the proof there. Your hands may be Kikuta, but your features are all Otori. Your father's mother worked as a spy for the Tribe. She was employed by the Tohan and sent to Hagi when Shigeru's father, Shigemori, was hardly more than a boy. A liaison occurred, apparently not one sanctioned by the Tribe. Your father was the result. Your grandmother must have been a woman of some ingenuity: she told no one; she was married to one of her cousins and the child was brought up as Kikuta.'

'Shigeru and my father were brothers? He was my uncle?'

'It would be hard for anyone to deny it, given the way you look. When Shigeru first set eyes on you, he was

230

struck by your resemblance to his younger brother, Takeshi. Of course, the two brothers were very alike. Now, if your hair were longer, you would be the image of Shigeru as a young man.'

'How did he discover this?'

'Some of it from his own family records. His father had always suspected that the woman had conceived a child and confided this to him before he died. The rest Shigeru worked out for himself. He traced your father to Mino and realized a son had been born after his death. Your father must have suffered some of the same conflict as you. Despite being raised as Kikuta and despite his skills, high even by the standards of the Tribe, he still tried to escape from them: in itself this suggests that his blood was mixed and that he lacked the fanaticism of the true Tribe. Shigeru had been compiling his records of the Tribe since he first became acquainted with Muto. Kenji. They met at Yaegahara; Kenji was caught up in the fighting and witnessed Shigemori's death.' He glanced down at Jato. 'He retrieved this sword and gave it to Shigeru. They may have told you this story.'

'Kenji once alluded to it,' I said.

'Kenji helped Shigeru escape from Iida's soldiers. They were both young men then; there was a liking between them. Apart from the friendship they were useful to each other. Over the years they exchanged information about many things, sometimes, it must be said, unwittingly. I don't believe even Kenji realized how secretive, even devious, Lord Shigeru could be.'

I was silent. The revelation had astonished me, yet on reflection it made perfect sense. It had been my Otori blood that had been so eager to learn the lessons of revenge when my family were massacred at Mino, that same blood that had formed the bond with Shigeru. I grieved for him anew, wished I had known earlier, yet rejoiced that he and I shared the same lineage, that I truly belonged to the Otori.

'This confirms that I have made the right choice,' I said finally, in a voice choked by emotion. 'But if I am to be one of the Otori, a warrior, I have so much to learn.' I gestured at the scrolls in the chest. 'Even my reading is poor!'

'You have the whole winter ahead of you,' the abbot replied. 'Makoto will help you with reading and writing. In the spring you should go to Arai to learn the practice of war. In the meantime you must study its theory, and keep up your training with the sword.'

He paused and smiled again. I could tell he had another of his surprises in store for me.

'I shall teach you,' he said. 'Before I was called to the service of the Enlightened One I was considered something of an expert in these matters. My name in the world was Matsuda Shingen.'

Even I had heard this name. Matsuda was one of the most illustrious Otori warriors of the previous generation, a hero to the young men of Hagi. The abbot chuckled as he read the astonishment on my face.

'I think we will enjoy the winter. Plenty of exercise to keep us warm. Take your possessions, Lord Otori. We will begin in the morning. When you are not studying you will join the monks in meditation. Makoto will rouse you at the hour of the Tiger.'

I bowed before him, overwhelmed by gratitude. He waved me away.

'We are just repaying our debt to you.'

'No,' I said. 'I am for ever in your debt. I will do anything you tell me. I am completely at your service.'

I was at the door when he called out, 'Maybe there is one thing.'

Turning, I fell to my knees. 'Anything!'

'Grow your hair!' he said, laughing.

I could still hear him chuckling as I followed Norio back to the guest room. He was carrying the chest for me but I held Jato. The wind had dropped a little, the snow had grown wetter and heavier. It dulled sound, blanketing the mountain, shutting off the temple from the world.

In the room the bedding had already been laid out. I thanked Norio and bade him goodnight. Two lamps lit the room. I drew Jato from its scabbard and gazed on the blade, thinking of the fire that had forged it into this combination of delicacy, strength and lethal sharpness. The folds in the steel gave it a beautiful wave-like pattern. It was Shigeru's gift to me, along with my name and my life. I held the sword in both hands and went through the ancient movements he had taught me in Hagi.

Jato sang to me of blood and war.

Eight

Kaede came back from afar, out of a red landscape, lapped by fire and blood. She had seen terrifying images during her fever; now she opened her eyes on the familiar light and shade of her parents' house. Often, when she had been a hostage with the Noguchi, she had had this dream of waking at home, only to wake properly a few moments later to the reality of life in the castle. She lay still now, eyes closed, waiting for the second waking, aware of something pricking her in the lower part of her belly, and wondering why she should dream of the smell of moxa.

'She has returned to us!' The man's voice, a stranger's, startled her. She felt a hand on her brow and knew it was Shizuka's, remembering feeling it there many times before, when its firm cool shape was the only thing that came between her mind and the terrors that assailed her. It seemed to be all she could remember. Something had happened to her, but her mind shied away from thinking about it. The movement reminded her of falling. She must have fallen from Takeo's horse, Raku, the little grey horse he had given her, yes, she had fallen, and she had lost his child.

Her eyes filled with tears. She knew she was not thinking clearly, but she knew the child was gone. She felt Shizuka's hand move and then it returned holding a cloth, slightly warmed, to wipe her face.

'Lady!' Shizuka said. 'Lady Kaede.'

Kaede tried to move her own hand, but it seemed to be immobilized and something pricked her there too.

'Don't try to move,' Shizuka said. 'Lord Fujiwara's physician, Dr Ishida, has been treating you. You are going to get well now. Don't cry, lady!'

'It's normal,' she heard the physician say. 'Those who come close to death always weep when they are brought back, whether from joy or sorrow I've never been able to tell.'

Kaede herself did not know. The tears flowed and when they finally stopped she fell asleep.

For several days she slept, woke, ate a little and slept again. Then she slept less, but lay with her eyes closed, listening to the household around her. She heard Hana's voice regaining its confidence, Ai's gentle tone, Shizuka singing and scolding Hana, who had taken to following her around like a shadow, trying to please her. It was a house of women – the men stayed away – women who were aware they had come close to the brink of disaster, were still not out of danger, but so far had survived. Autumn slowly turned to winter.

The only man was the physician, who stayed in the guest pavilion and visited her every day. He was small and deft, with long-fingered hands and a quiet voice. Kaede came to trust him, sensing that he did not judge her. He did not think her good or bad, indeed he did not think in such terms at all. He only wanted to see her recover.

He used techniques he had learned on the mainland: needles of gold and silver, a paste of mugwort leaves burned on the skin, and teas brewed from willow bark. He was the first person she had ever met who had travelled there. Sometimes she lay and listened to his voice telling Hana stories of the animals he had seen, huge whales in the sea and bears and tigers on land.

When she was able to get up and walk outside, it was Dr Ishida who suggested that a ceremony should be held for the lost child. Kaede was carried to the temple in a palanquin, and she knelt for a long time before the shrine to Jizo, the one who looks after the water children who die before they are born. She grieved for the child whose moment of life had been so brief, conceived and extinguished in the midst of violence. Yet it had been a child begun in love.

I will never forget you, she promised in her heart, and prayed it would have a safer passage next time. She felt its spirit was now safe until it began the journey of life again. She made the same prayer for Shigeru's child, realizing she was the only person apart from Shizuka who knew of its brief moment of existence. The tears flowed again, but when she returned home she did indeed feel that a weight had been lifted from her.

'Now you must take up life again,' Dr Ishida told her. 'You are young, you will marry and have other children.'

'I think I am destined not to marry,' Kaede replied.

He smiled, assuming she was joking. Of course, she thought, it was a joke. Women in her position, of her rank, always married, or rather *were* married to whoever seemed to offer the most advantageous alliance. But such marriages were arranged by fathers, or clan leaders, or other overlords, and she seemed suddenly to be free of all these. Her father was dead, as were most of his senior retainers. The Seishuu clan, to which both the Maruyama and Shirakawa families belonged, was fully occupied with the turmoil that had followed the downfall of the Tohan and the sudden unexpected rise of Arai Daiichi. Who was there to tell her what to do? Was it Arai now? Should she be making a formal alliance with him, recognizing him as her overlord, and what were the advantages or disadvantages of such a move?

'You have grown very serious,' he said. 'May I ask what is occupying your mind? You must try not to worry.'

'I have to decide what to do,' she said.

'I suggest doing nothing until you are stronger. Winter is nearly upon us. You must rest, eat well, and be very careful not to take a chill.'

And I must consolidate my lands, contact Sugita Hiroki at Maruyama and tell him I mean to take up my inheritance, and find money and food for my men, she thought, but did not speak this aloud to Ishida.

As she grew stronger she began to restore the house, before the snows began. Everything was washed, new matting laid, screens repaired, tiles and shingles replaced. The garden was tended again. She had little money to pay for anything, but she found men to work for her on the promise of payment in the spring, and every day she learned more of how a look or a tone of voice won her their devoted service.

She moved into her father's rooms where at last she had unrestricted access to his books. She read and practised writing for hours at a time, until Shizuka, fearing for her health, brought Hana to distract her. Then Kaede played with her sister, teaching her to read and use the brush like a man. Under Shizuka's strict care Hana had lost some of her wildness. She was as hungry for learning as Kaede.

'We should both have been born boys,' Kaede sighed.

'Father would have been proud of us then,' Hana said.

Her tongue was pressed against her upper teeth as she concentrated on the characters.

Kaede did not reply. She never spoke of her father and tried not to think about him. Indeed she could no longer clearly distinguish between what had actually happened when he died and the feverish imaginings of her illness. She did not question Shizuka and Kondo, afraid of their reply. She had been to the temple, performed the rites of mourning, and ordered a fine stone to be carved for his grave, but she still feared his ghost, which had hovered at the edge of the redness of her fever. Though she clung to the thought, *I have done nothing wrong*, she could not remember him without a twinge of shame which she masked with anger.

He will be more helpful to me dead than alive, she decided, and let it be known that she was reverting to the name of Shirakawa, since it had been her father's will that she should be his heir and should remain in the family home. When Shoji returned to the house after the period of mourning and began to go through the records and accounts with her she thought she detected some disapproval in his attitude, but the accounts were in such a terrible state she used her anger to cow him. It was hard to believe affairs had been allowed to deteriorate so badly. It seemed impossible to secure enough food for the men she had already and their families, let alone any others she might hope to employ. It was her main source of anxiety.

With Kondo she went though the armour and weapons and gave instructions for repairs to be done and replacements ordered. She came to rely more and more on his experience and judgment. He suggested she should re-establish the domain's borders, to prevent encroachment

238

and to maintain the warriors' fighting skills. She agreed, knowing instinctively she had to keep the men occupied and interested. For the first time she found herself grateful for the years in the castle, for she realized how much she had learned about warriors and weapons. From then on Kondo often rode out with five or six men, making use of these expeditions to bring back information too.

She told Kondo and Shizuka to let pieces of information fall among the men: an alliance with Arai, the campaign for Maruyama in the spring, the possibility of advancement and wealth.

She saw nothing of Lord Fujiwara, though he sent gifts, quail, dried persimmons, wine and warm quilted clothes. Ishida returned to the nobleman's residence and she knew the doctor would inform him of her progress, and certainly would not dare keep any secrets from him. She did not want to meet Fujiwara. It was shameful to have deceived him and she regretted the loss of his regard for her but she was also relieved not to see him face to face. His intense interest in her unnerved and repelled her, as much as his white skin and cormorant eyes.

'He is a useful ally,' Shizuka told her. They were in the garden, overseeing the replacement of the crushed stone lantern. It was a cool clear day of rare sunshine.

Kaede was watching a pair of ibises in the rice fields beyond the gate. Their pale pink winter plumage glowed against the bare earth.

'He's been very kind to me,' she said. 'I know I owe my life to him, through Dr Ishida. But it would not trouble me if I never saw him again.'

The ibises followed one another through the pools that had collected in the corner of the fields, their curved bills stirring up the muddy water.

'Anyway,' she added, 'I am flawed for him now. He will despise me more than ever.'

Shizuka had said nothing of the nobleman's desire to marry Kaede, and she did not mention it now.

'You must make some decisions,' she said quietly. 'Otherwise we will all starve before spring.'

'I am reluctant to approach anyone,' Kaede said. 'I must not seem like a supplicant, desperate and needy. I know I must go to Arai eventually, but I think it can wait till winter is over.'

'I believe the birds will begin to gather before then,' Shizuka said. 'Arai will send someone to you, I expect.'

'And what about you, Shizuka?' Kaede said. The pillar was in position and the new lantern in place. Tonight she would place a lamp in it; it would look beautiful in the frosty garden under the clear sky. 'What will you do? I don't suppose you will stay with me for ever, will you? You must have other concerns. What about your sons? You must long to see them. And what are your commands from the Tribe?'

'Nothing more at the moment than to continue looking after your interests,' Shizuka replied.

'Would they have taken the child as they took Takeo?' Kaede said, and then immediately added, 'oh, don't answer me, there is no point now.' She felt the tears threaten and pressed her lips firmly together. She was silent for a few moments and then went on, 'I suppose you keep them informed of my actions and decisions too?'

'I send messages from time to time to my uncle. When I thought you were close to death for instance. And I would tell him of any new developments: if you were to decide to marry again, that sort of thing.'

'I won't be doing that.' As the afternoon light began

to fade the pink plumage of the ibises glowed more deeply. It was very still. Now that the workmen had finished, the garden seemed more silent than ever. And in the silence she heard again the promise of the White Goddess. *Be patient.*

I will marry no one but him, she vowed again. *I will be patient.*

It was the last day of sunshine. The weather became damp and raw. A few days later Kondo returned from one of his patrols in a rainstorm. Dismounting rapidly he called to the women in the house, 'There are strangers on the road, Lord Arai's men, five or six, and horses.'

Kaede told him to assemble as many men as possible and give the impression there were many more at call.

'Tell the women to prepare food,' she said to Shizuka, 'Everything we have, make it lavish. We must seem to be prospering. Help me change my clothes, and bring my sisters. Then you must stay out of sight.'

She put on the most elegant robe that Fujiwara had given her, remembering as she always did the day she had promised it to Hana.

She will get it when it fits her, she thought, *and I swear I will be there to see her wear it.*

Hana and Ai entered the room, Hana chattering excitedly and jumping up and down to keep warm. Ayame followed, carrying a brazier. Kaede winced when she saw how full of charcoal it was: they would shiver more when Arai's men were gone.

'Who is coming?' Ai asked nervously. Ever since their father's death and Kaede's illness she had become more fragile, as if the combined shocks had weakened her.

'Arai's men. We have to make a good impression. That's why I've borrowed Hana's robe back again.'

'Don't get it dirty, older sister,' Hana said, groaning as Ayame began to comb out her hair. Usually she wore it tied back. Loose it was longer than she was tall.

'What do they want?' Ai had gone pale.

'I expect they will tell us,' Kaede replied.

'Do I have to be here?' Ai pleaded.

'Yes, put on the other robe Lord Fujiwara sent and help Hana dress. We must all be here together when they arrive.'

'Why?' Hana said.

Kaede did not answer. She herself hardly knew the reason. She had had a sudden image of the three of them in the lonely house, the three daughters of Lord Shirakawa, remote, beautiful, dangerous . . . that was how they must appear to Arai's warriors.

'All-merciful, all-compassionate one, help me,' she prayed to the White Goddess, as Shizuka tied her sash and combed out her hair.

She heard the tread of the horses' feet outside the gate, heard Kondo call a welcome to the men. His voice hit just the right note of courtesy and confidence, and she thanked Heaven for the Tribe's acting skills and hoped hers would be as great.

'Ayame, show our visitors to the guest pavilion,' she said. 'Give them tea and food. The best tea and the finest pottery. When they've finished eating ask their leader to come here to speak with me. Hana, if you are ready, come and sit down next to me.'

Shizuka helped Ai with her robe, and quickly combed her hair. 'I will hide where I can hear,' she whispered.

'Open the shutters before you go,' Kaede said. 'We will get the last of the sun.' For the rain had ceased and a fitful sun cast a silvery light over the garden and into the room.

'What do I have to do?' Hana said, kneeling beside Kaede.

'When the men come in you must bow at exactly the same moment I do. And then just look as beautiful as you can and sit without moving a muscle while I talk.'

'Is that all?' Hana was disappointed.

'Watch the men; study them without seeming to. You can tell me afterwards what you thought of them. You too, Ai. You must give nothing away, react to nothing – like statues.'

Ai came and knelt on Kaede's other side. She was trembling but was able to compose herself.

The sun's last rays streamed into the room, setting the dust motes dancing and lighting up the three girls. The newly cleared waterfall, made louder by the rain, could be heard from the garden. A shadow flashed blue as a kingfisher dived from a rock.

From the guest room came the murmur of the men's voices. Kaede imagined she could catch their unfamiliar smell. It made her tense. She straightened her back and her mind turned to ice. She would meet their power with her own. She would remember how easily they could die.

In a little while she heard Ayame's voice, telling the men Lady Shirakawa would receive them now. Shortly after, their leader and one of his companions approached the main house and stepped onto the veranda. Ayame dropped to her knees at the edge of the room and the retainer also knelt outside. As the other man crossed the threshold Kaede let him see the three of them, and then bowed to him, touching her forehead to the floor. Hana and Ai moved at exactly the same time.

The three girls sat up in unison.

The warrior knelt and announced, 'I am Akita

Tsutomu from Inuyama. I have been sent to Lady Shirakawa by Lord Arai.'

He bowed and stayed low. Kaede said, 'Welcome, Lord Akita. I am grateful to you for your arduous journey and to Lord Arai for sending you. I am eager to learn how I may serve him.' She added, 'You may sit up.'

He did so, and she gazed frankly at him. She knew women were supposed to keep their eyes cast down in the presence of men but she hardly felt like a woman any more. She wondered if she would ever be that sort of woman again. She realized Hana and Ai were staring in the same way at Akita, with opaque, unreadable eyes.

He was approaching middle age, his hair still black but beginning to thin. His nose was small, but slightly hooked, like a bird's, giving him a rapacious look, offset by a well-formed mouth with rather large lips. His clothes were travel-stained but of good quality. His hands were square, short-fingered, with strong, splayed thumbs. She guessed he would be a practical man, but also a conspirator, given to trickery. There was nothing there to trust.

'Lord Arai asks after your health,' he said, looking at each of the sisters, then returning his gaze to Kaede. 'It was reported that you were unwell.'

'I am recovered,' she replied. 'You may thank Lord Arai for his concern.'

He inclined his head slightly. He seemed ill at ease, as if he were more at home among men than among women and unsure of how to address her. She wondered how much he had heard of her situation, if he knew the cause of her illness.

'We heard with great regret of Lord Shirakawa's death,' he went on. 'Lord Arai has been concerned about your lack of protection and wishes to make it clear that he considers you to be in as strong an alliance with him as if you were part of his family.'

Hana and Ai turned their heads, exchanged a look with each other, and resumed their silent staring. It seemed to unnerve Akita even more. He cleared his throat. 'That being the case, Lord Arai wishes to receive you and your sisters at Inuyama to discuss the alliance and Lady Shirakawa's future.'

Impossible, she thought, though she said nothing for a few moments. Then she spoke, smiling slightly. 'Nothing would give me greater pleasure. However, my health is not strong enough to permit me to travel yet and, as we are still mourning our father, it is not fitting that we should leave home. It is late in the year. We will arrange a visit to Inuyama in the spring. You may tell Lord Arai that I consider our alliance unbroken and I am grateful to him for his protection. I will consult him as far as I am able and keep him informed of my decisions.'

Again the look between Hana and Ai flashed through the room like lightning. *It really is uncanny*, Kaede thought and suddenly wanted to laugh.

Akita said, 'I must urge Lady Shirakawa to return with me.'

'It is quite impossible,' she said, meeting his gaze and adding, 'it is not for you to urge me to do anything.'

The rebuke surprised him. A flush of colour spread around his neck and up to his cheekbones.

Hana and Ai leaned forward very slightly and their gaze intensified. The sun went behind clouds, darkening the room, and there was a sudden rush of rain on the roof. The bamboo wind chimes rang with a hollow note.

Akita said, 'I apologize. Of course you must do as seems fitting to you.'

245

'I will come to Inuyama in the spring,' she repeated. 'You may tell Lord Arai that. You are welcome to spend the night here, but I think you will need to leave in the morning to get back before the snow.'

'Lady Shirakawa.' He bowed to the floor. As he shuffled out backwards she asked, 'Who are your companions?' She spoke abruptly, allowing impatience to creep into her voice, knowing instinctively that she had dominated him. Something about the scene, her sisters, her own demeanour had cowed him. She could almost smell it.

'My sister's son, Sonoda Mitsuru, and three of my own retainers.'

'Leave your nephew here. He may enter my service for the winter and escort us to Inuyama. He will be a guarantee of your good faith.'

He stared at the ground, taken aback at the request, yet, she thought with anger, any man in her position would have demanded the same. If the young man were in her household his uncle would be less likely to misrepresent her or otherwise betray her to Arai.

'Of course, trust between us is a symbol of my trust in Lord Arai,' Kaede said, more impatiently, as he hesitated.

'I see no reason why he should not stay here,' Akita conceded.

I have a hostage, she thought, and marvelled at the sense of power it gave her.

She bowed to Akita, Hana and Ai copying her, while he prostrated himself before them. Rain was still falling when he left, but the sun had struggled out again, turning to fragmented rainbows the drops of water that clung to the bare branches and the last of the autumn leaves. She made a sign to her sisters not to move.

Before Akita entered the guest room he turned to look back at them. They sat motionless until he was out of sight. The sun vanished and the rain streamed down.

Ayame stood from where she had been kneeling in the shadows and closed the shutters. Kaede turned and hugged Hana.

'Did I do well?' Hana asked, her eyes lengthened and full of emotion.

'It was brilliant, almost like magic. But what was that look between you?'

'We should not have done it,' Ai said, ashamed. 'It's so childish. We used to do it when Mother or Ayame was teaching us. Hana started it. They never knew if they were imagining it or not. We never dared do it in front of Father. And to do it to a great lord . . .'

'It just seemed to happen,' Hana said, laughing. 'He didn't like it, did he? His eyes went all jumpy and he started to sweat.'

'He is hardly a great lord,' Kaede said. 'Arai might have sent someone of higher rank.'

'Would you have done what he asked then? Would we have gone back with him to Inuyama?'

'Even if Arai himself had come I would not,' Kaede replied. 'I will always make them wait for me.'

'Do you want to know what else I noticed?' Hana said.

'Tell me.'

'Lord Akita was afraid of you, older sister.'

'You have sharp eyes,' Kaede said, laughing.

'I don't want to go away,' Ai said. 'I never want to leave home.'

Kaede gazed at her sister with pity. 'You will have to

marry some day. You may have to go to Inuyama next year and stay for a while.'

'Will I have to?' Hana asked.

'Maybe,' Kaede said. 'Lots of men will want to marry you.'

For the sake of an alliance with me, she thought, saddened that she would have to use her sisters so.

'I'll only go if Shizuka comes with us,' Hana declared.

Kaede smiled and hugged her again. There was no point in telling her that Shizuka could never go in safety to Inuyama while Arai was there. 'Go and tell Shizuka to come to me. Ayame, you had better see what meal we can give these men tonight.'

'I'm glad you told them to leave tomorrow,' Ayame said. 'I don't think we could afford to feed them for longer. They are too used to eating well.' She shook her head. 'Though I have to say, Lady Kaede, I don't think your father would have approved of your conduct.'

'You don't have to say it,' Kaede retorted swiftly. 'And if you want to stay in this household you will never speak to me like that again.'

Ayame flinched at her tone. 'Lady Shirakawa,' she said dully, dropped to her knees and crawled backwards from the room.

Shizuka came in shortly, carrying a lamp, for dusk was now falling. Kaede told her sisters to go and change their clothes.

'How much did you hear?' she demanded when they had gone.

'Enough, and Kondo told me what Lord Akita said when he went back to the pavilion. He thought there was some supernatural power at work in this house. You terrified him. He said you were like the autumn spider,

248

golden and deadly, weaving a web of beauty to captivate men.'

'Quite poetic,' Kaede remarked.

'Yes, Kondo thought so too!'

Kaede could picture the ironic gleam in his eyes. One day, she promised herself, he would look at her without irony. He would take her seriously. They all would, all these men who thought they were so powerful.

'And my hostage, Sonoda Mitsuru, is he terrified too?'

'Your hostage!' Shizuka laughed. 'How did you dare suggest that?'

'Was I wrong?'

'No, on the contrary, it made them believe you are much stronger than was first thought. The young man is a little apprehensive about being left here. Where do you intend to put him?'

'Shoji can take him in his house and look after him. I certainly don't want him here.' Kaede paused, then went on with a trace of bitterness, 'He will be better treated than I was. But what about you? He will not be any danger to you, will he?'

'Arai must know I am still with you,' Shizuka said. 'I see no danger from this young man. His uncle, Lord Akita, will be careful not to upset you now. Your strength protects me – all of us. Arai probably expected to find you distraught and desperate for his help. He will hear a very different story. I told you the birds would gather.'

'So who do we expect next?'

'I believe someone will come from Maruyama before the onset of winter, in response to the messengers Kondo sent.'

Kaede was hoping for the same thing, her mind often turning to her last meeting with her kinswoman, and the promise that had been made then. Her father had told her she would have to fight for that inheritance, but she hardly knew who her adversaries would be or how to set about going to war. Who would teach her how to do it; who would lead an army on her behalf?

She said farewell the next day to Akita and his men, thankful that their stay was so short, and welcomed his nephew, summoning Shoji and handing him over. She was aware of her effect on the young man – he could not take his eyes off her and trembled in her presence – but he did not interest her at all, other than as her hostage.

'Keep him busy,' she told Shoji. 'Treat him well and with respect, but don't let him know too much of our affairs.'

Over the next few weeks men began to turn up at her gate. Some secret message had gone out that she was taking on warriors. They came singly or in twos and threes, never in large groups, men whose masters were dead or dispossessed, the straggling remnants of years of war. She and Kondo devised tests for them – she did not want rogues or fools – but they did not turn many away, for most were experienced fighters who would form the kernel of her army when spring came. Nevertheless, Kaede despaired of being able to feed and keep them all through the long winter.

A few days before the solstice Kondo came to her with the news she had been waiting for.

'Lord Sugita from Maruyama is here with several of his men.'

She welcomed them with delight. They revered the memory of Lady Maruyama and were accustomed to seeing a woman as a leader. She was especially glad to see Sugita, remembering him from the journey to Tsuwano.

He had left them there to return home, to ensure the domain was not attacked and taken over during Lady Maruyama's absence. Filled with grief at her death, he was determined her wishes should be fulfilled. A man of great practicality, he had also brought rice and other provisions with him.

'I will not add to your burdens,' he told Kaede.

'They are not so heavy that we cannot feed old friends,' she lied.

'Everyone is going to suffer this winter,' he replied gloomily. 'The storms, Iida's death, Arai's campaigns – the harvest is a fraction of what it should be.'

Kaede invited him to eat with her, something she did with none of the others, whom she left to Shoji and Kondo to look after. They talked briefly about the events at Inuyama, and then at length about the Maruyama inheritance. He treated Kaede with respect, coloured by an affectionate familiarity, as if he were an uncle or a cousin. She felt at ease with him: he was not threatened by her but he took her seriously.

When they had finished eating and the dishes had been cleared away he said, 'It was my lady's desire to see her domain in your care. I was delighted to receive your message that you intend to take up your inheritance. I came at once to tell you that I will help you: many of us will. We should start to plan our actions before spring.'

'It is my intention, and I'll need all the help I can get,' Kaede replied. 'I have no idea how to set about it. Will I be able simply to take the lands over? Who do they belong to now?'

'They belong to you,' he said. 'You are the next female heir, and it was our lady's express wish that the domain be yours. But several other people lay claim to it: the main contender is Lady Maruyama's stepdaughter, who is married to a cousin of Lord Iida. Arai has not been able to eradicate him and he has quite a large force – a mixture of Tohan, who fled from Noguchi castle when it fell, and disaffected Seishuu who see no reason why they should submit to Arai. They are wintering in the far west but they will march on Maruyama in the spring. If you do not move swiftly and boldly, the domain will be fought over and destroyed.'

'I promised Lady Naomi that I would prevent that happening,' Kaede said, 'but I didn't know what I was promising or how to achieve it.'

'There are many people willing to help you,' he said, leaning forward and whispering. 'I was sent by our council of elders to request that you come to us, and soon. The domain prospered under Lady Naomi; we all had enough to eat and even the poorest could feed their children. We traded with the mainland, mined silver and copper, established many small industries. The alliance between Lord Arai, Lord Otori Shigeru and the Maruyama would have extended that prosperity all the way into the Middle Country. We want to save what we can of the alliance.'

'I plan to visit Lord Arai in the spring,' Kaede said. 'I will formalize our alliance then.'

'Then one of your terms must be that he supports you in your claim to Maruyama. Only Arai is strong enough to dissuade the stepdaughter and her husband to retire without fighting. And if it comes to battle, only his army will be large enough to beat them. You must move quickly; as soon as the roads are open again you must go to Inuyama and then come to us, with Arai's backing.'

He looked at her, smiled slightly and said, 'I am sorry, I do not mean to seem to be commanding you in any way. But I hope you will take my advice.'

'I will,' she said. 'It is what I had already thought of doing, but with your support I am encouraged in it.'

They went on to talk of how many men Sugita could raise and he swore he would hand over the domain to no one but her. He said he would leave the next day, as he wanted to be back at Maruyama before the new year. Then he said casually, 'It's a shame Otori Takeo is dead. If you had married him, his name and the Otori connection would have made you even stronger.'

Kaede's heart seemed to stop beating, and fall from her chest to her stomach. 'I had not heard of his death,' she said, trying to keep her voice steady.

'Well, it's only what people are saying. I don't know any details. I suppose it's the obvious explanation for his disappearance. It may be only a rumour.'

'Maybe,' Kaede said, while thinking silently, *Or maybe he is dead in an open field or on the mountain and I will never know.* 'I am growing tired, Lord Sugita. Forgive me.'

'Lady Shirakawa.' He bowed to her and stood. 'We'll keep in touch as much as the weather allows. I will expect you at Maruyama in the spring; the clan's forces will support your claim. If anything changes, I will get word to you somehow.'

She promised to do the same, impatient for him to be gone. When he had left and she was sure he was safely inside the guest pavilion, she called for Shizuka, paced up and down, and when the girl came she seized her with both hands.

'Are you keeping something from me?'

'Lady?' Shizuka looked at her in surprise. 'What do you mean? What's happened?'

'Sugita said he'd heard Takeo was dead.'

'It's just a rumour.'

'But you've heard it?'

'Yes. I don't believe it though. If he were dead we would have been told. You look so pale! Sit down. You must not overtire yourself, you must not get sick again. I'll prepare the beds.'

She led her from the main room into the room where they slept. Kaede sank to the floor, her heart still thudding. 'I am so afraid he will die before I see him again.'

Shizuka knelt beside her, untied her sash, and helped her out of the formal robes she had been wearing.

'I'll massage your head. Sit still.'

Kaede was restlessly moving her head from side to side, clutching her hair, clenching and unclenching her fists. Shizuka's hands in her hair did not soothe her; they simply reminded her of the unbearable afternoon at Inuyama and the events that followed. She was shivering.

'You must find out, Shizuka, I must know for sure. Send a message to your uncle. Send Kondo. He must leave at once.'

'I thought you were beginning to forget him,' Shizuka murmured, her hands working at Kaede's scalp.

'I cannot forget him. I've tried, but as soon as I hear his name it all returns to me. Do you remember the day I first saw him at Tsuwano? I fell in love with him at that moment. A fever came over me. It was – it is – an enchantment, a sickness from which I can never be cured. You said we would get over it, but we never will.'

Her brow was burning beneath Shizuka's fingers. Alarmed, the girl asked, 'Shall I send for Ishida?'

'I am tormented by desire,' Kaede said in a low voice. 'Dr Ishida can do nothing for that.'

'Desire is simple enough to alleviate,' Shizuka replied calmly.

'But my desire is only for him. Nothing, no one else can relieve it. I know I must try to live without him. I have duties to my family that I must, I will, carry out. But if he is dead, you must tell me.'

'I will write to Kenji,' Shizuka promised. 'I'll send Kondo tomorrow, though we cannot really spare him . . .'

'Send him,' Kaede said.

Shizuka made an infusion from the willow twigs that Ishida had left, and persuaded Kaede to drink it, but her sleep was restless, and in the morning she was listless and feverish.

Ishida came, applied moxa and used his needles, rebuking her gently for not taking better care of herself.

'It's not serious,' he told Shizuka, when they stepped outside. 'It will pass in a day or two. She is too sensitive and makes too many demands on herself. She should marry.'

'She will only agree to marry one man – and that is impossible,' Shizuka said.

'The father of the child?'

Shizuka nodded. 'Yesterday she heard a rumour that he was dead. The fever started then.'

'Ah.' His eyes had a thoughtful, faraway look. She wondered what or whom he was remembering from his youth.

'I fear the coming months,' she said. 'Once we are closed in by snow I am afraid she will begin to brood.'

'I have a letter for her from Lord Fujiwara. He would like her to visit him and stay for a few days. The change of scene may help to lift her spirits and distract her.'

'Lord Fujiwara is too kind to this house, pays us too great an attention.' Shizuka used the formal words of thanks automatically as she took the letter. She was acutely aware of the man next to her, of their hands touching briefly. The distant look in his eyes had sparked something in her. During Kaede's illness they had spent many hours together and she had come to admire his patience and skill. He was kind, unlike most men she had known.

'Will you come again tomorrow?' she said, glancing at him.

'Of course. You can give me Lady Kaede's reply to the letter. You will accompany her to Lord Fujiwara's?'

'Of course!' She repeated his words playfully. He smiled and touched her again, deliberately, on the arm. The pressure of his fingers made her shiver. It was so long since she had slept with a man. She had a sudden strong desire to feel his hands all over her body; she wanted to lie down with him and hold him. He deserved it for his kindness.

'Till tomorrow,' he said, his eyes warm, as if he had recognized her feelings and shared them.

She slipped into her sandals and ran to call the servants with the palanquin.

Kaede's fever subsided, and by evening she had recovered some of her energy. She had lain still all day, warm under a huge pile of quilts, next to the brazier that Ayame had insisted on lighting, thinking about the future. Takeo might be dead, the child certainly was: her heart wanted only to follow them to the next world, but her reason told her it would be sheer weakness to throw her life away and abandon those who depended on her: a woman might act like that, a man in her position never would.

Shizuka is right, she thought, *there is only one person I know who can help me now. I must see what arrangement I can come to with Fujiwara.*

Shizuka gave her the letter that Ishida had brought that morning. Fujiwara had also sent gifts for the new year, specially shaped rice cakes, dried sardines and sweetened chestnuts, rolled kelp and rice wine. Hana and Ai were busy in the kitchen helping to prepare for the festival.

'He flatters me; he writes in men's language saying he knows I understand it,' Kaede said. 'But there are so many characters I don't know.' She sighed deeply. 'There's so much I need to learn. Is one winter going to be enough?'

'Will you go to Lord Fujiwara's?'

'I suppose so. He might teach me. Do you think he would?'

'There's nothing he'd like more,' Shizuka said dryly.

'I thought he would want nothing more to do with me, but he says he has been waiting for my recovery. I am better – as well as I will ever be.' Kaede's voice was doubtful. 'I must be better. I have to look after my sisters, my land, my men.'

'As I've said many times, Fujiwara is your best ally in this.'

'Maybe not the best: the only. But I don't really trust him. What does he want from me?'

'What do you want from him?' Shizuka replied.

'That's simple. On the one hand, learning, on the other money and food to raise an army and feed it. But what do I offer him in return?'

Shizuka wondered if she should mention Fujiwara's desire for marriage, but decided against it, fearing it would disturb Kaede to the point of fever again. Let the nobleman speak for himself. She was sure he would.

'He addresses me as Lady Shirakawa. I am ashamed to face him, after deceiving him.'

'He will have learned of your father's wishes regarding your name,' Shizuka said. 'Everyone knows that your father named you as his heir before his death. We have made sure of that.'

Kaede glanced at her to see if she was mocking her, but Shizuka's face was serious. 'Of course, I had to do as my father requested,' she agreed.

'There is nothing else Lord Fujiwara needs to know, then. Filial obedience comes before everything.'

'So K'ung Fu-Tzu tells me,' Kaede said. 'Lord Fujiwara *needs* to know nothing else but I suspect he *wants* to know a great deal more. If he is still interested in me, that is.'

'He will be,' Shizuka assured her, thinking that Kaede was more beautiful than ever. Her illness and grief had removed the last traces of childishness from her and had given her expression depth and mystery.

They celebrated the new year with Fujiwara's gifts, and ate buckwheat noodles, and black beans that Ayame had put away at the end of the summer. At midnight they went to the temple and listened to the priests' chanting and the bells' tolling for the extinction of human passions. Kaede knew she should pray to be freed from them all and to be purified, but found herself asking for what she most desired, for Takeo to be alive, and then for money and power.

The following day the women of the household took

candles, incense and lanterns, wrinkled mandarins, sweet chestnuts and dried persimmons, and went to the caves where the Shirakawa river emerged from a series of underground caverns. Here they performed their own ceremonies before the rock that the water had turned into the shape of the White Goddess. No men were ever supposed to come into this place; if they did the mountain might fall, and the Shirakawa be extinguished. An aged couple lived behind the shrine at the entrance to the cave – only the old woman went inside to take offerings to the goddess. Kaede knelt on the damp rock listening to the ancient voice mumble words she hardly knew the meaning of. She thought of her mother and Lady Maruyama and asked for their help and their intercession. She realized how much this holy place meant to her, and she felt that the goddess was watching over her.

The next day she went to Lord Fujiwara's. Hana was bitterly disappointed at being left behind and wept when she had to say goodbye not only to Kaede but also to Shizuka.

'It's only for a few days,' Kaede said.

'Why can't I come with you?'

'Lord Fujiwara did not invite you. Besides, you would hate it there. You would have to behave properly, speak in formal language, and sit still most of the day.'

'Will you hate it?'

'I expect I will,' Kaede sighed.

'At least you will eat delicious food,' Hana said, adding longingly, 'quail!'

'If we are eating his food, there will be more for you here,' Kaede replied. It was in fact one of the reasons why she was happy to be away for a while, for no matter how many times she looked at the food stores and calculated the days of winter, it remained obvious that they would run out of food before spring.

'And someone has to entertain young Mitsuru,' Shizuka added. 'You must make sure he is not too home-sick.'

'Ai can do that,' Hana retorted. 'He likes Ai.'

Kaede had noticed the same thing. Her sister had not admitted any affection in return, but she was shy about such matters – And anyway, Kaede thought, what differ-ence did her feelings make? Ai would have to be betrothed soon. The new year had seen her turn fourteen. It might be that Sonoda Mitsuru, if his uncle were to adopt him, would be a good match, but she would not relinquish her sister cheaply.

In a year they will be lining up for marriages with the Shirakawa, she told herself.

Ai had coloured a little at Hana's remark. 'Take care of yourself, older sister,' she said, embracing Kaede. 'Don't worry about us. I'll look after everything here.'

'We are not far away,' Kaede replied. 'You must send for me if you think I am needed.' She could not help adding, 'And if any messages come for me, if Kondo returns, let me know at once.'

They arrived at Lord Fujiwara's in the early afternoon. The day had begun mild and overcast, but even as they travelled the wind swung to the north-east and the tem-perature dropped.

Mamoru met them, conveyed the nobleman's greet-ings, and led them, not to the guest rooms where they had stayed before, but to another smaller pavilion, less ornately decorated but to Kaede's eyes even more beauti-ful, with its elegant simplicity and muted colours. She was grateful for this thoughtfulness, for she had been dreading seeing her father's angry ghost in the room where her secret had been revealed to him.

'Lord Fujiwara thought Lady Shirakawa would prefer to rest this evening,' Mamoru said quietly. 'He will receive you tomorrow, if that is agreeable to you.'

'Thank you,' Kaede said. 'Please tell Lord Fujiwara I am completely at his service. I will do whatever he desires.'

She was already aware of tension. Mamoru had used her name without hesitation, had glanced at her swiftly when she arrived, as if trying to discern any change in her, but since then had not looked at her at all. However, she knew already how much he saw of her without appearing to. She straightened her back and gazed at him with a hint of disdain in her expression. Let him study her all he liked as a subject for the roles he played on stage. He would never be other than a counterfeit of what she was. She did not care what he thought of her. But she did care what Fujiwara thought. *He must despise me*, she told herself, *but if he shows it by so much as a flicker of one eyebrow, I'll leave and never see him again, no matter what he might do for me.*

She was relieved that the meeting was to be postponed. Ishida paid them a call and checked her pulse and eyes. He told her he would prepare a new sort of tea that would purify the blood and strengthen the stomach, and asked her to send Shizuka to his rooms the following day to collect it.

A hot bath had been prepared, making Kaede warm not only from the water, but also with envy at the amount of wood available to heat it. Afterwards food was brought to their room by maids who hardly spoke at all.

'It is the traditional ladies' winter meal,' Shizuka

exclaimed when she saw the delicacies of the season, raw sea bream and squid, broiled eel with green perilla and horseradish, pickled cucumbers and salted lotus root, rare black mushrooms and burdock, laid out on the lacquer trays. 'This is what they would eat in the capital. I wonder how many other women in the Three Countries are eating something this exquisite tonight!'

'Everything is exquisite here,' Kaede replied. *How easy it is*, she thought, *to have luxury and taste when you have money!*

They had finished eating and were thinking about retiring when there was a tap outside the door.

'The maids have come to prepare the beds,' Shizuka said and went to the door. But when she slid it open, it was Mamoru who stood outside. There was snow on his hair.

'Forgive me,' he said, 'but the first snow of the year has begun to fall. Lord Fujiwara wishes to visit Lady Shirakawa. The view from this pavilion is particularly fine.'

'This is Lord Fujiwara's house,' Kaede said. 'I am his guest. Whatever is his pleasure is mine also.'

Mamoru left and she heard him speak to the maids. A few moments later two of them came to the room with warm red quilted robes which they dressed her in. Accompanied by Shizuka, she went out onto the veranda. Animal skins had been placed over cushions for them to sit on. Lanterns had been hung from the trees, lighting the falling flakes. The ground was already white. A garden of rocks lay under two pine trees that grew in low, beautifully trained patterns, framing the view. Behind them the dull mass of the mountain was just visible through the swirling snow. Kaede was silent, transfixed by the beauty of the scene, its silent purity.

Moving so quietly that they hardly heard him, Lord Fujiwara approached them. They both knelt before him.

'Lady Shirakawa,' he said. 'I am so grateful to you. First for condescending to visit my humble place and secondly for indulging my whim to share the first snow viewing with you.

'Please sit up,' he added. 'You must wrap yourself up well; you must not catch cold.'

Servants filed behind him bringing braziers, flasks of wine, cups and furs. Mamoru took one of the furs and placed it over her shoulders, then wrapped another around Fujiwara as he sat beside her. Kaede stroked the pelt with a mixture of delight and revulsion.

'They come from the mainland,' Fujiwara told her after they had exchanged formal greetings. 'Ishida brings them back when he goes on his expeditions there.'

'What animal is it?'

'Some kind of bear, I believe.'

She could not imagine a bear so large. She tried to picture it in its native land, so distant and foreign to her. It would be powerful, slow moving, ferocious, yet men had killed and skinned it. She wondered if its spirit still dwelt somehow in the skin and if it would resent her wearing its warmth. She shivered. 'Dr Ishida is brave as well as clever, to go on such dangerous journeys.'

'He has an unquenchable thirst for knowledge, it seems. Of course it has all been rewarded by Lady Shirakawa's recovery.'

'I owe him my life,' she said in a low voice.

'Then he is even more precious to me than on his own account.'

She detected his usual irony, but no contempt. Indeed, he could hardly be more flattering.

'How lovely the first snow is,' she said. 'Yet by the end of winter we long for it to melt.'

'Snow pleases me,' he said. 'I like its whiteness and the way it wraps the world. Beneath it everything becomes clean.'

Mamoru poured wine and passed it to them. Then he vanished into the shadows. The servants withdrew. They were not really alone yet there was an illusion of solitude as though nothing existed but the two of them, the glowing braziers, the heavy animal furs and the snow.

After they had watched it in silence for a while Fujiwara called to the servants to bring more lamps.

'I want to see your face,' he said, leaning forward and studying her in the same hungry way he had gazed on his treasures. Kaede raised her eyes and looked past him at the snow, now falling more thickly, swirling in the light from the lanterns, blocking out the mountains, blurring the outside world.

'Possibly more beautiful than ever,' he said quietly; she thought she detected a note of relief in his voice. She knew that if her illness had marred her in any way he would have withdrawn politely and would never have seen her again. They could all have starved to death at Shirakawa with no gesture of compassion or help from him. *How cold he is,* she thought, and felt her own body chill in response, yet she made no sign of it, just continued to gaze past him, letting the snow fill her eyes and dazzle her. She would be cold, like ice, like celadon. And if he wanted to possess her he would pay the highest price.

He drank, filled his cup and drank again, his eyes never leaving her face. Neither of them spoke. Finally he said abruptly, 'Of course you will have to marry.'

'I have no intention of marrying,' Kaede replied, and then feared she had spoken too bluntly.

'I imagined you would say that since you always hold a different opinion to the world. But in all practical terms you must be married. There is no alternative.'

'My reputation is very unfavourable,' Kaede said. 'Too many men connected with me have perished. I do not want to be the cause of any more deaths.'

She felt his interest deepen, noticed the curve of his mouth increase slightly. Yet it was not with desire for her, she knew that. It was the same emotion she had caught a whiff of before, a burning curiosity, carefully controlled, to know all her secrets.

He called to Mamoru, telling him to send the servants away and retire himself.

'Where is your woman?' he said to Kaede. 'Tell her to wait for you inside. I want to speak to you privately.'

Kaede spoke to Shizuka. After a pause Fujiwara went on, 'Are you warm enough? You must not be ill again. Ishida tells me you are prone to sudden fevers.'

Of course, Ishida would tell him everything about me, Kaede thought as she replied, 'Thank you, I am warm enough for the moment. But Lord Fujiwara will forgive me if I do not stay up long. I become tired very easily.'

'We will talk for a little while,' he said. 'We have many weeks before us, I hope. All winter in fact. But there is something about this night, the snow, your presence here . . . it's a memory that will stay with us all our lives.'

He wants to marry me, Kaede thought with a sense of shock, followed by deep unease. If he offered marriage how could she refuse? To use his own phrase 'in all practical terms', it made perfect sense. It was a far greater honour than she deserved, it would solve all her problems of money and food, it was a highly desirable alliance. Yet she knew his preference was for men; he neither loved nor desired her. She prayed he would not speak, for she did not see how she could refuse him. She was afraid of the strength of his will which always took what it wanted and always had its own way. She doubted her own strength to deny him. Not only would it be an unthinkable insult to someone of his rank, but he fascinated her as much as he alarmed her and this gave him a power over her that she barely understood.

'I have never seen a bear,' she said, hoping to change the subject, drawing the heavy skin closer around her.

'We have small bears here in the mountains – one came to the garden once after a particularly long winter. I had it captured and caged for a while but it pined and died. It was nothing like this size. Ishida will tell us of his travels one day. Would you like that?'

'Very much. He is the only person I know who has ever been to the mainland.'

'It's a dangerous voyage. Quite apart from the storms there are often encounters with pirates.'

At that moment Kaede felt she would rather meet a dozen bears or twenty pirates than remain with this unnerving man. She could think of nothing else to say. Indeed she felt powerless to move at all.

'Mamoru and Ishida have both told me what people say about you, that desire for you brings death.'

Kaede said nothing. *I will not be ashamed,* she thought. *I have done nothing wrong.* She lifted her eyes and looked at him directly, her face calm, her gaze steady.

'Yet from what Ishida tells me, one man who desired you escaped death.'

She felt her heart twist and jump, like a fish when it finds its living flesh pierced by the cook's knife. His eyes flickered. A small muscle twitched in his cheek. He looked away from her at the snow. *He is asking what should not be asked*, she thought, *I will tell him, but he will pay a price for it*. As she saw his weakness she became aware of her own power. Her courage began to return.

'Who was it?' he whispered.

The night was silent, apart from the soft drift of snow, the wind in the pines, the murmur of water.

'Lord Otori Takeo,' she said.

'Yes, it could only be him,' he replied, making her wonder what she had given away before and what he knew about Takeo now. He leaned forward, his face moving into the lamplight. 'Tell me about it.'

'I could tell you many things,' she said slowly. 'About Lord Shigeru's betrayal and death and Lord Takeo's revenge and what happened the night Iida died and Inuyama fell. But every story comes at a price. What will you give me in return?'

He smiled and in a tone of complicity said, 'What does Lady Shirakawa desire?'

'I need money to hire men and equip them, and food for my household.'

He came close to laughing. 'Most women your age would ask for a new fan or a robe. But you are always able to surprise me.'

'Do you accept my price?' She felt she had nothing to lose now from boldness.

'Yes, I do. For Iida, money, for Shigeru, bushels of rice. And for the living one – I assume he still lives – what shall I pay you for Takeo's story?'

His voice changed as he spoke the name, as though he

were tasting it in his mouth, and she wondered again what he had heard about Takeo.

'Teach me,' she said, 'There are so many things I need to know. Teach me as if I were a boy.'

He inclined his head in agreement. 'It will be a pleasure to continue your father's instruction.'

'But everything must be kept secret between us. Like the treasures of your collection, nothing must be exposed. I will divulge these things only for your gaze. No one else must ever be told them.'

'That makes them all the more precious, all the more desirable.'

'No one else has ever heard them,' Kaede whispered. 'And once I have told you I will never speak of them again.'

The wind had risen a little and a flurry of snow blew onto the veranda, the flakes hissing as they hit the lamps and the braziers. Kaede could feel cold creeping over her, meeting her coldness of heart and spirit. She longed to leave him, yet knew she could not move until he released her.

'You are cold,' he said, and clapped his hands. The servants appeared out of the shadows and helped Kaede to her feet, lifting the heavy fur from her.

'I look forward to your stories,' he said, wishing her goodnight with unusual warmth. But Kaede found herself wondering if she had not made a pact with a demon from hell. She prayed he would not ask her to marry him. She would never allow him to cage her in this luxurious beautiful house, concealed like a treasure, to be gazed on only by him.

At the end of the week she returned home. The first snow had melted and frozen and the road was icy but passable. Icicles hung from the eaves of the houses, dripping in the sun, glistening and brilliant. Fujiwara had kept his word. He was a rigorous and demanding teacher and he had set her tasks to practise before she returned to his house again. He had already dispatched food for her household and men.

The days had been spent in study and the nights in story-telling. She knew by instinct what he wanted to hear and she told him details she had not known she remembered: the colour of flowers, the birds' song, the exact condition of the weather, the touch of a hand, the smell of a robe, the way lamplight fell on a face. And the undercurrents of desire and conspiracy that she had both known and not known, and that only now became clear to her with the telling. She told him everything, in a clear measured voice, showing no shame, grief or regret.

He was reluctant to allow her to return home but she used her sisters as an excuse. He wanted her to stay there for ever, she knew, and she fought that desire silently. Yet it seemed that everyone shared it. The servants expected it and their treatment of her changed slightly. They deferred to her as though she were already more than a specially favoured guest. They sought her permission, her opinion, and she knew they would only do so if he had so ordered.

She felt deep relief when she left him and she dreaded returning again. Yet when she was home, she saw the food, the firewood and the money he had sent and was grateful that he had kept her family from starving. That night she lay thinking, *I am trapped. I shall never escape him. Yet what else can I do?*

It was a long time before she slept and she was late rising the next morning. Shizuka was not in the room when she woke. Kaede called to her and Ayame came in with tea.

She poured Kaede a cup. 'Shizuka is with Kondo,' she said. 'He returned late last night.'

'Tell her to come to me,' Kaede said. She looked at the tea as though she did not know what to do with it. She sipped a mouthful, placed the cup on the tray, then picked it up. Her hands were icy. She held the cup between them, trying to warm them.

'Lord Fujiwara sent this tea,' Ayame said. 'A whole box of it. Isn't it delicious?'

'Fetch Shizuka!' Kaede cried angrily. 'Tell her to come to me at once!'

A few minutes later Shizuka came into the room and knelt in front of Kaede. Her face was sombre.

'What is it?' Kaede said. 'Is he dead?' The cup began to shake in her hands, spilling the tea.

Shizuka took it from her, and held her hands tightly. 'You must not be distressed. You must not become ill. He is not dead. But he has left the Tribe and they have issued an edict against him.'

'What does that mean?'

'You remember what he told you at Terayama? If he did not go with them they would not allow him to live. It is the same.'

'Why?' Kaede said, 'Why? I don't understand.'

'It's the way the Tribe are. Obedience is everything to them.'

'So why would he leave them?'

'It's not clear. There was some altercation, some disagreement. He was sent on a mission and never came back from it.' Shizuka paused. 'Kondo thinks he may be at Terayama. If he is, he will be safe there for the winter.'

270

Kaede pulled her hands away from Shizuka and stood. 'I must go there.'

'It's impossible,' Shizuka said. 'It's already closed off by snow.'

'I must see him!' Kaede said, her eyes blazing in her pale face. 'If he has left the Tribe he will become Otori again. If he is Otori, we can marry!'

'Lady!' Shizuka stood too. 'What madness is this? You cannot just take after him like that! Even if the roads were open it would be unthinkable. Better by far, if you want what you say you want, to marry Fujiwara. It is what he desires.'

Kaede struggled to regain control of herself. 'There is nothing to stop me going to Terayama. Indeed, I should go there . . . on a pilgrimage . . . to give thanks to the all-merciful one for saving my life. I have promised to go to Inuyama, to Arai, as soon as the snows melt. I shall go to the temple on the way. Even if Lord Fujiwara does want to marry me, I can do nothing without consulting Lord Arai. Oh, Shizuka, how long is it till spring?'

Nine

The winter days crawled past. Every month Kaede went to Lord Fujiwara's residence, stayed for a week and, at night while the snow fell or the moon shone coldly on the frozen garden, recounted the story of her life. He asked many questions and made her repeat many parts.

'It could be the subject of a drama,' he said more than once. 'Maybe I should try my hand at writing such a thing.'

'You would never be able to show it to anyone,' she replied.

'No, the delight would be in the writing alone. I would share it with you, of course. We might have it acted once for our pleasure and then have the actors put to death.'

He often made comments like this, with no trace of emotion, alarming her more and more, though she kept her fears hidden. With each retelling her face became more mask-like, her movements more studied, as though she were endlessly acting out her life on a stage he had created as carefully as the perfectly constructed theatre where Mamoru and the other young men played their roles.

During the day he kept his promise to teach her as if she were a boy. He used men's language with her and made her speak it to him. It amused him sometimes to see her dressed in Mamoru's clothes, with her hair tied back. The role-playing exhausted her. But she learned.

Fujiwara kept his other promises, having food delivered to her house and money handed over to Shizuka at the end of each visit. Kaede counted it with the same avidity with which she studied. She saw them both as equal currency for her future, giving her freedom and power.

In early spring there was a bitter snap of cold weather that froze the plum blossom on the branches. Kaede's impatience grew with the lengthening days; the increased cold and harder frosts, followed by fresh snow, nearly drove her mad. She could feel her mind, frantic like a bird trapped inside the house, yet she did not dare share her feelings with anyone, not even with Shizuka.

On sunny days she went to the stables and watched Raku when Amano let the horses out to gallop in the water meadows. The horse often seemed to look questioningly towards the north-east, tasting the sharp wind.

'Soon,' she promised him. 'Soon we will be on our way.'

Finally the full moon of the third month turned and brought with it a warm wind from the south. Kaede woke to the sound of water dripping from the eaves, trickling through the garden, racing down the waterfalls. In three days the snow was gone. The world lay bare and muddy, waiting to be filled with sound and colour again.

'I have to go away for a while,' she told Fujiwara on her last visit. 'I have been summoned by Lord Arai to Inuyama.'

'You will seek his permission to marry?'

'It is something that must be discussed with him before I can make any decisions,' she murmured.

'Then I will let you go.' His lips curved slightly but the smile did not reach his eyes.

For the last month she had been making preparations, waiting for the thaw, thankful for Fujiwara's money. Within a week she left on a cold, bright morning, the sun appearing and disappearing behind racing clouds, the wind from the east, keen and bracing. Hana had begged to be allowed to come and at first Kaede had intended to take her. But a fear grew in her that once they were at Inuyama Arai might keep her sister as a hostage. For the time being Hana was safer at home. She hardly admitted even to herself that if Takeo were at Terayama she might never go on to the capital. Ai did not want to come, and Kaede left her hostage, Mitsuru, with Shoji, as a guarantee for her own safety.

She took Kondo, Amano and six other men. She wanted to move quickly, always aware of how short a life might be and how precious every hour was. She put on men's garments and rode Raku. He had wintered well, hardly losing any weight, and he stepped out with an eagerness that equalled hers. He was already shedding his winter coat and the rough grey hair clung to her clothes.

Shizuka accompanied her, along with one of the maids from the house, Manami. Shizuka had decided she would go at least as far as Terayama and, while Kaede went on to the capital, she would visit her grandparents' home, in the mountains behind Yamagata, to see her sons. Manami was a sensible and practical woman who quickly took it upon herself to supervise their meals and lodging at the inns along the road, demanding hot food and water, disputing prices, cowing innkeepers and always getting her own way.

'I won't have to worry about who'll look after you when I leave you,' Shizuka said on the third night, after hearing Manami scold the innkeeper for providing inferior, flea-ridden bedding. 'I think Manami's tongue would stop an ogre in its tracks.'

'I'll miss you,' Kaede said. 'I think you are my courage. I don't know how brave I can be without you. And who will tell me what is really happening beneath all the lies and the pretence?'

'I think you can discern that well enough for yourself,' Shizuka replied. 'Besides, Kondo will be with you. You will make a better impression on Arai without me!'

'What should I expect from Arai?'

'He has always taken your part. He will continue to champion you. He is generous and loyal, except when he feels he has been slighted or deceived.'

'He is impulsive, I thought,' Kaede said.

'Yes, to the point of rashness. He is hot in every sense of the word, passionate and stubborn.'

'You loved him very much?' Kaede said.

'I was only a girl. He was my first lover. I was deeply in love with him, and he must have loved me after his own fashion. He kept me with him for fourteen years.'

'I will plead with him to forgive you,' Kaede exclaimed.

'I don't know which I fear most, his forgiveness or his rage,' Shizuka admitted, thinking of Dr Ishida and the discreet, entirely satisfactory affair they had been conducting all winter.

'Then maybe I should not mention you at all.'

'It's usually best to say nothing,' Shizuka agreed. 'Anyway, his main concern will be with your marriage and the alliances that may be made by it.'

'I will not marry until I have secured Maruyama,' Kaede replied. 'First he must assist me in that.'

But first I must see Takeo, she thought. *If he is not at Terayama, I will forget him. It will be a sign that it is not meant to be. Oh, merciful Heaven, let him be there!*

As the road ascended further into the mountain range, the thaw was less apparent. Drifts of unmelted snow still covered the paths in places and often there was ice underfoot. The horses' feet were wrapped in straw but their progress was slow and Kaede's impatience intensified.

Finally, late one afternoon, they arrived at the inn at the foot of the holy mountain, where Kaede had rested when she had first visited the temple with Lady Maruyama. Here they would stay the night before making the final ascent the next day.

Kaede slept fitfully, her mind full of the companions from her previous journey, whose names were now entered in the ledgers of the dead. She recalled the day they had ridden out together, how light-hearted everyone had seemed, while they had been planning assassination and civil war. She had known nothing of that; she had been a green girl, nursing a secret love. She felt a wave of scornful pity for that innocent, guileless self. She had changed completely, but the love had not changed.

The light was paling behind the shutters and birds were calling. The room seemed unbearably stuffy. Manami was snoring slightly. Kaede got up quietly, pulled on a quilted robe, and slid open the door to the courtyard. From behind the wall she could hear the horses stamping on their lines. She heard one of them give a whicker of recognition. *The men must be up already,* she thought, and heard footsteps turn through the gate. She stepped behind the shutter again.

Everything was misty and indistinct in the dawn light. A figure came into the courtyard. She thought, *It's him.* She thought, *It cannot be.*

Takeo came out of the mist towards her.

She stepped onto the veranda and, as he recognized her, she saw the look that swept across his face. She thought, with gratitude and relief, *It's all right. He's alive. He loves me.*

He came up onto the veranda silently and fell on his knees before her. She knelt too. 'Sit up,' she whispered.

He did so, and they stared at each other for several moments, she as if she would drink him in, he obliquely, not meeting her gaze. They sat awkwardly, so much between them.

Takeo said finally, 'I saw my horse. I knew you must be here but I couldn't believe it.'

'I heard you were here. In great danger, but alive.'

'The danger is not so great,' he said. 'My greatest danger is from you – that you cannot forgive me.'

'I can't not forgive you,' she replied simply. 'As long as you don't leave me again.'

'I was told you were to be married. I have been afraid of it all winter.'

'There is someone who wants to marry me: Lord Fujiwara. But we are not married yet, not even betrothed.'

'Then we must marry immediately. Are you here to visit the temple?'

'That was my intention. Then I was to go on to Inuyama.' She was studying his face. He looked older, the bones more pronounced, the mouth more determined. His hair, shorter than it had been, was not pulled back in the warrior style, but fell against his forehead, thick and glossy.

'I'll send men to escort you up the mountain. I'll come to the women's rooms in the temple this evening. We have so much to plan. Don't look in my eyes,' he added. 'I don't want you to fall asleep.'

'I don't mind,' she replied. 'Sleep rarely comes to me. Send me to sleep until this evening, then the hours will pass quickly. When I slept before the White Goddess came to me in a vision. She told me to be patient, to wait for you. I am here to thank her for it and for saving my life.'

'I was told you were dying,' he said, and could not continue. After a few moments he spoke with an effort. 'Is Muto Shizuka with you?'

'Yes.'

'And you have a retainer from the Tribe, Kondo Kiichi?'

She nodded.

'They must be sent away. Leave your other men here for the time being. Do you have another woman to accompany you?'

'Yes,' Kaede said. 'But I don't think Shizuka would do anything to harm you.' Even as she spoke she thought, *But how do I know? Can I trust Shizuka? Or Kondo, come to that. I have seen his ruthlessness.*

'I am under sentence of death from the Tribe,' Takeo said. 'Therefore any one of them is a danger to me.'

'Isn't it dangerous for you to be out, like this?'

He smiled. 'I've never let anyone confine me. I like to explore places at night. I need to know the terrain, and if the Otori are planning to attack me across the border. I was on my way back when I saw Raku. He recognized me. Did you hear him?'

'He has been waiting for you too,' she said, and felt

sorrow uncurl in her belly. 'Does everyone want your death?'

'They are not going to succeed. Not yet. I'll tell you why tonight.'

She longed for him to hold her. She could feel her body leaning towards him. In the same moment he responded, and took her in his arms. She felt his heart beat, his lips against her neck. Then he whispered, 'Someone's awake. I must go.'

She could hear nothing. Takeo pulled gently away from her. 'Till this evening,' he said.

She looked at him, seeking his gaze, half-hoping to be plunged into sleep, but he had gone. She cried out in alarm. There was no sign of him in the courtyard or beyond. The wind chimes rang out sharply as if in the breath of someone passing beneath them. Her heart was pounding. Had it been his ghost that had come to her? Had she been dreaming and what would she find when she woke?

'What are you doing out here, lady?' Manami's voice was shrill with concern. 'You'll catch your death of cold.'

Kaede pulled the robe around her. She was indeed shivering. 'I could not sleep,' she said slowly, 'I had a dream . . .'

'Go inside. I'll send for tea.' Manami stepped into her sandals and hurried away across the courtyard.

Swallows darted to and from the eaves. Kaede smelled wood smoke as the fires were lit. The horses whinnied as they were fed. She heard Raku's voice as she had heard it earlier. The air was sharp, but she could smell blossom. She felt her heart swell with hope. It had not been a dream. He was here. In a few hours they would be together. She did not want to go inside. She wanted to stay where she was, remembering his look, his touch, his smell.

Manami came back, carrying a tray with tea and cups on it. She scolded Kaede again, and chivvied her into the room. Shizuka was getting dressed. She took one look at Kaede and exclaimed, 'You've seen Takeo?'

Kaede did not reply immediately. She took a cup of tea from Manami and drank it slowly. She felt she had to be careful what she said: Shizuka was from the Tribe, who had placed Takeo under sentence of death. She had assured Takeo that Shizuka would not harm him but how could she be certain of that? However, she found she could not control her expression, could not stop smiling, as if the mask had cracked and fallen away.

'I am going to the temple,' she said. 'I must get ready. Manami will come with me. Shizuka, you may leave now to see your sons and you can take Kondo with you.'

'I thought Kondo was to go with you to Inuyama,' Shizuka said.

'I have changed my mind. He must go with you. And you must both leave at once, now.'

'These are Takeo's orders, I suppose,' Shizuka said. 'You cannot pretend to me. I know you have seen him.'

'I told him you would not harm him,' Kaede said. 'You would not?'

Shizuka said sharply, 'Better not to ask that. If I do not see him, I cannot harm him. But how long do you intend to stay at the temple? Don't forget, Arai is waiting for you at Inuyama.'

'I don't know. It all depends on Takeo.' Kaede could not prevent herself from continuing. 'He said we must marry. We must, we will.'

'You must not do anything before you have seen Arai,'

Shizuka said urgently. 'If you marry without his approval you will insult him. He will be deeply offended. You cannot afford to incite his enmity. He is your strongest ally. And what about Lord Fujiwara? You are as good as betrothed to him. Will you offend him too?'

'I cannot marry Fujiwara,' Kaede cried. 'He of all people knows that I can marry no one but Takeo. To all other men I bring death. But I am Takeo's life and he is mine.'

'This is not the way the world works,' Shizuka said. 'Remember what Lady Maruyama told you, how easily these warlords and warriors can crush a women if they think that you question their power over you. Fujiwara expects to marry you: he must have already consulted Arai. It is a match Arai can only be in favour of. Apart from that, Takeo has the entire Tribe against him; he cannot survive. Don't look at me like that: it distresses me to hurt you. It's because I care so much for you that I must say this to you. I could swear to you never to harm him but it would make no difference; there are hundreds out there who will try. Sooner or later one of them will succeed. No one can escape the Tribe for ever. You have to accept that this will be his fate. What will you do after his death when you have insulted everyone who takes your part? You will have no hope of Maruyama and will lose Shirakawa. Your sisters will be ruined with you. Arai is your overlord. You must go to Inuyama and accept his decision on your marriage. Otherwise you will enrage him. Believe me. I know how his mind works.'

'Can Arai prevent the coming of spring?' Kaede replied. 'Can he order the snow not to thaw?'

'All men like to believe they can. Women get their own way by indulging this belief, not by opposing it.'

'Lord Arai will learn differently,' Kaede said in a low

voice. 'Make yourself ready. You and Kondo must be gone in an hour.'

She turned away. Her heart was beating wildly, excitement building up in her belly, her chest, her throat. She could think of nothing other than being joined with him. The sight of him, his closeness, awoke the fever in her again.

'You are mad,' Shizuka said. 'You have gone beyond reason. You are unleashing disaster on yourself and your family.'

As if in confirmation of Shizuka's fears there was a sudden noise; the house groaned, the screens rattled, the wind chimes sounded as the ground shook beneath their feet.

Ten

As soon as the snow began to melt and the thaw came, word spread like running water that I was at Terayama and was going to challenge the Otori lords for my inheritance. And like running water, first in a trickle, then in a flood, warriors began to make their way to the mountain temple. Some were masterless, but most were Otori who recognized the legitimacy of my claim as Shigeru's heir. My story was already a legend, and I seemed to have become a hero, not only to the young men of the warrior class, but also to the farmers and villagers of the Otori domain, who had reached a state of desperation after the bitter winter, the increased taxation and the ever harsher laws imposed by Shoichi and Masahiro, Shigeru's uncles.

The air was full of the sounds of spring. The willows put on their gold-green fronds. Swallows darted over the flooded fields and crafted their nests under the eaves of the temple buildings. Every night the noise of frogs grew louder, the loud call of the rain frog, the clacking rhythm of the tree frog and the sweet tinkling of the little bell frog. Flowers bloomed in a riot along the dykes: bitter cress, buttercups and bright pink vetch. Herons, ibises and cranes returned to the rivers and the pools.

The abbot, Matsuda Shingen, made the considerable

wealth of the temple freely available to me and with his help I spent the early weeks of spring organizing the men who came to me, equipping and arming them. Smiths and armourers appeared from Yamagata and elsewhere and set up their workshops at the foot of the holy mountain. Every day horse dealers came, hoping to make a good sale, and they usually did for I bought all the horses I could. No matter how many men I had and how well they were armed, my main weapons would always be speed and surprise. I did not have the time or the resources to muster a huge army of foot soldiers like Arai. I had to rely on a small, but swifter, band of horsemen.

Among the first to arrive were the Miyoshi brothers, Kahei and Gemba, with whom I had trained in Hagi. Those days when we had fought with wooden swords now seemed impossibly distant. Their appearance meant a great deal to me, far more than they suspected when they fell to their knees and begged to be allowed to join me. It meant that the best of the Otori had not forgotten Shigeru. They brought thirty men with them and, just as welcome, news from Hagi.

'Shoichi and Masahiro are aware of your return,' Kahei told me. He was several years older than me and had some experience of war, having been at Yaegahara at the age of fourteen. 'But they don't take it very seriously. They feel it will only take one quick skirmish to rout you.' He grinned at me. 'I don't mean to insult you, but they've formed the impression that you're something of a weakling.'

'That's the only way they've seen me,' I replied. I remembered Iida's retainer, Abe, who had thought the same thing and had been taught differently by Jato. 'They are correct in some ways. It is true that I am young and know only the theory of war, not its practice. But I have right on my side and am fulfilling Shigeru's will.'

'People say you are touched by Heaven,' Gemba said. 'They say you have been given powers that are not of this world.'

'We know all about that!' said Kahei. 'Remember the fight with Yoshitomi? But he considered the powers to be from Hell, not Heaven.'

I had fought a bout against Masahiro's son with wooden swords. He was a better swordsman than I was then, but I had other skills that he thought cheating and I had used them to prevent him killing me.

'Have they taken my house and land?' I asked. 'I heard they intended to.'

'Not yet, mainly because our old teacher, Ichiro, has refused to hand them over. He's made it clear he won't give in without a fight. The lords are reluctant to start a brawl with him and Shigeru's – your – remaining men.'

It was a relief to me to know that Ichiro was still alive. I hoped he would leave soon and come to the temple, where I could protect him. Since the thaw I had been expecting him daily.

'Also, they are not certain of the townspeople,' Gemba put in. 'They don't want to provoke anyone. They're afraid of an uprising.'

'They always preferred to plot in secret,' I said.

'They call it negotiation,' Kahei said dryly. 'Have they tried to negotiate with you?'

'I've heard nothing from them. Besides, there is nothing to negotiate. They were responsible for Shigeru's death. They tried to murder him in his own house and when that failed they handed him over to Iida. I cannot come to an agreement with them, even if they offer it.'

'What will be your strategy?' Kahei asked, narrowing his eyes.

'There's no way I can attack the Otori in Hagi. I'd need far greater resources than I have now. I am thinking I must approach Arai . . . but I'll do nothing until Ichiro gets here. He said he would come as soon as the road was clear.'

'Send us to Inuyama,' Kahei said. 'Our mother's sister is married to one of Arai's retainers. We can find out if winter has changed Arai's attitude towards you.'

'When the time is right, I will,' I promised, glad to have a way to approach Arai indirectly. I did not tell them or anyone else yet what I had already decided: to go first to Kaede wherever she was and marry her and then to take over the Shirakawa and Maruyama lands with her, if she would still have me, if she were not already married . . .

With every spring day my restlessness increased. The weather was fickle, sun one day, icy winds the next. The plum trees blossomed in a hailstorm. Even when the cherry buds started to swell it was still cold. But there were signs of spring everywhere, especially, it seemed, in my blood. The disciplined life of the past winter had left me fitter than I had ever been, physically and mentally. Matsuda's teaching, his unfailing affection for me, the knowledge of my Otori blood had all given me new self-confidence. I was less ridden by my split nature, less troubled by conflicting loyalties. I made no outward show of the restlessness that tormented me. I was learning to show nothing to the world. But at night my thoughts turned to Kaede and my desire followed. I longed for her, fearing that she was married to someone else and lost to me for ever. When I could not sleep I slipped from the room and left the temple, exploring the surrounding district, sometimes going as far as Yamagata. The hours of meditation, study and training had honed all my skills; I had no fear of anyone detecting me.

Makoto and I met every day to study together but by silent agreement we did not touch each other. Our friendship had moved on to another plane, which I felt would last a lifetime. Nor did I sleep with any women. None was allowed in the temple itself, fears of assassination kept me from the brothels, and I did not want to start another child. I often thought of Yuki. I could not stop myself passing in front of her parents' house one moonless night late in the second month. The plum tree's blossom gleamed white in the darkness but there were no lights within and only one guard on the gate. I'd heard that Arai's men had ransacked the house in the autumn. Now it seemed to be deserted. Even the smell of the fermenting soybeans had faded.

I thought about our child. I was sure it would be a boy, brought up by the Tribe to hate me and in all probability destined to fulfil the blind woman's prophecy. Knowing the future did not mean that I could escape it: it was part of the bitter sadness of human life.

I wondered where Yuki was now – possibly in some distant secret village north of Matsue – and I often thought about her father, Kenji. He probably would be not so far away, in one of the Muto villages in the mountains, not knowing that the secret network of the Tribe's hiding places had all been revealed to me in the records which Shigeru had left and which I had spent the winter learning by heart. I was still not sure what I would do with this knowledge, whether I would take advantage of it to buy forgiveness and friendship from Arai or use it myself to eradicate the secret organization that had sentenced me to death.

A long time ago Kenji had sworn to protect me as long as I lived. I had discounted this promise as part of the deviousness of his nature and I had not forgiven him for his part in Shigeru's betrayal. But I also knew that without him I would not have been able to carry out the work of revenge and I could not forget that he had followed me back into the castle that night. If I could have chosen anyone's help, it would have been his, but I did not think he would ever go against the rulings of the Tribe. If we met it would be as enemies, each seeking to kill the other.

Once when I was coming home at dawn I heard an animal's sharp panting and surprised a wolf on the path. He could smell me but could not see me. I was close enough to see the bright reddish hair behind his ears, close enough to smell his breath. He snarled in fear, backed away, turned and slipped into the undergrowth. I could hear him stop and sniff again, his nose as sharp as my ears. Our worlds of the senses overlapped, mine dominated by hearing, his by smell. I wondered what it would be like to enter the wolf's wild and solitary realm. In the Tribe I was known as the Dog, but I preferred to think of myself like this wolf, no longer owned by anyone.

Then the morning came when I saw my horse, Raku. It was late in the third month, when the cherry blossoms were on the point of flowering. I was walking up the steep track as the sky lightened, my eyes on the mountain peaks, still snow covered, turning pink in the sun. I saw the unfamiliar horses on their lines outside the inn. No one seemed to be up though I heard a shutter slide open from the other side of the courtyard. My gaze drifted over the horses as it always does and, at the same time as I recognized Raku's grey coat and black mane, the horse turned his head, saw me and whickered in delight.

He had been my gift to Kaede; he was almost my only possession left after the fall of Inuyama. Could she have sold him or given him away? Or had he brought her here to me?

Between the stables and the guest rooms of the inn was a small courtyard, with pine trees and stone lanterns. I stepped into it. I knew someone was awake; I could hear breathing behind the shutters. I went towards the veranda, desperate to know if it was Kaede, and at the same time certain that in the next moment I would see her.

She was even lovelier than I remembered. Her illness had left her thinner and frailer, but it had brought out the beauty of her bones, the slenderness of her wrists and neck. The pounding of my heart silenced the world around me. Then, realizing that for a few moments we would be alone before the inn awoke, I went and knelt before her.

All too soon I heard the women wake inside the room. I took on invisibility and slipped away. I heard Kaede's gasp of fear and realized I had not yet told her about my Tribe skills. There was so much we needed to talk about: would we ever have enough time? The wind chimes rang out as I passed beneath them. I could see my horse looking for me, but he did not see me. Then my shape returned. I was striding up the hill, filled with energetic joy as if I had drunk some magic potion. Kaede was here. She was not married. She would be mine.

As I did every day, I went to the burial ground and knelt before Shigeru's grave. At this early hour it was deserted, the light dim beneath the cedars. The sun was touching their tips; on the opposite side of the valley the mist hung along the sides of the slopes so the peaks seemed to be floating on foam.

The waterfall kept up its ceaseless babble, echoed by the softer trickle of water flowing through gutters and pipes into the pools and cisterns of the garden. I could hear the monks at prayer, the rise and fall of the sutras, the sudden clear peal of a bell. I was glad Shigeru dwelt in this peaceful place. I spoke to his spirit asking for his strength and wisdom to be transferred to me. I told him what he no doubt already knew, that I was going to fulfil his last requests to me. And, first of all, I was going to marry Shirakawa Kaede.

There was a sudden heavy shaking as the earth trembled. I was gripped by certainty that I was doing the right thing, and also by a sense of urgency. We must marry immediately.

A change in the note of the water made me turn my head. In the large pond carp were threshing and milling just below the surface of the water, a flickering mat of red and gold. Makoto was feeding them, his face calm and serene as he watched them.

Red and gold filled my eyes, the colours of good fortune, the colours of marriage.

He saw me looking at him and called, 'Where were you? You missed the first meal.'

'I'll eat later.' I got to my feet and went towards him. I could not keep my excitement to myself. 'Lady Shirakawa is here. Will you go with Kahei and escort her to the women's guest house?'

He threw the last of the millet into the water. 'I will tell Kahei. I prefer not to go myself. I don't want to remind her of the pain I caused her.'

'Maybe you are right. Yes, tell Kahei. Let them bring her here before noon.'

'Why is she here?' Makoto asked, glancing sideways at me.

'She came on a pilgrimage, to give thanks for her recovery. But now that she is here I intend to marry her.'

'Just like that?' He laughed without mirth.

'Why not?'

'My experience of marriages is very limited, but I believe in the case of great families like the Shirakawa or, come to that, the Otori, consent has to be given, the clan lords have to agree.'

'I am the lord of my clan and I give my consent,' I replied lightly, feeling he was raising unnecessary problems.

'Your case is slightly different. But who does Lady Shirakawa obey? Her family may have other plans for her.'

'She has no family.' I could feel anger beginning to simmer.

'Don't be a fool, Takeo. Everyone has family, especially unmarried girls who are the heir to great domains.'

'I have both the legal right and a moral duty to marry her, since she was betrothed to my adopted father.' My tone was hotter now. 'It was Shigeru's express will that I should do so.'

'Don't be angry with me,' he said, after a pause. 'I know your feelings for her. I'm only saying what everyone will tell you.'

'She loves me too!'

'Love has nothing to do with marriage.' He shook his head, looking at me as if I were a child.

'Nothing's going to stop me! She is here. I will not let

her slip away from me again. We will be married this week.'

The bell tolled from the temple. One of the older monks walked across the garden, looking disapprovingly at us. Makoto had kept his voice low throughout our exchange but I had been talking loudly and forcefully.

'I must go to meditation,' he said. 'Maybe you should too. Think about what you are doing before you act.'

'My mind is made up. Go and meditate! I'll tell Kahei. And then I'll speak to the abbot.'

It was already past the time when I usually went to him every morning for two hours of swordsmanship. I hurried to find the Miyoshi brothers, and caught up with them on their way downhill to speak to an armourer.

'Lady Shirakawa?' Kahei said, 'Is it safe to go near her?'

'Why do you say that?' I demanded.

'No offence, Takeo, but everyone knows about her. She brings death to men.'

'Only if they desire her,' Gemba added. Then taking a quick look at my face went on, 'That's what people say!'

'And they also say that she's so beautiful it's impossible to look at her without desiring her.' Kahei looked gloomy. 'You're sending us to certain death.'

I was in no mood for their clowning but their words brought home to me even more how essential it was that we should marry. Kaede had said that she was safe only with me and I understood why. Only marriage to me would save her from the curse she seemed to be under. I knew that she would never be any danger to me. Other men who desired her had died, but I had joined my body to hers and lived.

I was not going to explain all this to the Miyoshi brothers.

'Bring her to the women's guest rooms as soon as possible,' I said shortly. 'Make sure none of her men come and also that Kondo Kiichi and Muto Shizuka leave today. She will bring one woman with her. Treat them with the utmost courtesy. Tell her I will call on her around the hour of the Monkey.'

'Takeo is truly fearless,' Gemba muttered.

'Lady Shirakawa is going to be my wife.'

That startled them. They saw I was serious and kept their mouths closed. They bowed formally to me and walked silently to the guardhouse where they collected five or six other men. Once they were beyond the gate they made a few jokes at my expense, not realizing that I could hear them, about the praying mantis that devours her mate. I thought about going after them to teach them a lesson, but I was already late for the abbot.

Listening to their laughter fade away down the slope, I hurried to the hall where our sessions took place. He was already there, dressed in his priest's robes. I was still in the rough garb I wore on my night-time wanderings: a sort of adaptation of the Tribe's black uniform – knee-length trousers, leggings and split-toed boots – which did as well for sword fighting as for leaping up walls and running over roofs.

Matsuda did not seem to be at all encumbered by his long skirts and deep sleeves. I usually finished the sessions out of breath and pouring with sweat. He remained as cool and unruffled as if he had spent those same two hours in prayer.

I knelt before him to apologize for my lateness. He looked me up and down, a quizzical expression on his face, but said nothing, indicating the wooden pole with his head.

I took it from the rack. It was dark in colour, almost black, longer than Jato and much heavier. Since I had been practising daily with it the muscles in my wrists and arms had increased in strength and flexibility and I finally seemed to be over the injury to my right hand that Akio had caused me in Inuyama. At first the pole had felt like an obstinate horse, slugging against the bit; little by little I had learned to control it until I could manipulate it as deftly as a pair of eating sticks.

In practice that precision was as necessary as in real combat, for a false move could crack a skull or crush a breastbone. We did not have enough men to risk killing or injuring each other in training.

A wave of tiredness swept over me as I raised the pole into the challenge position. I had barely slept the night before and had not eaten since the evening meal. Then I thought of Kaede, saw her form as I'd seen her earlier, kneeling on the veranda. Energy flowed back into me. I realized in that split second how completely necessary she was to me.

Normally I was no match for Matsuda. But something had transformed me, had taken all the elements of training and melded them into a whole: a tough, indestructible spirit that sprang from the core of my being and flowed into my sword arm. For the first time I realized I was forty years younger than Matsuda. I saw his age and his vulnerability. I saw I had him at my mercy.

I checked my attack and let the pole drop. In that instance his staff found the unguarded space, catching me on the side of the neck with a blow that left me dizzy. Luckily he had not struck with full force.

His normally serene eyes were blazing with genuine anger.

'That's to teach you a lesson,' he growled. 'First, not to be late and, second, not to let your softness of heart emerge while you're fighting.'

I opened my mouth to speak but he cut me off. 'Don't argue. You give me the first inkling I'm not wasting my time with you and then you throw it away. Why? Not because you felt pity for me, I hope?'

I shook my head.

He sighed. 'You can't fool me. I saw it in your eyes. I saw the boy who came here last year and was moved by Sesshu. Is that what you want to be? An artist? I told you then that you could come back here and study and draw – is that what you want?'

I was disinclined to answer but he waited until I did. 'A part of me might want it, but not yet. First I have to carry out Shigeru's commands.'

'Are you sure of that? Will you commit yourself to it with a whole heart?'

I heard the utter seriousness of his tone and answered in the same way. 'Yes, I will.'

'You will be leading many men, some to their death. Are you sure enough of yourself to do that? If you have any weakness, Takeo, it is this. You feel too much pity. A warrior needs more than a dash of ruthlessness, of black blood. Many will die following you and you will kill many yourself. Once you launch yourself on this path you must pursue it to the end. You cannot check your attack or drop your guard because you feel pity for your opponent.'

I could feel the colour mounting to my face. 'I will not do it again. I did not mean to insult you. Forgive me.'

'I'll forgive you if you can achieve that move again and follow it through!'

He took up the challenge position, his eyes fixed on mine. I had no qualms about meeting his gaze: he had never succumbed to the Kikuta sleep and I had never tried to impose it on him. Nor did I ever intentionally use invisibility or the second self with him, though sometimes, in the heat of combat, I felt my image begin to slide away.

His staff moved like lightning through the air. I stopped thinking then about anything except the opponent in front of me and the thrust of the pole, the floor beneath our feet, the space around us that we filled almost like a dance. And twice more I came to the point where I saw my dominance over him, and neither time did I fail to follow the move through.

When we had finished even Matsuda was glowing slightly, perhaps due to the spring weather. As we were wiping the sweat from our faces with towels Norio brought, he said, 'I did not think you would ever make a swordsman but you have done better than I expected. When you concentrate you are not bad, not bad at all.'

I was speechless at such high praise. He laughed. 'Don't let it go to your head. I'll meet you again later this afternoon. I hope you have prepared your study on strategy.'

'Yes, sir. But there is something else I need to talk to you about.'

'Something to do with Lady Shirakawa?'

'How did you know?'

'I'd already heard that she was on her way to visit the temple. Arrangements have been made for her to stay in the women's guest house. It is a great honour for us. I will go and see her later today.'

It all sounded like casual chat about an ordinary guest but I knew Matsuda well enough by now: he did nothing casually. I was afraid he would have the same misgivings about my marriage to Kaede that Makoto had voiced, but I had to tell him my intentions sooner or later. All this flashed through my head in an instant and then it occurred to me that if I should seek anyone's permission, it should be his.

I fell to my knees and said, 'I wish to marry Lady Shirakawa. May I have your permission and may the ceremony be held here?'

'Is that the reason she came here? Does she come with the permission of her family and clan?'

'No, she came for a different purpose – to give thanks for recovering from an illness. But it was one of Lord Shigeru's last commands to me, that I should marry her, and now fate seems to have brought her here to me . . .' I heard a note of pleading in my voice.

The abbot heard it too. Smiling, he said, 'The problem is not going to be on your side, Takeo. For you it is the right thing to do. But for her to marry without approval from her clan, from Lord Arai . . . Be patient, seek his permission. He was in favour of the marriage last year. There's every reason to think he still will be.'

'I may be murdered at any moment!' I exclaimed. 'I have no time to be patient! And there is someone else who wishes to marry her.'

'Are they betrothed?'

'There is nothing official. But apparently he has expectations of the marriage taking place. He is a nobleman, his estate lies alongside hers.'

'Fujiwara,' Matsuda said.

'You know him?'

'I know who he is. Everyone does, apart from half-literates like you. It's a very suitable alliance. The estates will be joined, Fujiwara's son will inherit them both, and more importantly, since Fujiwara will almost certainly return to the capital soon, Arai will have a friend at court.'

'Arai will not, because she will not marry Fujiwara. She will marry me, and before the end of the week!'

'Between them they will crush you.' His eyes were fixed on my face.

'Not if Arai thinks I can help him destroy the Tribe. And when we marry we will move at once to Maruyama. Lady Shirakawa is the legal heir to that domain as well as to her father's. It will give me the resources I need to challenge the Otori.'

'As a strategy, it's not bad,' he said. 'But there are grave risks. You could completely antagonize Arai. I'd thought it better for you to serve under him for a while and learn the art of war. And you do not want to make an enemy of a man like Fujiwara. This move, for all its boldness, could destroy your hopes utterly. I don't want to see that happen. I want to see all of Shigeru's desires fulfilled. Is it worth the gamble?'

'Nothing will prevent me from marrying her,' I said in a low voice.

'You are infatuated with her. Don't let that affect your judgment.'

'It's more than infatuation. She is my life and I am hers.'

He sighed. 'We all think that at some age about some woman or other. Believe me, it doesn't last.'

'Lord Shigeru and Lady Maruyama loved each other deeply for years,' I dared to say.

'Yes, well, it must be some madness in the Otori blood,' he retorted, but his expression had softened and his eyes took on a musing look.

'It's true,' he said finally. 'Their love did last. And it illuminated all their plans and hopes. If they had married, and brought about the alliance they dreamed of between the Middle Country and the West, who knows what they might not have achieved?' He reached down and patted me on the shoulder. 'It's as if their spirits have brought about a second chance in you and Lady Shirakawa. And, I can't deny it, to make Maruyama your base makes a great deal of sense. For that reason, as much as for the sake of the dead, I will agree to this marriage. You may start making the necessary preparations.'

'I've never been to this sort of wedding,' I confessed, after I had bowed to the ground in gratitude. 'What needs to be done?'

'The woman that came with her will know. Ask her. I hope I haven't reached my dotage,' he added, before dismissing me.

It was nearly time for the midday meal. I went to wash and change my clothes. I dressed with care, putting on another of the silk robes with the Otori crest on the back that had been given to me when I arrived at Terayama after my journey through the snow. I ate distractedly, hardly tasting the food, listening all the time for her arrival.

Finally I heard Kahei's voice outside the eating hall. I called to him, and he came in to join me.

'Lady Shirakawa is at the women's guest rooms,' he said. 'Fifty more men have come from Hagi. We'll billet them in the village. Gemba is arranging it.'

'I'll see them tonight,' I said, my heart lifting from

both pieces of news. I left him eating and went back to my room, where I knelt at the writing table and took out the scrolls the abbot had told me to read. I thought I would die of impatience before I saw Kaede again, but gradually I became absorbed in the art of war: the accounts of battles won and lost, strategy and tactics, the roles played by Heaven and Earth. The problem he had set me was how to take the town of Yamagata. It had been a theoretical problem, no more; Yamagata was still under the control of Arai through his interim governor, though there had been reports that the Otori planned to retake their former city and were assembling an army on their southern border near Tsuwano. Matsuda had intended to approach Arai on my behalf and make peace between us, whereupon I would serve Arai while pursuing the Otori inheritance. However, I was now acutely aware that if I risked inciting Arai's enmity anew by marrying Kaede I might well need to take Yamagata at once. It added a certain sense of reality to my studies of strategy.

I knew the town so well; I'd explored every street; I'd climbed into the castle. And I knew the terrain around it, its mountains, valleys, hills and rivers. My main difficulty was having so few men at my command: a thousand at most. Yamagata was a prosperous town, but the winter had been hard on everyone. If I attacked in early spring could the castle withstand a long siege? Would diplomacy bring about a surrender where force would not? What advantages did I have over the defenders?

While I was brooding over these problems my thoughts turned to the outcaste, Jo-An. I had said I would send for him in the spring but I was still not sure if I wanted to. I could never forget the hungry, passionate look in his eyes, in the eyes of the boatman and the other outcastes. 'He's your man, now,' Jo-An had said of the boatman. 'We all are.' Could I add outcastes to my army, or the farmers who came daily to pray and make offerings at Shigeru's grave? I had no doubt that I could count on these men if I wanted them. But was this what the warrior class did? I had never read of battles where farmers fought. Usually they stayed well clear of the combat, hating both sides equally and afterwards stripping the dead impartially.

As it often did, the face of the farmer I had murdered in his secret field in the hills behind Matsue floated before my mind's eye. I heard his voice call again, 'Lord Shigeru!' As much as anything else, I wanted to lay his ghost to rest. But he also brought into my mind the courage and determination of his fellows, resources that were wasted at the moment. If I used them would he stop haunting me?

The farmers in the Otori lands, both in the existing ones around Hagi, and those that had been ceded to the Tohan – Yamagata included – had loved Shigeru. They had already risen in fury after his death. I believed they would also support me, but I feared using them would weaken the loyalty of my warriors.

Back to the theoretical problem of Yamagata: if I could get rid of the interim lieutenant Arai had placed in the castle, there was a much greater chance of the city surrendering without a long siege. What I needed was an assassin I could trust. The Tribe had admitted I was the only person who could have climbed alone into Yamagata castle, but it did not seem like a good scheme for the commander-in-chief to undertake. My thoughts began to drift a little, reminding me I'd hardly slept the night before. I wondered if I could train young boys and girls in the way the Tribe trained them. They might not have innate skills, yet there was much that was simply a matter of teaching. I could see all the advantages of a network of spies. Might there not be some disaffected Tribe members who could be persuaded to serve me? I put the thought away for the time being, but it was to return to me later.

As the day warmed up, time slowed even more. Flies, woken from their winter sleep, were buzzing against the screens. I heard the first bush warbler calling from the forest, the glide of the swallows' wings and the snap of their beaks as they took insects. The sounds of the temple murmured around me: the tread of feet, the swish of robes, the rise and fall of chanting, the sudden clear note of a bell.

A light breeze was blowing from the south, full of the fragrance of spring. Within a week Kaede and I would be married. Life seemed to rise around me, embracing me with its vigour and energy. Yet I was kneeling here, rapt in the study of war.

And when Kaede and I met that evening we did not talk of love, but of strategy. We had no need to talk of love; we were to be married, we were to become husband and wife. But if we were to live long enough to have children, we needed to act swiftly to consolidate our power.

I had been right in my instinct, when Makoto first told me that she was raising an army, that Kaede would make a formidable ally. She agreed with me that we should go straight to Maruyama; she told me of her meeting with Sugita Haruki in the autumn. He was waiting to hear from her and she suggested sending some of her men to the domain to let him know of our intentions. I agreed, and thought the younger of the Miyoshi brothers, Gemba, might go with them. We sent no messages to Inuyama: the less Arai knew of our plans the better.

'Shizuka said our marriage will enrage him,' Kaede said.

I knew it probably would. We should have known better. We should have been patient. Perhaps if we had approached Arai through the proper channels, through Kahei's aunt or through Matsuda or Sugita, he would have decided in our favour. But we were both seized by a desperate sense of urgency, knowing how short our lives might be. And so we were married a few days later, before the shrine, in the shadow of the trees that surrounded Shigeru's grave, in accordance with his will but in defiance of all the rules of our class. I suppose I might say in our defence that neither of us had had a typical upbringing. We had both escaped, for different reasons, the rigid training in obedience of most warriors' children. It gave us freedom to act as we pleased, but the elders of our class were to make us pay for it.

The weather continued warm under the south wind. On our wedding day the cherry blossoms were fully open, a mass of pink and white. Kaede's men had now been allowed to join mine and the highest-ranking warrior among them, Amano Tenzo, spoke for her and on behalf of the Shirakawa clan. When Kaede was led forward by the shrine maiden, in the red and white robes Manami had somehow managed to find for her, she looked beautiful in a timeless way, as if she were a sacred being. I spoke my name as Otori Takeo and named Shigeru and the Otori clan as my ancestors. We exchanged the ritual cups of wine, three times thrice, and as the sacred branches were offered a sudden gust of wind sent a snow storm of petals down on us.

It might have seemed like a chilly omen, but that night after the feasting and the celebrations when we were finally alone together we had no thoughts of omens. In Inuyama we had made love in a sort of wild desperation, expecting to die before morning. But now, in the safety of Terayama, we had time to explore each other's bodies, to give and take pleasure slowly – and besides since then Yuki had taught me something of the art of love.

We talked about our lives since we had been separated, especially about the child. We thought about its soul, launched again into the cycle of birth and death, and prayed for it. I told Kaede about my visit to Hagi and my flight through the snow. I did not tell her about Yuki, and she kept secrets from me, for though she told me a little about Lord Fujiwara, she did not go into details as to the pact they had made. I knew he had given her large amounts of money and food, and it worried me, for it made me think his views on the marriage were more fixed than hers. I felt a slight chill in my spine that may have been a premonition but I put the thought away for I wanted nothing to spoil my joy.

I woke towards dawn to find her sleeping in my arms. Her skin was white, silky to my touch, both warm and cool at the same time. Her hair, so long and thick it covered us both like a shawl, smelled of jasmine. I had thought her like the flower on the high mountain, completely beyond my reach, but she was here, she was mine. The world stood still in the silent night as the realization sank in. The backs of my eyes stung as tears came. Heaven was benign. The gods loved me. They had given me Kaede.

For a few days Heaven continued to smile on us, giving us gentle spring weather, every day sunny. Everyone at the temple seemed happy for us, from Manami who beamed with delight when she brought us tea the first morning, to the abbot who resumed my lessons, teasing me unmercifully if he caught me yawning. Scores of people made the climb up the mountain to bring gifts and wish us well, just as the village people would have done in Mino.

Only Makoto sounded a different note. 'Make the most of your happiness,' he said to me. 'I am happy for you, believe me, but I fear it will not last.'

I already knew this: I had learned it from Shigeru. *Death comes suddenly and life is fragile and brief,* he had told me, the day after he had saved my life in Mino. *No one can alter this either by prayers or spells.* It was the fragility of life that made it so precious. Our happiness was all the more intense for our awareness of how fleeting it might be.

The cherry blossoms were already falling, the days lengthening as the season turned. The winter of preparation was over: spring was giving way to summer and summer was the season of war. Five battles lay ahead of us, four to win and one to lose.

Acknowledgments

I would like to thank the Asialink Foundation and all my friends in Japan and Australia who have helped me in researching and writing Tales of the Otori.

In *Grass for his Pillow* I particular want to thank Ms Sugiyama Kazuko for her calligraphy and Simon Higgins for his advice on martial arts.

鼻びしびし……長く

かき撫でて　我を除きて　人はあらじ

と誇ろへど　寒くしあれば

麻衾　引き被り　布肩衣

のしくしくに　服襲へども

……後略

『万葉集　巻五

八九二